KE
THE
MOUNTAIN
MAN

GEMMA WEIR

Megan,

*For fictional men in all their forms, because sometimes they're
so much better than the real life ones.*

#KeptbyGranger

Cz 27x

Warning

This book contains an over the top, jealous, unreasonable, possessive asshole.

If you consider unapologetic alphaholes unacceptable, or feel their behavior is in some way abusive, then this isn't the book or series for you.

If you're a nay sayer who thinks what I write is romanticizing domestic violence and abuse then please, please stop reading now.

This book isn't a guide to dysfunctional relationships, it's fiction. My books are fantasy, this isn't real life, it's a romance novel and should be read as such.

We all know in the real world throwing a woman over your shoulder, messing with her birth control or stalking her and letting yourself into her home is a one way ticket to either a restraining order or the mental hospital. But I'd like to think that in fiction it's okay to agree that these things are incredibly sexy. Please do not kink shame me or my enthusiastic readers for finding these extreme alphahole behaviors hot, maybe if you read this book with the pinch of romantic salt it was intended to come with, you might like it too.

So if, like me, you love a guy who is so obsessively in love with his girl that he will snarl, demand, punish and fuck her until she gives herself to him completely, then read on and welcome to the world of my Montana Mountain Men.

KEPT BY THE MOUNTAIN MAN

ONE

ALICE

Teeth gritted, I tip my head back and blink up at the bright winter sun taunting me in the sky above. Why did my stupid shit heap of an RV have to break down here? I mean, yes, I'm in Montana which is the state I wanted to get to, but I'd planned to head for one of the bigger, more popular ski resorts hoping to find a job at a hotel or in a café.

Instead, I'm in Rockhead Point, population, not enough, and my car has stopped, literally just stopped. I have money, I could maybe get it fixed, but the last time I paid to get it patched up, the guy told me the engine was on its last legs and if it broke down again it'd end up costing me much more than the RV's worth to fix it.

When my dad bought this crap heap RV back in the eighties, he was so proud to own a brand new vehicle. Unfortunately for my dad, this was a shining example of his bad decision making, and the RV I inherited when he was sent to jail for fraud, is a pile of crap and always has been.

Silver lining to Dad being incarcerated – we at least had a vehicle to move all our stuff in when we lost our house and had to move in with my grandparents.

I smile as I think about the time we spent living with Gram Gram and Pops, those were some of the happiest times of my life. Gram Gram baked almost every day and when me and Serenity came back from school, the house always smelled like sugar and vanilla.

Those two years were so calm and normal, I wish we'd stayed. Instead, Mom met Wayne, a long-distance truck driver from Florida, and dragged us half way across the country to move into his trailer with him. We only got to see Gram Gram and Pops every couple of years after that.

Tears try to fill my eyes, but I blink them away. I can't lose my shit on the side of the road; tears don't solve problems and I'm nothing if not a great problem solver, after all, I learned from the very best. I think Serenity became our family fixer around the time we moved to Florida. She was thirteen, I was eight, and when Mom decided she'd lose Wayne if she had to stay behind and look after us, it made total sense that Serenity could step up and take care of both me and her while Mom toured the country in Wayne's truck.

The first few weeks were scary, but honestly my sister was amazing, Gram Gram taught us how to cook when we lived with her, she also taught us how to be thrifty, how to make each dollar stretch. The things we didn't already know about how to take care of ourselves, we figured out pretty quickly.

We made friends with the sweet old lady who lived in the trailer next door, and once she figured out that Mom wasn't always around, she kept an eye on us and never told anyone that two kids were essentially living alone.

The years we lived in Florida weren't the greatest, but me and my sister were a family. If I had any problems, Serenity fixed them for me.

In the years that followed, Mom met three other Waynes and so we moved whenever she fell in love, bouncing about across the country until we finally ended up in Missouri. That's when everything kind of went to shit.

Bob, the pharmaceuticals sales rep, became Mom's third husband when I was thirteen and Serenity was eighteen. By then, my sister was more like a mom to me than my actual mom. She was the one who helped me with my homework, gave me tampons when I started my period, and nursed me through the failure of my first crush. If I had a problem my sister fixed it, until she didn't anymore.

The day she came home from school and announced that she'd enrolled in the military and was leaving for basic training, was one of the worst days of my life. Serenity was my world, my one constant, my big sister and my sole support network.

She packed her stuff, kissed me goodbye, and told me she couldn't sacrifice any more of her life to take care of me and had to do something for herself for once. And then she was gone. She has an apartment in West Virginia that she and her boyfriend share somewhere close to the military base they work out of. She sometimes sends me a text on my birthday if she's not on deployment, but I haven't seen her in person since the day she left.

Pops passed away when I was fifteen, Gram Gram a year later, and somehow by the time I was sixteen I had literally no one who cared about me in my life. The day I graduated from Highschool, I loaded my dad's shitty RV—that thankfully Serenity kept running till she left—with a case full of my clothes and a handful of other things, and left while Mom and Bob were on a yet another business trip, their tenth that year. It took her nearly six months to call me and ask me where I was.

Since then, I've spent the last five years following the seasons and seasonal jobs. In summer I head for the beach, I waitress or tend bar and make the most of the seaside towns and tourists. In the fall I follow the leaves, almost always ending up in a place with spectacular color changing trees and nature, then in the winter I find the snow. Spring is usually a quiet time, but there's always a job to be found if you're not picky about what you do.

Shitty and falling apart as it might be, this RV has been my home and transport for years and without it, I'm pretty damn screwed.

I Lift the hood and peer at the engine, wishing it had a big arrow pointing to the broken bit so I could attempt to fix it without having to find a mechanic, but unfortunately one of the things Gram Gram never taught us was how to fix a car. Serenity knew, but she left before I could drive, and good old Bob had no interest in spending time with his wife's annoying teenage daughter.

After I left Missouri, I did think about tracking down my dad. He got out of jail right about the time we moved in with Bob, but he never made any effort to contact us over the years, so it seemed stupid to reach out to someone who had about as much interest in being a father as Mom did in being a mother.

Giving up on my futile engine inspection, I shut the hood and lean my ass against it, pulling my cell out of my jeans pocket and looking down at it. For a moment I think about clicking into the contact section and calling someone, but even after five years on my own, I still only have three numbers listed in there. Mom, Bob and Serenity, and none of them would care that my RV had died in a small town in Montana. Not that I'd ever call them to burden them with my problems anyway.

It took me a long time growing up to understand that I was a generally unlikable person. I'm not rude, or mean, I just don't have the type of personality that people like. As a kid I tried to change, I tried to make friends, but the ones who did tolerate me for the short term were soon repulsed by my needy nature and tendency to cling.

The high school guidance counselor, that the school insisted I saw, said that no one liked someone who was incapable of looking after themselves and unless I wanted to be alone for the rest of my life, I should learn to become independent and self-sufficient.

That meeting with Mrs. Geraldine Colburn was an enlightening experience. In less than an hour, she made me understand why I struggled to make friends, why my mom had always picked her boyfriends over me and why Serenity left. Her words changed everything for me and I'll always be grateful for her honesty.

Since the day I left home I haven't attempted to force my company on anyone, I know who I am, so I don't contact my mom or Serenity. I'm not a burden anymore, and with that realization came a freedom I wasn't expecting.

I've lost count of the number of jobs I've had in the past five years, but I never try to form bonds or set down roots. I move with each season, never settling anywhere for more than three months. I'm a nomad, but I don't mind.

Sighing, I switch to my internet tab and start to type in 'Mechanics shops near me' but a car slows to a stop beside me before I can hit enter.

"You having some car troubles?" a low, rumbling voice asks.

"I'm fine, I'm just about to call a mechanic," I say, not looking at the person as I hold out my cell to indicate my readiness to make a call.

"My brothers own the only mechanics shop in town, I'll give them a ring, tell them to get the tow out here."

"No that's fine, I can handle making the call, thanks though," I say politely, still not acknowledging the man.

"I'll wait for them to arrive."

"I appreciate you stopping to check on a stranger on the side of the road, that's very nice of you, but honestly I'll be just fine. Thank you."

The road crunches beneath tires and I'm pleased when the car starts to pull away, only instead of leaving, he pulls ahead of me, slowing to a stop on the side of the road and killing the car's engine. Either this guy is a super helper that just won't take no for an answer, or he's a creep and I'm going to have to lock myself in my stationary RV while I call the cops or hope I'm a faster runner than he is.

His car door swings open and I see his head appear, followed by a broad back. More and more of him curls from the car and I feel my eyes widen, because this guy must be well over six foot tall. I'm not a short girl at five foot eight and he's at least a head taller than me.

I'm moving before I even realize I'm doing it, circling my RV and opening the driver's door to climb back inside. I know some basic self-defense, but against a guy this big, I'm not sure any of it would help me.

Closing the door behind me, I press the button to lock it, suddenly glad that my ancient RV doesn't have central locking and that all the other doors are already locked shut. When he appears at my window, I have to swallow past my shock as my eyes take in his appearance.

A shock of barely tamed dark brown hair covers his head, his chin coated in dark stubble almost thick enough to be called a beard. His jaw is square, his features masculine, leading to warm brown eyes that are focused on me like I'm a wild animal ready to attack.

His chest is massive, thick and broad with what I suspect is hard muscle, although I can't see for sure through his Henley and thick padded bodywarmer. His lips are tipped at the corners in an almost smile, but the friendly expression doesn't seem to reach his eyes.

"Hi ma'am, my name is Granger Barnett. I can see you're a little freaked out, so here's what you're going to do. Take out your cell and type in 911. I'm not going to attempt to touch or open your vehicle, I'm just going to stay right here until one of my brothers gets here to recover you from the side of the road. If at any point you feel unsafe, I want you go right ahead and call the sheriff. Rockhead Point is a pretty safe town, but I can't think of a single roadside I'd consider safe enough for one of my sisters to be stranded on, and I wouldn't be able to live with myself if I were to leave you here alone."

Nodding, I do as he suggests and type 911 into my cell, my thumb poised over the call button. Maybe I'm being naïve, but he doesn't seem dangerous. I'm still not going to unlock my door or get out of the RV though.

He watches me as I type into my cell, then nods approvingly. "I'm gonna give my brother Bay a call, him and my brother Penn run the shop and they should be able to get out here pretty quick."

I nod again, and he clicks into his cell then lifts it to his ear. "Hey Bro, I'm out on Sunderland Ave and there's a woman broken down in a…" Pausing, he glances down at the RV and wrinkles his brow. "It's an old dodge RV."

He stops speaking, and I'm assuming whoever is on the other end of the line is talking.

"Okay, yeah, I'm gonna stay with her till you get here. Okay. Thanks." Ending the call, he slides his cell and his hands into his pockets in what I think he's hoping is non-threatening body language.

"How many sisters do you have?" Shoot, why did I just ask him that? It's none of my business and I know better than to try to engage people in unnecessary conversation.

"Two. Bonnie is married to my oldest brother, and Cora is engaged to my brother Huck and expecting my first niece or nephew."

I nod. Looking down at the cell in my hands and hoping he goes and sits back in his car. I don't want him to feel obliged to talk to me just because he's playing the good Samaritan.

"Do you have a name?"

Lifting my gaze, I don't smile, I don't need to look eager. "Alice."

"Well, Miss Alice, it's nice to meet you. Do you have any siblings?"

"One older sister." A short and sweet answer, he doesn't want to chat, he's just being polite after I asked him about his sisters, that's all.

"I'm one of seven, nine now with the girls," he laughs. "I couldn't imagine only having one sibling. Are you and your sister close?"

"Not really," I shake my head.

"That's a shame, my family is very close, my brothers are my best friends and I'd be lost without them. So, are you on vacation?"

"Just passing through."

"You don't say much, do you?"

I allow my lips to tip up at the sides in an attempt at a smile, but don't say anything.

"So where are you passing through to?"

"Big Mountain."

"Oh, do you ski?"

I shake my head.

"Snowboard?"

I shake my head again.

"You're heading to one of the most popular ski resorts in the state, but you don't ski or snowboard?" he asks, a little bemused.

"There's always plenty of work during ski season," I admit reluctantly, not wanting to force him to engage with me anymore than he has to. He's obviously feeling awkward just standing here without talking.

"What kind of work are you looking for?"

I shrug. "I don't really mind."

"Do you live in Montana?"

"No."

"So where have you come from?"

I'm saved from answering when a large black tow truck appears beside us, a guy who looks similar to Granger behind the wheel, smiling widely, his arm hanging out the window. "Hiya, let me just get turned round and I'll get that beast hooked up. Granger, can you move your car out the way?"

Granger nods, then walks to his car. When his engine starts, I expect him to drive away and a twinge of sadness that he's leaving hits me. Only instead of pulling onto the road, he drives forward a hundred yards then stops again, getting back out of his car just in time to guide the tow truck toward the front of my RV.

Once the tow truck's in position, Granger's brother jumps out of the cab and Granger walks over to him, slapping him on the shoulder and pointing at me. I startle a little when they both move to toward me.

"Miss Alice, this is my brother Bay."

"Nice to meet you, Miss Alice, I'm gonna need you to jump out so I can hook your RV up to the truck. Then we can recover you back to the shop so we can see what's going on with this beast. You can go jump into the cab of my truck, the heaters are on and this won't take a minute."

Nodding, I unlock the RV, my cell still gripped tightly in my hand as I grab my purse and then open the door. Both men step back to allow me to climb out. When my feet are firmly on the floor, I look up, and up again at the brothers who are both well over six feet tall.

"Thanks," I mumble as I bypass them both and head for the tow truck.

TWO

GRANGER

Fuck, this is her. Her. My woman. Mine. All mine. How is this possible? How can it happen just like that? One glance and I knew, unequivocally knew without any element of doubt that I'm going to make this woman mine, that I'm going to marry her, fill her with my baby and keep her forever.

I really try hard not to watch her leave but I just can't help myself, Alice is the most curious woman I've ever met. She's tall, her frame slim and almost athletic, with small breasts and narrow hips. Her hair is a shiny blonde, the color of straw on a warm summer day, and it's long, reaching right down her back in the loose braid she's got it twisted into.

She's dressed plainly in simple blue jeans, a long sleeve white t-shirt and brown leather boots. She'd be completely average if you only looked at her from the neck down, because her face is almost angelic. I'm not a fucking poetic guy, but this woman is ethereal. Her features are almost elfin, a tiny nose, high cheek bones and full pouty lips, she's quite simply the most beautiful creature I've ever seen in my life.

There doesn't seem to be a scrap of makeup on her face, nor anything to accentuate her bright green eyes. I'm not sure I've ever seen anyone with naturally blonde hair and green eyes before, but on her it's stunning.

I've met a lot of beautiful women, but usually they come complete with a sense of entitlement that's completely missing from Alice. She doesn't move like a woman who's aware of the power of her beauty either. Her steps are long, but she's not strutting, she's just trying to get to where she's going as fast as she can and right now, where she wants to be seems to be away from us.

"Woo, she is—" Bay starts

"Mine," I snap the word out before I even realize I was thinking it.

"What?"

"Mine," I say again under my breath. "She's mine."

"Do you know her?" Bay asks, his brow furrowed as

he looks at me in confusion.

"Nope, met her ten minutes ago, right before I called you."

"Fuck, that must have been some ten minutes. What the hell did she say to you to make you go all gaga like Beau and Huck?"

"She barely said ten words to me." I laugh.

"Then..." he trails off.

"I have no fucking clue, but I know she's mine. Don't ask me how I know, I just do."

"Do you even know her last name?"

"Nope."

"Is she even single?"

"Not anymore, she's mine," I say single-mindedly.

"You can't just—"

"I just did," I interrupt him. "She's alone, hardly anything in the RV and not wearing a ring, if she has a boyfriend then he's doing a shitty job looking after her and he doesn't deserve her. Either way, she's mine now and I'm keeping her."

Bay's chuckle starts off low and quiet, building in volume until he's straight out laughing. "Fuck, that poor girl."

I smile to myself, Alice has an aura of sadness around her, but I'll fix that, she's mine now, even though it makes very little sense to me how this happened. I should have taken notice when my dad told us about meeting Mom, I should have been less skeptical when first Beau, then Huck fell for their women, because now it's happening to me. Suddenly, it makes complete sense to feel this way about a woman I don't know at all, even though it shouldn't.

If I were in my right mind, I'd get in my car and drive away, but it's like the moment I saw her, my world narrowed and now all I want is to talk to her, to learn everything there is to know about her.

Something about Alice is calling to my baser instincts, telling me that she needs to be cared for, coddled and protected. Maybe it's because she wouldn't look me in the eye, maybe it's because she almost seemed to be upset with herself for asking me a question, or maybe it's just the air of hopelessness that seems to be following her. Whatever it is, I want her, need her, need to take care of her in a way I've only ever heard my brothers try to explain and now makes perfect sense.

Bay slaps me on the shoulder, still chuckling as he quickly hooks Alice's clapped out RV to the tow truck. "I take it you're following me back to the shop?"

"Yep."

Scoffing, he shakes his head. "We got to start putting bets on who falls next now it's gotten you. My money's on Teddy, he's got hearts in his eyes watching Cora getting bigger with Huck's baby, I think he's got the urge to be a daddy, not just an uncle."

"The mac truck analogy that Daddy, Beau and Huck said, makes total sense now. Don't say anything to piss off my woman," I warn, as I walk around the truck, climb back into my car and then pull onto the road after Bay and follow them back to garage.

My mind is spinning at a hundred miles an hour as we drive the short distance into town to my brothers' shop. Penn and Bay love restoring classic cars, as well as maintaining the town's mixture of new and ancient vehicles. When Bay backs Alice's RV into the building, the shit heap of a RV doesn't look too out of place next to Winston Jones' farm truck and his wife's Cadillac, which are both in for their yearly service.

When Bay kills the engine on the tow, his door opens and he frowns at me as he moves to unhook the RV so he can move the tow truck round the back of the shop and out of the way.

"What's up?" I ask as I close the distance between us.

"She's not much of a talker, is she? I asked her a few questions and she barely muttered two words to me."

"Tell me you weren't a dick to her," I snarl.

"I wasn't a dick, I just asked her how long she'd had the RV and where she was headed. You sure she's the one? She's pretty, but she's not exactly a chatty Cathy."

"Yes, I'm sure. Ever thought she's just shy?"

He shrugs. "I mean there's shy and there's non-communicative."

"So she doesn't want to answer a load of questions from a stranger, that's not that weird. We're just used to women we meet having known us or at least known of us all our lives. Alice isn't from here, she's probably terrified."

Walking away from Bay before he has a chance to respond, I circle the truck just as Alice is closing the door behind her, her purse clutched to her chest, her eyes downcast and still filled with a sadness that I wish I knew how to eradicate.

"So it's gonna take a little while for Bay to look over your RV, did you want to come grab some lunch with me?"

She lifts her eyes to me, purses her lips, then shakes her head. "I can just wait here, you don't need to entertain me."

"You've still got to eat though, I mean it's lunchtime, and there's a great little diner just around the corner, I'd enjoy having some company," I coax, frantically trying to force down the caveman urge that's telling me to just throw her over my shoulder and take her home with me.

"Don't you have to go to work?"

Her voice is sweet and low, but I get the feeling she's making it sound deliberately monotone, like she doesn't want to sound too interested.

"Nope, joys of running my own business, I can set my own hours. Come on, let's go eat, I'm starving." Placing my palm flat against the base of her spine, I guide her forward, not giving her a chance to deliver the rejection to my invite that I can see on the edge of her lips.

She freezes beneath my touch but I don't move my hand. I want her to get used to me touching her, I want her to want it, to crave it, and that will only come once she gets used to me being around. There's plenty of people on the sidewalk as I lead her toward Granny Annie's diner, and despite us not being alone she doesn't relax, her back taut and ramrod straight even as I push open the door to the diner and let her walk in first.

Annie waves at me from behind the counter, I come into the diner at least a couple of times a week, and Annie was my mama's friend so she's known me and my brothers literally our entire lives.

"Granger, take that booth over there, Tasha will be out in just a minute to bring you some coffee."

"Thanks Annie," I call, replacing my hand on Alice's back as I propel her toward a small booth in the middle of the busy restaurant. I gesture for Alice to slide into one side of the booth and I sit opposite her, hating that I'm no longer able to touch her, but glad that I can look her in the face from here.

"Hey Granger," Tasha our waitress says, pushing

the loose strands of dark hair that have fallen from her tight bun behind her ears as she pulls out two menu's from beneath her arm and hands one to Alice then one to me. Turning the coffee cups that are already set up on the table the right way up, she immediately fills mine. "Coffee?" she asks Alice.

"No, thank you, could I just get some water please?" Alice asks in her soft, quiet voice.

"Sure thing, you take a look at the menu and I'll be right out with your drink," Tasha says, flashing Alice a big motherly smile, touching her shoulder as she leaves.

"Not a coffee drinker?"

Shrugging, she lifts the menu in front of her, effectively blocking her from my view.

There's something adorably childish about the action and I smile at the menu, leaning back in my seat and watching her, waiting for her to drop the cover and see me sitting here staring at her. I wish I knew her better, or at all, then I'd know how to go about making her mine in every way possible. She's skittish, that much is obvious and I don't want to scare her off, even if my brother is currently holding her getaway vehicle hostage.

"Here you go, sweetie," Tasha says, reappearing at the side of the table and placing a large glass of ice water in front of Alice. "You 'bout ready to order?"

I wait as my girl slowly emerges from behind her menu

shield. "I'll have a ham and mustard on rye please, with a side of fries."

Tasha nods then turns to me. "Granger?"

"Chili cheese burger, extra fries, extra onion rings please."

"Any more drinks?"

Both Alice and I shake our heads and Tasha nods, scribbling down on her little pad before taking our menus and scurrying away, taking an order from another table on her way to the kitchen.

"So, you never finished telling me where you're from," I say, lifting my coffee mug and taking a sip.

"All over really."

I wait for her to expand, but she doesn't and her gaze drops to her hands as she picks at the napkin in front of her.

"So where were you last?"

"Vermont."

"You drove that RV from Vermont to Montana?" I ask incredulous.

"Yes."

Another one-word answer. It's starting to drive me a little crazy.

"What were you doing in Vermont?

"I was working as a walking guide showing the tourists the fall leaves."

"Is that what you're hoping to do up in Big Mountain?"

"No, in winter I usually look for work at one of the resorts."

I try not to look too shocked, even though I think that's the longest sentence she's said to me so far. "Were you in Vermont long?"

She shakes her head. "About three months."

"And before Vermont?"

"I was in the Hampton's for the summer, working as a waitress."

"Is that where you're from then?"

"No, I was just there for the summer."

"So where's home?"

For the first time, her gaze lifts and she looks as me quizzically like I've asked an odd question. "My RV."

"No, I mean home home, where your family and friends are."

"My mom lives in Missouri with her husband, my sister lives in West Virginia with her boyfriend and I'm not sure where my dad is, I haven't seen him since I was a kid."

An ache blooms in my chest for the beautiful woman in front of me. She's telling me where her family live, but it's clear she doesn't consider any of those places as home. Does she not have a home? Does she just move aimlessly from place to place living out of a beat up RV with nowhere permanent to put down roots? The thought sickens me. I know not everyone lives in the town they were born in, but Rockhead Point is my home and I can't ever imagine wanting to be anywhere else. Everything I love is here and even though I went away to college, I never felt settled until I was back here and surrounded by my family.

"So, The Hamptons in the summer, Vermont in fall and Montana in winter, what about spring?"

"Spring, I usually just pick a small city halfway between where I've been for the winter and where I plan to go in summer and take whatever job I can find, usually bar work, occasionally in a factory or office, I'm not picky, work's work."

"How long have you been living like that? Moving every few months?"

She shrugs again, and I'm starting to hate that dismissive little gesture. "Five years, I guess. I don't mind moving around, I'll be on my way again as soon as your brother figures out what's wrong with my RV this time."

"This time?"

She laughs and it's the first real, honest sound she's made. Her laugh is nothing like her deliberately toned down voice. It's high and free and real, and my dick twitches in my pants just from the sound.

"The engine's pretty much shot, but I just keep getting it fixed and it keeps plodding along. I don't actually know what I'll do once it dies for good."

I part my lips to speak just as Tasha arrives with our food. Placing it in front of us, she checks we're good, then leaves to tend to the rest of her customers. "You could always get a job here, we're not as big a ski town as Big Mountain, but we have plenty of tourists up here in the winter and I could ask around to see if there's any jobs going."

She shakes her head so fast I worry she's going to give herself whiplash. "No. No, that's fine, as soon as my RV's fixed, I'll be leaving."

A ball of fear and anger lodges in the center of my chest. She can't leave, if she does I might never see her again, and now I know she exists there'll never be anyone for me but her. When she tentatively starts to eat, I slide my cell from my pocket and type out a message to Bay.

Me

I don't care what you have to do, make sure that RV won't run. I can't let her leave.

Lifting my burger, I take a bite, not reacting when my cell buzzes beside me. After a moment, I place my burger back on the plate, wipe my fingers on a napkin, then open my cell, smiling as I read his reply.

Bay

> Not a problem, engine's fucked
> anyway, could have done a temporary
> fix to get her going again, but no
> saying how long it would hold.
> Best she stay in town and I'll do a
> complete overhaul on it.
> Could take months ☺

A sigh of relief slips past my lips, and I hide it by taking a drink of my coffee. Glancing over at her, I notice she's picking at her food, playing with it more than eating it. "Is your food okay?"

"It's fine thanks."

We fall into a thick silence that seems to become more dense with every minute that passes. "So, Alice, what's your surname?"

"Lowe."

"How old are you?"

"Twenty-Three"

One word answers again, either she really has zero interest in speaking to me, or she's forgotten how to have a conversation. I know we just met, but I want her to have some interest in me and right now, it's pretty obvious she'd be as happy to sit here alone as she would to have me for company.

We eat the rest of our lunch in relative quiet, I ask occasional questions and she answers them with as little information as she can possibly give.

"Are you on the run from the police?" I blurt, wishing I could swallow the words back the moment I say them.

"What? No. Of course I'm not, why on earth would you think that?" she gasps, her voice showing a little more animation than it has up to now.

"Well, you're just not exactly engaging. I've only asked you basic questions and you've given me almost nothing."

"I'm being polite, it's weird to bombard people with your entire life story the moment you meet them," she says, her voice back to the monotone mousiness of before.

"I'd rather have your life story," I say eagerly.

"Why?" Her eyes lift and there's a genuine curiosity and confusion in her expression, like it's odd to her that someone would show real interest in her.

"Because I want to know you better."

Her lips part, but no words come out.

"So, Alice Lowe, from everywhere and nowhere in particular, tell me about you."

THREE

ALICE

Granger is staring at me like I'm the most fascinating person in the world, and I don't know why. This close, without the safety of a car door between us, he seems almost dangerous. There's an intensity to him that's both terrifying and achingly familiar, even though I know I've never met him before today.

Normally, it's easy to distance myself from others. They ask the basic questions to be polite and that's where any association ends. They recognize me as the type of person not worth knowing and I don't ever force my company on people who so obviously don't want it.

But Granger is different. I don't remember the last

time I didn't eat alone, but he basically forced me to go to lunch with him and I can still feel the residue of the heat from his touch on my back. He hasn't stopped asking me questions since the moment we sat down, and for the first time in years, I'm almost tempted to really talk to someone. I won't, because I hate the moment when someone regrets being nice to me and I never want to see that look on Granger's face, but it's nice to be tempted.

He's waiting expectantly for me to speak, but I have no idea what he wants me to say.

"How about I tell you a little about me," he smiles. "My name is Granger Barnett, which you know. I'm thirty-five years old, my birthday is February 12th, I own my own carpentry business building bespoke furniture. I have six brothers and two sisters. Both my parents have passed away and I live right here in Rockhead Point, about half way up the mountain in a big ole house my daddy built for my mama when they first got married. I'm single, I share that big ole house with my whole family and I'd really like to take you out tonight on a date."

Gob smacked, I let my mouth fall open as I sit and stare at him.

"Your turn," he says with a smug grin.

"I'm not that interesting."

"I'll be the judge of that. You know loads about me now, it's only fair that you give me equal amounts of stuff about you."

"Alice Lowe, twenty-three, June 2nd, I already told you about my family. I was born in Pennsylvania and now I move from place to place with the seasons."

"And the date?" he asks, smiling.

"I'm hoping to be on my way to Big Mountain by then."

The smile doesn't fall from his lips. "But if you're not, I can take you out?"

"Maybe we should get back and check on your brother and my RV."

"Finish your food and then we'll go, no rush."

Looking down at my plate, I realize I've hardly eaten anything. A warmth bursts to life in my chest, but I tamp it down. Granger doesn't care about me, he's just being polite. I Lift my sandwich and finish it as quickly as I can, not really tasting it as I remind myself over and over that he's just a nice man, that he'd do this for anyone, that nothing about me is the cause of his behavior. People can't like me, because I'm not likeable.

"I'll be right back," he says, pushing up from the table and heading toward the counter. I force myself not to stare after him like a fool and instead take a sip of my water, running my finger over the condensation that's pooled on the side of the glass.

Most people struggle to sit alone in a restaurant,

needing their cell phones to act as a buffer between them and the loneliness of their own company, but not me, being alone is one of the things I'm truly exceptional at.

"You ready?" Granger asks when he slides into the seat opposite me again.

"Yep. Just need to get the bill."

"I already paid it."

"What? Well how much was mine?"

"My treat."

"I can pay my own way, I don't need you to buy my food."

Instead of answering, Granger stands, and blocks my exit, holding his hand out for me to take. I stare at it, then up at him. "I can get up on my own and I want to pay for my lunch."

"And I said, it was my treat. Now take my hand so we can go." His tone is stern, but not angry. I comply because he told me to and for some reason, that feels completely right.

Lifting my hand, I place it in his outstretched one and the moment my skin touches him, he closes his grip around me and gently urges me to stand. I expect him to release his hold on me once I'm up, but he doesn't, instead he takes the lead and tows me along behind him through the maze of tables and out onto the sidewalk.

Once we're outside I tug my hand, but instead of

relinquishing me, his grip tightens as he slows to walk at my pace, my hand still held tightly in his. Glancing down, I furrow my brow, not sure what to make of him and his desire to hold my hand. The last time I did this with anyone was when I was a kid and Serenity would walk me to the bus stop. She'd hold my hand all the way down the street until we got on the bus, then she'd sit by my side while the bus went to my school, dropping the little kids off before it went to the middle school for the older ones.

Something about Granger's hold on me feels familiar to the safety and security I always felt when my sister was there, and I have to fight my natural urge to enjoy being protected by him. Granger isn't looking to protect me. I have no idea what he wants with me, but it's definitely not the responsibility of someone who can so easily become completely dependent on anyone who shows an ounce of interest in her.

I'm not completely naïve, men have wanted to have sex with me before, and twice, I've let them. On both occasions, I instantly became overly clingy and needy before the sweat had even cooled and knowing who I am and how I behave, I decided that sex wasn't for me. I have a vibrator for when I need it, which honestly isn't that often, apparently my personality issues also come with almost zero sex drive.

I try in vain to tug my hand free, but a scathing glare

from Granger stills my movements and I turn my attention forward, forcing myself not to overthink his probably innocent touch. I'm grateful when he doesn't try to speak to me on the short walk to his brother's garage, we've spent almost an hour together now and that's about the amount of time I'm tolerable to other people. From now on, he'll start to figure out who I am and his attention will disappear just as fast as it appeared.

When we get to the garage, Bay and another man are leaning into the engine bay of the RV, talking between themselves as they reach in and touch parts of the engine.

"Hey," Granger says, announcing our arrival.

Both men straighten and emerge from beneath the hood, stepping away from my home on wheels and crossing the asphalt to come toward us.

"Alice, this is my other brother Penn, Penn this is Alice Lowe, the owner of this here RV."

"Nice to meet you, Alice."

"You too," I say quietly, wishing Granger would let go of my hand now we're here with his family.

"Bay and I were just talking about this beast," Penn says, slapping his hand against the side of the RV.

"What's the prognosis?" I ask.

"Alternator and starter have gone, timing belt needs changing, your radiator's been patched so many times it's almost completely made of aluminum foil, and the gear box is on its last legs," Penn says apologetically, glancing between his brothers as he gives me the bad news.

"How much do you think it would cost to fix all that?"

"More than it would to put in a reconditioned engine."

"Damn," I sigh, not resisting when Granger reels me into him, releasing my hand to wrap a comforting arm around my shoulders.

"Far as we can see, you've got a couple of options. We can try and source all the replacement parts, or we can try to find you a whole new engine," Bay says, his eyes sympathetic.

Sighing, I reluctantly nod. "The last time I had it patched up they warned me it wouldn't last too much longer, but I hoped it'd at least get me to Big Mountain where I could park it up on a campsite for the winter."

"Can you afford to have it fixed?" Granger asks me quietly.

"Yeah, I just don't want to end up spending more money fixing it up than it's worth. It might be time to think about replacing it."

Granger tenses beside me and I turn to look at him, wondering what I said or did to make him uncomfortable.

"Why don't you let Bay and Penn find out how much the repairs or a new engine would cost first, before you make any big decisions."

I nod and Granger relaxes. "Do you need to keep the

RV here or could you tow it to a local campsite for me? I don't need the engine to run to sleep in it."

The men seem to have a silent conversation before Granger speaks. "Why don't you stay with us for a few days, it's the Snow bunny festival this weekend and the campsite and hotels will have been booked solid for months in advance, on a count of all the visitors that come to watch the mountain open for the season.

"I'm sure I can find somewhere," I say, a little panicked.

"Not this weekend. We've got a spare room and if our sisters find out we've let you stay in this RV without heat or lights, they'll skin us alive." Bay laughs.

"That's very sweet but I couldn't—"

"Come on, Cora's at work, I'll take you over to meet her now," Granger says, steering me away from the garage, his brothers and my RV before I have a chance to argue.

"Granger," I start.

"You're gonna love Cora, she's a bit full on, actually more than a bit full on since she got pregnant, but she's a great girl," he says, as he guides me up the sidewalk, his arm still wrapped around me, holding me in a firm but gentle one-armed embrace.

My feet start to slow as I plan my escape, the excuse to get away from him and find a hotel to hold up in for a few days already formed on my lips, but before I get a chance, he's holding open a door to a clothing store and ushering me inside.

A stunning red head is behind the counter, chatting happily to a customer, but when she spots Granger, she practically shoves the clothing bag at the person she's serving in her rush to dart around the counter. Bouncing over to us, her beachball pregnant belly protruding from her shirt makes it pretty obvious that this is the sister Cora he was talking about.

"Granger, the crib," she shouts, throwing her arms around his neck.

"You like it?" he asks softly.

"I love it. It's so perfect, thank you, thank you so much."

"You're welcome. Cora, I'd like you to meet someone. This is Alice Lowe, and she's going to be staying up at the house with us."

Cora's eyes widen as she steps back from Granger and turns her gaze in my direction. "She's staying at our house?"

"Yes," Granger nods, his expression calm.

Cora's eyes widen and her lips form into an O shape before she practically launches herself at me. "Oh my god, Alice, it's so nice to meet you. Are you from Rockhead Point? I don't recognize you, but I mean I don't know everyone. So how long have you and Granger known each other?"

"We just met today and no, I'm just passing through, Granger stopped to help when my RV broke down."

Cora's smile never wavers as she looks between me and Granger, her eyes landing on his arm over my shoulder.

"What time are you finishing today?" Granger asks her.

Lifting her wrist, she glances at her watch. "In an hour, Huck's insisting he get off work to come pick me up. I told him I can just hang out with Bonnie or at my mom's, but since he put this baby in my belly he thinks I suddenly became incapable of coping a minute without him," she laughs, rolling her eyes dramatically.

"I'll give him a call, tell him I'll give you a ride home, Alice just needs to pack a bag and then I'm taking her to get settled too."

Cora's smile becomes shrewd and she sidles over to me, looping her arm through mine. "This is awesome, Bonnie is going to be so excited to meet you. We're so outnumbered with all the testosterone at home, with all the guys, plus the construction crew. Having another girl around to even the numbers a little is just perfect. I'll call Huck and tell him you're going to take me home while you go help Alice pack."

Releasing me, her cell is out of her pocket and at her

ear a moment later as I stare after her, a little too shocked to do anything but gawp.

"Let's go get some of your stuff and then we can come back and pick Cora up," Granger says, herding me back out of the store and toward the garage again.

"Look..." I start.

"I can see you want to argue, but honestly, honey, it's not going to work. This is a small town packed full of good old-fashioned values. There's no way we're gonna let you stay in an RV with no power or heat when it's cold and dark out and you're in an unfamiliar place. In normal circumstances, I'd happily help you find a hotel, but you picked the one weekend in the winter months here in Rockhead Point where every hotel, motel, guest house and campsite will be fully booked because of the festival. Now we have space at our house and I assure you, you're one hundred percent safe with me and my family, hell, I'll even take you to the sheriff's office and have them vouch for me if that'll put your mind at ease. But there's not a single scenario in the whole goddamn world that I'd allow you to put yourself at risk when I know I can help and keep you safe."

He's not shouting, but the tone of his voice and the stern expression on his face has me swallowing down my argument and nodding my agreement.

"Good, now shall we go to the sheriff's office?"

I take a moment to consider, then nod again. Truthfully, I don't feel in any danger in Granger's company now, but better he think I don't trust him. That way he won't want to get to know me and I won't have to watch that like turn to loathe, just like it always does.

Instead of being annoyed, he nods, smiling brightly. "Good girl, you don't know me, best to be safe before you put yourself at risk."

His words almost sound like praise, but that can't be right. Why would he praise me for not trusting that he doesn't want to hurt me?

Reaching for my hand, he weaves his fingers with mine, holding tight and stopping me from pulling free as he turns us in the opposite direction and starts to lead me away. He doesn't bother speaking as we walk down the busy sidewalk, eventually reaching an ugly squat building with a sign above the door declaring itself as Rockhead Point Sheriff's office.

Granger holds open the door for me and I step inside, His grip on me is sure and unrelenting, his fingers warm and oddly reassuring. I should be appalled at his touch, at allowing him to break so many of my rules, so why do I suddenly want him to twirl me, to pull me into his arms and dip me while his lips find mine? What the hell is happening? How is this complete stranger breaking all of my rules about staying aloof?

"Hey Granger, how's it going? Is everything okay?" a guy in a deputy's uniform asks, getting up from an office desk and making his way over to the wooden counter that divides the space.

"Hi Cam, this here is Alice Lowe, her RV broke down and with the festival being this weekend and the town fit to burst with tourists, she's gonna come stay at our place. I suggested she come over here to the sheriff's office so you can vouch for her safety in my home," Granger says casually, like having to prove he's not a dangerous rapist or murderer is a completely normal thing for him.

Cam's eyes take me in, his gaze running over me as his lips twitch into a warm smile. "Nice to meet you, Miss Alice. I'm deputy Cameron Cunningham and I can one hundred percent vouch for Granger and the rest of his family, you'll be safe there, but if you'd prefer, I've got a spare bedroom in my apartment that you'd be welcome to use."

The noise that comes from Granger sounds almost like a growl, but I must have misheard, because why would he be growling? That's a possessive thing, right?

"She's staying with me," Granger says, dragging me slightly behind him, hiding me from the other man's gaze.

Cam laughs loudly, slapping his palm against the wood of the counter. "Well, I'll be damned."

Confused, I try to step around Granger, but he blocks

me, pulling me into his back and almost pinning me in place, the warmth of his body surprising me.

"Miss Alice, I promise you, you're safe and if you have any problems just call me." There's a shuffling of paper and when I peer around Granger's huge frame, the deputy is pushing a small business card to the edge of the counter.

Granger picks it up, then hands it to me. As I take it, he twists, effectively pushing me ahead of him as he ushers us both out of the building and onto the street again. "Granger," I say, trying to drag my hand free as he moves to my side and marches at a too fast a pace for me to keep up with. "Granger, stop, you're going too fast."

He immediately slows his pace, but he doesn't turn to look at me, or speak, his jaw clenched tightly, his hold on me a little too firm. We make it back to the garage in a couple of minutes and he finally releases me when we're beside my RV. "Pack your stuff, do you need me to get you a packing box?"

"I'll just grab a change of clothes, hopefully your brothers will be able to fix my RV quickly."

"No, I'll get you some boxes, pack up all your clothes, with no heat they'll get damp pretty quick," Granger says sternly.

Opening the back doors, I step up into the RV and drop to my knees, lifting the bench seat to get to my small collection of clothes. My life is simple, and storage space in my compact RV is scarce, so I don't really have too much and his suggestion that I'll need boxes to pack up all my stuff is almost laughable. Grabbing my old duffle that I brought with me from my mom and Bob's place, I stuff all my clothes inside, then grab the charger for my cellphone, my ID, the paperback I'm in the middle of reading, my toiletries bag and finally my bunny stuffy I've had since I was a kid. It's kind of pathetic that almost all my worldly possessions fit into one bag, but when you live a nomadic lifestyle, you don't have time or space to worry about nonessential belongings.

Granger comes back out of the garage carrying two huge cardboard boxes, but he pauses when he sees me sat of the step of the RV with my duffle at my feet. "I've got these two, I can go get some more boxes if these aren't enough."

"I'm packed," I say motioning to my bag.

"I told you, *all* your clothes, honey."

Dipping my chin, I point to the bag again.

His eyes narrow and his lips spread into a hard line. "That's not all your clothes."

"I live in an RV, I travel light, this is all my clothes," I say quietly, not quite able to lift my eyes to his again.

"What about other important stuff? We live about twenty minutes out of town, obviously we can come back for anything you've forgotten, but it's not a quick journey."

"I have everything I'll need," I say again, suddenly realizing how much time and attention he's giving me. My eyes lift and I enjoy the way he's watching me, and I see what looks to be genuine concern on his face.

Somehow this gorgeous stranger is interested in me and even though I know it won't last, I can't help but want to bask in his attention while I can. I'm so used to pushing people away before they become sick of me, that I don't remember the last time I spent this long in anyone's company when I haven't been forced on them for a job. It's as nice as it is unnerving, especially because Granger seems to be one of those tactile people, always touching me, holding my hand or putting his arm around me. I'd never admit it, but I love the contact, the way it feels to have his fingers entwined with mine, the weight of his arm over my shoulder, it's addicting, especially from him.

His eyes move from me, to the clean and relatively empty RV behind me. "Is all your stuff hidden in the cupboards?"

"Kitchen stuff is stored beneath the little hotplate, cleaning stuff beneath the sink. I keep my clothes beneath the bench seat and other than some books, there's not much else in here. I don't need much."

"What about a tv or a laptop or iPad or whatever?"

"I don't have any of those things."

His lips purse again and he stiffens, as if the idea of me not having what most people consider normal, essential devises, is inconceivable.

"Most places I stay don't have Wi-Fi and I've never really watched a lot of tv. My life is quiet, I work, I read, that's about it," I confess, not realizing how pathetic that sounds until the words are out of my mouth.

"Come on, I'll put your stuff in the car, then we can go get Cora, she should be about done now," he says, his voice gruff and low.

Standing, I close the door to the RV behind me, pushing down the lock as I hold the handle and click the lock into place. It feels strange to be leaving it behind and knowing I won't be sleeping in my lumpy fold out bed tonight, the place I've slept every night for the last five years, and a wave of melancholy hits that I don't expect. I've thought about scrapping the bag of crap before, but now given that the engine is shot it's more of a reality than ever, and that makes me more sad than I'm prepared to admit, even to myself. This RV, as shitty as it is, is the last link to my family. My dad bought it, my mom moved us across the country in it more than once, and my sister used it to drive me to school and back for years when the house we lived in wasn't on the school bus route. If the RV goes, I'll have nothing that ties me to them anymore.

Granger picks up the duffel with one hand and

entwines our fingers together with the other, leading me to his car where he puts my stuff in the trunk. "Jump in, we'll drive over to Cora's store," he orders softly, opening the passenger door for me and then leaning in to buckle the seatbelt once I'm sitting down.

Closing the door, he circles the car and I wrinkle my nose in confusion. Why isn't he annoyed with me yet? Maybe he's just a really, really nice, patient person, but still, he should be starting to get pissed with me by now. Only Granger isn't showing any of the normal signs I'd expect from someone after spending a couple of hours in my company.

I almost ask him why he's still being nice, but swallow down the words as he opens the driver's door and climbs in beside me. I've tried asking people what about me makes me so dislikeable in the past and it never ends well, there's no way I'm going to ask him why he can still tolerate me, that's even more ridiculous.

The drive to Cora's store takes less than a minute and she bounds out of the door and climbs into the car before Granger can even release his seatbelt. "Huck says thank you for giving me a ride, but that he's coming home anyway because he wants to meet Alice," Cora says the moment her butt hits the back seat.

"Are you okay back there? You should sit up front," I suggest, eager to put a little distance between me and this confounding man.

"I'm fine, I've got plenty of room back here," she waves me off.

Granger glances back at her, then smoothly pulls away from the curb and into traffic.

"So what do you do for work?" Cora asks.

"Whatever's available," I answer.

"Do you live locally? You said you were just passing through, were you heading home?"

"I move around a lot," I say noncommittally. "I was on my way to Big Mountain."

"Oh, do you ski?"

"No."

Cora laughs lightly. "Well, this is a great place to breakdown, I've been here my whole life and I can't imagine wanting to live anywhere else."

"I'll be on my way as soon as my RV's fixed."

"Oh," she says with a frown, glancing to Granger in the rear-view mirror. "Well, I'm sure once you've spent a few days here we'll convince you to stay," she says, her voice bright and cheery again.

She spends the next twenty minutes asking me a stream of almost unrelenting questions, that I answer with my usual one word replies, but by the time we pull off the main road and onto a driveway, just like Granger, she doesn't seem annoyed or bored with me.

"Did Granger warn you that we're under construction at the moment? Please try and ignore the chaos, it's all outside at the minute and they don't plan to break through to the main house till all the wings are water tight and have all the basic amenities."

"I really would have been happy staying in my RV."

"No," Cora says a little too loudly. "No, you're better off up here warm and comfortable than in a cold RV on the side of the road somewhere."

We pull to a stop outside a huge log home, like Cora warned, there's construction work happening on both sides of the main house with construction workers all over the place. Granger slows to a stop behind a shiny black vintage looking muscle car and a huge truck. Killing the engine, he opens his door and climbs out, circling the car and opening my door before I get a chance to.

Holding out his hand to me, he waits patiently for me to take it and when I don't, he leans down and grabs mine, entwining our fingers as he gently pulls me from the car. Guiding me to the side, he closes the door behind me, then looks down at me, his eyes warm and full of something I don't recognize.

"Welcome home, Alice."

FOUR

GRANGER

The moment the words are out of my mouth, I hear how right they sound. This is her home now, here with me, I just need to figure out how to make her realize it too. I only met this woman less than three hours ago, but she's already mine beyond question. Though she's skittish and more closed off than any other person I've ever met.

On a couple of occasions, she's looked at me with these wide hopeful eyes, but in the next instant her gaze is on the floor and she's hiding, as if she's remembered she's trying her best not to engage with anyone.

I'm not a virgin, I've had more than my fair share of women, but unlike my brothers I've never felt the urge to shit where I eat and when the urge for a woman takes me, I like to go a bit further afield to find someone to entertain me for a night. I've met all kinds of women, but never has anyone intrigued me as much as she does.

Her eyes are filled with secrets and I want to know every single one. I've always enjoyed puzzles, and Alice is most definitely a puzzle I plan on solving.

Her wide, slightly horrified eyes find mine, before she quickly looks away and I know if we weren't miles away from town, she'd be trying to run right now. Her fingers are still entwined with mine and I tighten my hold a little as I turn and open Cora's door, ignoring the smug way she's looking between me and Alice with barely restrained glee. Both her and Bonnie have been looking forward to the next brother being hit by what they like to call the caveman love bug and I know she's overjoyed that Alice is here with me, even if it's not exactly the way I'd like to bring my woman home for the first time.

My teeth are already clenching with the fact that Alice isn't going to be in my bed with me tonight, that I won't be sliding between her thighs and tasting her pussy for the first time, but she's here and at least for a few days she won't be going anywhere. I know I can't keep her stranded up here forever, but at least I have the long weekend to start to convince her that she belongs to me.

She tries to pull her hand free, but I ignore her

attempts, grabbing her bag from the truck before following Cora into the house. The moment we step inside and I close the door behind us, I exhale a long, silent breath of relief. She's here, in my home with me and no matter what, unless she's married with a couple of kids squirrelled away, I never plan to let her go.

Cora walks ahead of us, dropping her purse on the kitchen counter as Huck closes the distance between him and his woman and embraces her, kissing her thoroughly as Alice and I watch.

"That's my brother Huck," I laugh. "Let me show you around."

Alice nods, but she's still watching Huck devour Cora like he hasn't seen her in years, not the couple of hours since he took her to work this morning.

"The living space is open, so kitchen, living, dining," I say, motioning to the large space. "All the doors lead off to a bedroom, I'm this one," I say pointing to the second door to the right. "And you'll be in here," I say, guiding her to the door next to mine. It leads to the room that used to be our parent's suite but hasn't really been used since Mama died. I'm thankful now that Bonnie and Cora redecorated in here last month, so at least it's bright and clean, and not full of my parents' flowery shit.

Opening the door, I lead her into the space, through the small sitting area and into the bedroom. "Are you sure it's okay for me to stay in here, this is beautiful," Alice says, taking in the room the girls painted in a warm cream, with pale pink and cream bedding and bold black and pink soft furnishings.

"Yeah, this was our parents' room, but it's mainly just been empty since our mama died years ago. It's a guest suite now, the girls completely redecorated it fairly recently and you're the first person to use it."

Reluctantly, I place her bag on the bed and then try to think of an excuse to stay with her, but when nothing apart from ripping off her clothes and fucking her until she understands who she belongs to comes to mind, I release her hand and take a step back. "I'll leave you to get settled and unpack, come on back into the living room once you're done, I'll give you the rest of the tour and properly introduce you to the family."

Without looking at me, she nods, gives me a polite half smile, then waits with her hands clutched together in front of her for me to leave. Walking away and leaving her is much harder than it should be, but I force my feet to move until I'm closing the door to the room behind me and fighting the urge to barge back in and take what's mine.

Huck, Cora, Beau and Bonnie are all sitting on the couch staring at me, my brothers are both looking on with sympathy, while the girls have matching expressions of amused enthusiasm.

"Sooo," Bonnie gushes, the first to speak.

"So?"

"Tell us about her."

"Her name is Alice, she's twenty-three, I met her this afternoon and she's going to be staying here," I say succinctly.

Rolling her eyes dramatically, Bonnie tips her head to the side and waits for me to elaborate.

"She yours?" Beau asks.

"Yep," I nod.

"She gonna have a problem with that?"

"I have absolutely no idea, I've never met anyone so closed off who hides everything the way my Alice does."

"Your Alice," Cora sighs sweetly.

"I have no idea what the hell I'm going to do," I admit, crossing the room and sitting down on the coffee table in front of the two couples. "She barely speaks, answers every question with one word or the absolute minimum she can say. She tries not to look at me, even though when she does I can see she knows there's something between us. She acts like she's either on the run or hiding from something, but she doesn't seem scared, more like she's so used to being distant she's forgotten how not to be."

"Where does she live? How long do you have before she wants to go home?" Huck asks.

"From what little I've managed to pry out of her, she doesn't really have a home, she moves with the seasons, finding temporary jobs doing whatever's needed. She was headed up to Big Mountain hoping to get a job in one of the resorts when she broke down. She lives in her shitty RV, but when I asked if she could afford to get it repaired, she said she could without thinking about it, even said she might have to buy a new RV instead, so I don't think it's a money thing."

"What about her family?" Bonnie asks.

"Mom and step-dad live in Missouri, sister lives in west Virginia, hasn't seen her dad since she was a kid, I get the impression they aren't close. I think she's all alone."

"Oh no," Cora says, her eyes welling with tears.

"Calm down, Peaches, she's not alone anymore," Huck coos, pulling her into his lap and wrapping his arms around her. Since Cora got pregnant, she has been an emotional mess, all films and shows have been banned from the living room tv unless they're comedies, because everything else makes her cry... and every time she cries, Huck loses his shit.

"You need to woo her," Cora says, her voice full of emotion.

"I'm a fucking man, Cora, I don't woo," I say.

"Well, the caveman bullshit your brothers used on us won't work on someone who will barely look at you,"

Bonnie says pointedly. "Try using that *Mine* crap on her and watch her run as quick as she can away from you."

"Where's she going to go?" I ask arrogantly. "We're halfway up a fucking mountain and she's got no car and no way of leaving. She's mine and I won't let her go."

"Kidnap isn't okay," Cora and Bonnie say in unison.

"Worked for me," Huck mutters beneath his breath.

Cora's eyes turn glacial and she slowly turns to glare at her fiancé. "Kidnapping is not okay. You're lucky that I was already in love with you at that point else I'd have stabbed you in your sleep and then had you arrested when I called the cops."

Instead of looking even remotely concerned, my brother grabs his woman's chin with his fingers and snarls, "Mine," before kissing her roughly.

Rolling my eyes, I ignore the PDA and look to Beau and his wife. "It's not kidnapping if she's here already."

"Why don't you try spending some time with her, get to know her," Bonnie suggests.

"Claim her, she'll be putty in your hands, that's why we only fall for one woman, so when we do they're unable to resist, because we're all in from moment one. Alice will be the same, just show her how much she's already yours," Beau tells me, his low, confident voice making complete sense to the caveman that apparently lives inside of me.

My eyes go to the door behind my siblings and the

almost overwhelming need to go to her, to touch her, to claim her, to own her; hits me like a freight train. Having her here but not being able to touch her feels like torture, but as much as what Beau said feels right, if Alice freaks out and runs, I might never see her again. Unlike Bonnie and Cora, Alice has no ties to Rockhead point, she's only passing through and if she leaves, I don't even have a direction to chase her in.

Somehow, I need to find a way to satisfy my baser urges to claim her while not scaring the hell out of her, but also not letting her leave.

Huck and Cora come up for air, and start making suggestions that range between me barging my way into the room she's staying in and making her come until she's unable to live without the orgasms I give her, and leaving her alone tonight to give her a chance to get used to being here and feeling comfortable.

Honestly, I prefer the orgasm idea, but considering I'm a complete stranger, I'm not sure Alice would be as onboard. Throughout the entire conversation, my eyes stay fixed on her door that's still closed and I imagine what she's doing in there. It's been over half an hour now, more than enough time for her to unpack and freshen up, but she's still in there.

A wave of panic washes over me when I wonder if she's run, if she's climbed out the window and ran away, until I remember that it's cold and we live in the middle of nowhere. Fleeing isn't an option even if she wanted to.

The front door opens and Cody and Teddy walk in looking windswept, both of them in workwear. "Hey," I call, "Come sit down, I need to talk to you guys."

Cody takes one look at me and starts to laugh. "Oh fuck, you too?"

Teddy smiles, but manages not to laugh as they both drop down onto the couch. "So, who is she? Is she at least legal? Cora and Bonnie are practically babies. Let me guess, yours is a senior in high school," Cody mocks.

"Shut up, asshole. Her name's Alice and she's twenty-three. She's here, in Mama's old room, she's gonna be staying with us."

Cody's eyes widen and his mouth falls open. "Do we know her? Is she from town?"

"No, you don't know her and no she's not from town," I say tersely, not sure why his questions are pissing me off when I'd be asking the exact same thing if he were in my position.

"She was on her way to Big Mountain for work when her RV broke down today, Granger stopped to help, she's his, so she's here," Beau says succinctly.

"Fuck," Teddy laughs. "That's fast work, even for one of us. You only met her today and she's moved in already," he laughs, whistling.

"It's not like that… yet," I snarl, forcing the words from my lips and hating that it's true when all I want is to own her completely.

"Oh," Teddy says, his expression turning serious. "So…?"

"So don't do anything to fuck this up, I just need to make her understand. She's skittish, a real flight risk until I get things straightened out with her," I confess.

"So, what you're saying is that she has no fucking clue that she's here because you plan to marry her?" Cody laughs, still clearly amused despite how serious everyone else has become.

"She's mine, she won't be leaving. She just doesn't know it yet," I tell him, meaning every single word.

FIVE

ALICE

I walk to the door, pause, then turn around and scurry back to sit on the bed again, it's the fifth time I've done the same thing but somehow, I can't convince myself to actually open the door and leave this room. Granger's on the other side and I feel this need to be close to him, even though the more time I spend with him, the sooner he'll be sick of me. A part of me must be a closet masochist because I still want to go to him even knowing I'll see that look in his eyes, the same look I've seen a million times in my life.

He's gorgeous and nice and I don't know what to do with that. I'm not a virgin, I let a guy take me out on a date and then take my virginity in the back seat of his car when I was a junior in high school. Back then, I thought that maybe giving him what he wanted would make him like me for longer than it usually takes for people to realize how toxic I am, but sex actually had the opposite affect and I'd barely pulled my panties back on before he was driving me home and telling me he didn't think we were gonna work out. The second time I picked a guy to have sex with worked out the same way. I even tried a woman once, but despite her kisses being nice, I couldn't get sexually aroused enough to make it fun. Turns out, not being able to get wet makes women hate you almost as quickly as having actual sex with a guy.

No, my dating track record is pitiful and it's been nearly two years since I've even bothered to look at a guy. Being celibate doesn't really bother me, and generally I'm happier alone. Constantly trying to make people like me is exhausting, especially when it never, ever works.

Getting up from the bed, I cross to the door and press my ear to the wood. I can hear the muffled sounds of voices, but not clearly enough to be able to make out what they're saying. This time I don't rush back to the bed, I slowly retreat, knowing that more than likely they're discussing how to get rid of the stranger in their home. Cora is probably telling them how awful I am, and questioning Granger as to why he insisted on bringing me home.

A knock on the door makes me jump and I grip the comforter I'm sitting on tightly beneath my fingers. For a second, I contemplate lying down on the bed and pretending to be asleep, but before I can move, the door inches open and Granger's handsome face peers around the edge.

"Hey," he says when he sees me sitting on the bed.

"Hi."

"Is everything okay? Do you need anything? Is the room okay?"

"The room's beautiful," I say quietly, focusing my attention on my hands on the bed and not on him.

"I thought I said to come back out once you were settled?" His words are a statement disguised as a question. We both know he told me to come out to the living room, and now he's found me just sitting here, we both know that I've ignored his suggestion and stayed hidden, but I'm hoping he's too polite to call me out on my cowardice.

"Come on, most of my family apart from Bay and Penn, who you've already met, are home, they're excited to meet you," he says, suddenly sounding much closer and when I look up, he's standing beside me, really close as his hand lifts mine from the comforter and he entwines our fingers together, tugging me gently up from the bed.

"I—"

"I swear they're not all like Cora," he laughs, deflecting my attempt at arguing as he tows me effortlessly from the room, his thumb rubbing circles on my hand like he's trying to reassure me.

He opens the door for us and I turn my head and stare wistfully behind me at the sanctuary the beautiful room had afforded me, as he leads me into the living space and toward the group of people on the sofa, all watching me expectantly.

Granger tows me around a huge corner couch and drags me to sit right next to him on the other side, facing the five unfamiliar faces that are staring back at me. In normal circumstances, I'd be concerned about the fact that Granger is sitting so close I'm practically pressed into him from my hip to my knee, our hands still tightly held together resting on his thigh, but for this moment it's reassuring being next to him when there's so many strangers staring at me.

"Okay so you know Cora, next to her is Huck, then Beau and his wife Bonnie, and this is Cody and Teddy," he says, pointing to each person in turn. "Everyone, this is Alice," he says magnanimously.

All six faces are smiling back at me and I try to return the gesture, fighting the internal survival instinct I've built up; the one that tells me to nod politely then leave any situation where I'm forced to be around groups of friends. "Hi," I say dumbly.

The two younger guys both smirk at me and I feel myself shrink back a little, only to find Granger's huge body blocking my retreat.

"It's nice to meet you, Alice," the other woman, Bonnie says, her expression open and honest, and unlike most women my age when I meet them.

"You too," I say politely. "Thank you all for offering me a place to stay, I really would have been fine in my RV but Granger kind of insisted," I say on a rush.

"There's no way we'd have let you stay alone in your RV with no power or heat," the big guy sitting with Bonnie growls menacingly.

"Hopefully my RV will be fixed soon and I'll be out of your hair. I've been considering upgrading to something newer for a while now, so it might be time to get something more reliable anyway," I mutter to no one in particular.

"So you live alone?" one of the guys asks.

"Yes."

"Is that safe?" someone else asks.

I shrug. "As safe as living anywhere alone, I imagine."

"Don't you get lonely?" Cora questions.

"No," I say, shrugging. "I've been living alone for the last five years, I prefer it," I lie. I don't prefer it, but it's better than forcing yourself on people who don't like you and feel obliged to tolerate you.

"Wow, I couldn't imagine living alone, I lived in a house with three other people in college and I hated it because it was too quiet," the youngest looking brother laughs.

One of the other brothers jumps up from the couch and heads to the refrigerator. "Beer, Alice? Or we have fruity wine cooler things, soda, juice and water."

"A beer is great, thanks," I say politely. He grabs bottles out and quickly returns to the couch, handing a bottle of juice to Cora, then beers to me and Bonnie, before he throws bottles to his brothers and settles back into his spot again.

I try to pull my hand free from Granger's, but instead of releasing me, he takes my bottle from me, opens it with one hand then hands it back to me with a wink.

"So, Granger tells us you were on your way up to Big Mountain for a job? What do you normally do up there?" The big guy beside Bonnie asks, his tone gruff as he pulls Bonnie onto his lap and she immediately snuggles into him.

I shrug again. "The resorts normally take on seasonal staff during ski season, waitresses, maids, sometimes reception staff. I'll do whatever, I'm not picky, work is work."

"You ever done any office stuff, answering the phone,

filing, that kind of thing?" he asks.

"Yeah," I say elongating the word, unsure where he's going with this.

"Well, the woman who does all my paperwork quit last week so she could go on tour with her waste of space husband, and I was gonna advertise her job but this works out perfectly," big guy says.

"What works out?" I ask stupidly.

"You're looking for a job, I have a job available."

"Oh, Beau, that's such a good idea," Bonnie says happily. "He was trying to get me to quit my job and go work for him, but now you're here I don't have to," she laughs, slapping the guy who I now know is Beau on the chest playfully.

"You're quitting that job the moment my baby's in your belly," he tells her, pulling her into him even closer and kissing her.

"Err, thank you for the offer, but I'm going to be leaving as soon as my RV's fixed, or as soon as I can buy a new one if mine's not fixable. I won't be here, so you'd be better looking for someone permanent."

"How long were you planning on staying in Big Mountain?" Beau asks.

"Probably till the end of February, maybe March if there's a lot of snow," I say, glancing at all the others who are watching me intently as Granger sits stiffly behind me.

"So stay here and work for me till then. By that point, Marlene will probably have realized her husband is a waste of space and will have come back without him," Beau offers.

I'm shaking my head before my lips manage to form words. "I appreciate the offer but—"

"Thanks, Beau, that'd be great," Granger answers from behind me, his fingers gripping mine tightly in some kind of silent gesture that I don't understand in the least. "Alice can stay here with us for the winter, got to be better than staying in an RV at a trailer park on your own."

"Wait," I blurt, twisting around to glare at Granger.

As if sensing my anger, the guy who got the beers jumps up from the couch again. "I should get dinner started. Alice, you're not a vegan or a vegetarian or anything, are you? Any allergies or things you just hate?"

"You don't have to make me dinner," I argue.

"Nonsense, you live here, you eat here, house rules. And I'm Cody by the way, I know you had a lot of names fired at you earlier," he smiles. "So, veggie?"

"Err no, I'm not a picky eater," I say weakly.

With a wink he strides toward the kitchen area, and I wonder what he's making that would need him to start cooking now when it's barely four in the afternoon.

Cora yawns loudly and Huck scoops her off the couch. "Nap time, Peaches," he announces, as he carries her toward one of the doors that lead off the main living space, and just as quickly, Bonnie announces she wants to go check on her horse and she and Beau leave.

Again, I try to yank my hand free of Granger's hold, but instead of releasing me, he gets up from the couch and pulls me up with him.

"Granger," I say, planting my feet and trying to hold my ground.

"You obviously have something you want to say to me, I'd rather do that in private," he growls, his voice low.

I nod, because I do need to ask him why he thinks it's okay to accept a job on my behalf. I rarely get mad, but he's right, I'd rather do it in private than in front of his family, who so far have all been very nice to me.

Instead of leading me back to the room I'm staying in, he opens a different door and I find myself being led into a different bedroom, this one is masculine and almost rustic in appearance. A big bed dominates the space that looks like it's been carved out of the trunk of a tree. A gorgeous dresser is set against a wall that's painted a rich navy blue, while the other walls are a stark white that only seems to accentuate the beautiful grains in the wooden furniture.

"Is this your room?" I ask.

Nodding, he pulls me further into the room and closes the door behind us, until it's just me, him, and the huge bed. Swallowing thickly, I try to step back, but his hold on me stops me and instead he reels me in closer until barely an inch separates us.

This close, he seems even taller and I have to tip my head back to look up into his beautifully handsome face.

"You're going to take that job," he says suddenly, shocking me.

"No, I'm not."

"Yes, you are. I want to get to know you and I can't do that if you're hours away in Big Mountain. You're going to take the job for my brother, you're going to stay here in this house and you're going to be mine," he tells me a moment before his lips close over mine.

Shocked, for the longest second I do nothing, just stand there as his lips devour mine, his tongue pushing his way into my mouth as his arms surround me, holding my body tight against his. When I'm finally released from my shock induced stupor, I slap at his chest, closing my mouth and denying his kiss.

"Alice," he growls, his hand cupping my cheek and tilting me to how he wants me as he attacks my mouth again.

"No," I cry against his lips shoving at him again. "No."

He stops and reluctantly pulls back, not letting me go, but no longer trying to kiss me.

"What are you doing?" I demand.

"Kissing you," he smirks.

"Why?"

"Because I wanted to."

"That's not a good enough reason."

"How about because you're beautiful, because I can't stay away from you, because from the moment I saw you I knew you were mine, and I don't think I can let you go now I know you exist."

My eyes widen and my lips fall open as I stare at him in utter, baffled shock. "What?"

"You're mine, Alice."

"That's ridiculous," I say, bursting into loud laughter, my eyes actually closing as I laugh so hard I bend at the waist when a stitch forms in my side.

My laughter abruptly dissolves when I'm airborne for a moment, my back hitting the bed with an umph as Granger crawls over me, grabbing my hands and pinning them above my head.

I should be terrified, but for some reason I'm not scared of this very odd, possibly crazy, stunningly gorgeous stranger pinning me to his bed. I really don't think he's going to hurt me or rape me, plus we're in his home, that's full of his family who don't seem like the type who'd be okay with their brother forcing himself on a girl only feet from where they're cooking in the kitchen.

"I don't appreciate you laughing at me," he growls,

not letting me go but not getting any closer either."

"If you don't want to be laughed at you shouldn't say ridiculous things," I taunt, wishing I could swallow back the words the moment they're free. I know better than to engage with people, I know better than to be engaging and interested. This is my first time being pinned down for inciting a conversation, but regardless, I don't do this. Attempting to make friends or engage always backfires on me.

"You being mine isn't ridiculous."

"Granger, we met three hours ago."

"When you know, you know, and I know you're meant to be mine, that us meeting this morning wasn't a coincidence. My family has a history of finding their women and knowing in that exact moment. That's what happened when I saw you this morning. I knew."

"Wow, does your family also have a history of mental instability?" Oh my god, what is wrong with me? Why am I taunting him? Why am I speaking to him at all?

His laugh is low, rough and full of amusement, he's not in the least bit offended that I just suggested him and his family are all crazy. "Not crazy, just single minded and confident in their ability to know who their women are the moment they find them."

Sighing, I close my eyes for a second and silently remind myself why this can't happen.

People don't like me.

My likeability has a timescale.

I'm needy.

I'm pathetic

I'm toxic.

Each thought feels like a physical blow, but each hit is a much needed reminder. When I open my eyes, my mind is clearer and my armor is firmly fixed back in place. "Look, Granger, it's very sweet that you think I'm this fabled person you've been searching for, but I promise you I'm not. I'm nobody, I belong to no one, I'm a loner, a wanderer, and that's what suits me. Your family seem great, you seem great, but I need to buy a new RV and get on my way. I think it'd be best if you just take me back down into town and I promise you'll never see me again. That way, when you meet your actual person, I won't even be a footnote in your happy ever after." Forcing a smile to my lips, I wait for his weight to lift, for his hold on me to loosen, but it doesn't.

"You're my person, Alice, you might not feel it yet, but I do. Maybe before today you were nobody's, but now you're mine and I plan on keeping you. I'm not taking you to town, I'm not helping you leave. Nothing has ever felt as right to me as you do beneath me, and I'll do whatever it takes to help you understand what this is between us."

Suddenly my arms are free, but he doesn't get up,

instead his hand carefully cups my cheek and he leans down. He presses his lips to mine, kissing me softly, reverently and with so much feeling that I can't help but kiss him back.

In the past, kisses have just been an empty movement, lips pressed to lips, but what Granger is doing seems like so much more. He's reaffirming all he just said and branding it into my skin, he's telling me with his mouth, his hands, his tongue that I'm his, that this is us now, that we share this connection that's different to anything I've felt before.

His body is on top of mine, his weight holding me down, but he's not forcing this on me, I'm just as much a willing participant as he is and I feel tears that I don't understand filling my eyes. How can a kiss make me cry?

Pulling back, his lips leave mine and I blink my eyes open and stare up at him. His brow furrows when he see the tears I can feel rolling down my cheeks and he quickly uses his thumbs to wipe them away.

"Please don't be scared of me, I'll never hurt you, I just don't think that now I've found you I can live without you. I'm a Barnett and I know I'm throwing a lot at you right now, I know I'm a lot to deal with, but I swear if you let me I'll be your everything. I wasn't searching for you and I know you don't think you were looking for me either, but I promise we're both exactly where we're meant to be and I'll prove that to you, if you give me the chance."

"What if I don't want to."

His eyes darken and his lids hood as his mouth curls into a cruel grin. "I'll convince you."

Rolling upwards, his weight lifts from me and he sits back between my thighs, that until this moment I hadn't noticed he'd parted. Heavy hands settle on my legs and he squeezes gently, making sure I'm more than aware of his hands on me.

"Are you wet, my Alice? You say I'm not yours and you're not mine, but if I slid my fingers into your cunt right now would I find you dry and as uninterested as your words pretend to be, or as soaked as your body is telling me you are?"

His hands slowly start to inch up my thighs toward my core, and my breathing becomes ragged. It's been so long since I've felt even a flutter of desire, and right now there's a herd of butterflies doing the can-can in my stomach, heating me from within.

"Tell me to stop and I will, I'll never take what you haven't freely given," Granger assures me, his fingers inching higher, making my skin pebble with awareness the closer he gets to my swollen and needy sex.

I should tell him to stop, I'm a bag of mixed signals, my head is warning him off, but my brain can't convince the words to come out of my mouth and right now, I'm just lying here on his bed not even trying to get away from him.

Maybe this is the easiest way of getting rid of him. Sex has worked in the past, it'll work again. He'll lose all interest once he's touched me and then I can leave, hopefully with a few orgasms to remember him by, but with no hard feelings on his side and a reminder that nobody ever wants me again once I give myself to them on mine.

"Tell me to stop, Alice," he warns, as his fingers reach the apex between my thighs, mere millimeters from my jean-covered pussy.

I should, I know I should, but I don't, instead I push my hips up off the bed and arch into his touch, daring him to do what he's threatening to; to touch me. A salacious grin spreads across his mouth as he confidently unbuttons my jeans and peels them over my butt until they're resting just below my knees, leaving me bare except for my boring black cotton panties.

For the first time in years, I wish I wore sexy underwear. If he'll lose interest after this, I'd rather he remember me for the plain, unlikable woman in the sexy red crotchless panties, rather than the plain Target black ones that are a little wrinkled where the elastic is starting to sag.

I expect him to rip my underwear down, but instead he leans down and presses his nose against the fabric and inhales. I'm not sure if that's sexy or weird, but for the first time ever I wonder what I smell like down there, and hope it's nice and not nasty.

The question forms on my lips but it dissolves again when he grips the waistband of my panties and slowly starts to reveal me. When my panties are around my knees with my jeans, I start to feel self conscious. My mom insisted I get laser hair removal when I was in high school, so thankfully I'm smooth and I don't have an eighties raging bush, but maybe he likes hair, or maybe he thinks I have so much sex I keep myself clean shaven and ready to go.

"So wet," Granger growls, pulling me from my internal freak out as he runs his fingers over my pussy, sliding easily through my very aroused folds. "I can't wait to watch you come."

My mind goes blank at the first stroke of his tongue.

No one has ever given me oral before, it's not really a car sex possibility, or at least not in my limited experience, and the sensation of him licking me almost has me blacking out at how amazing it feels.

Hot, wet, awesome, this is literally the best thing I've ever felt and I've not even had an orgasm yet. His fingers join in on the fun and I'm lost, my mind blown as he's in me, over me, licking me, sucking me and fucking me all in one and when my orgasm hits, I know I scream as much in surprise as in pleasure.

I won't survive.

I was fine without sex, I've never thought I was missing out on anything by being alone and not having someone to touch me or for me to touch in return. But now, knowing someone can make me feel like this, I'm not sure I can live never feeling this again.

I expect him to get up, to get his dick out and shove it at my face, to want to fuck me, but instead of any of those things, his mouth is on my sex again and he's eating me like I'm his favourite desert. I moan like a porn star every time his fingers thrust deep inside of me, every time his tongue laps at my clit, every time his teeth scrape over my sensitive flesh that feels like it's been heightened until every minute touch is a mini explosion of pleasure.

"Scream, Alice, scream for me," he demands, a moment before his tongue does something that makes my eyes roll into the back of my head and an orgasm hit me like a tornado, picking me up, spinning me around and around, then spitting me back out the other side, forever changed from the experience.

Panting, I cover my face with my hands, trying to stifle the sounds I can hear myself making but have zero control over. I should be embarrassed, but honestly, I just don't care. I don't care if he hears, I don't care if the entire house hears. That. Was. Amazing.

My hands are ripped from my face and his lips find mine. He's kissing me, after he just had his mouth on my pussy and it tastes... okay. I expect him to realize that he just gave me mouth to sex resuscitation and pull back to get a drink or something, but if anything, he just kisses me harder, more intensely, and I realize that I don't care. All I can taste now is him, and I'm kissing him back, and it's so good that I know this will be almost as hard to give up as my sudden new awareness of oral and how fantastic it is.

"Has anyone ever told you how sexy you look when you come?" he rasps against my mouth.

Shaking my head, I lift off the pillow and try to reclaim his lips, with talking comes the inevitable rejection and I don't want to hear that yet, I want a few more perfectly blissful moments before reality takes over.

"I can't wait to watch you come on my dick. I want to feel you clamp down on my cock as your lips part and you scream out my name as I claim your cunt."

My brow furrows and I can feel the confusion on my face. Are we going to have sex now? I'm down for that, I've already had two orgasms but it's only fair he gets his. I don't have any condoms, but Granger must have. With how good he is at eating pussy, he probably has an industrial sized party pack in his bedside cabinet to keep the constant flow of women who find themselves in his bed protected.

Wiggling, I try to work my jeans down my legs, but his hands find them and instead of removing them, he's pulling my panties back up.

"I thought you wanted to have sex?" I ask, my voice raspy from all the screaming.

"I want you more than you'll ever understand, but if I fuck you now, you're mine. I won't let you leave me, ever, and I know you're not ready for that. Your cunt belongs to my fingers and my tongue already, but the moment my dick gets inside of you, I'm keeping you and I need you to fully understand that before I claim you."

"Don't be absurd, you want me, I want you, let's just have some fun before I leave," I coax, trying to sound alluring and sexy, and instead just becoming needy and pathetic as I beg this stranger to fuck me.

Chuckling lowly, he drags my jeans over my butt and fastens the button at my waist covering me completely, before he possessively cups my sex over my clothes. "I've touched you, I've tasted you and you already belong to me, Alice. But the moment I get inside of you, I'm keeping you as my property. I'll fucking kill anyone who tries to take what's mine, who tries to touch what's mine, or taste what's mine."

I feel shock tinged with fear creep into my expression, as my eyes widen and I push myself back into the cushions trying to find some distance from him when I'm still beneath him on his bed.

"I'm trying really hard not to sound like a fucking psycho and I can see I'm doing a shitty job. I want you, Alice, not for a one-night stand, or a fling while you're in town. I want you to be mine."

"You don't even know me."

"I don't need to know you; I feel that you're mine. I know that doesn't make any sense right now, but speak to Bonnie and Cora and they'll tell you this is how it is for us Barnett's. We find our woman and that's it, she's ours, we're hers, nothing else is an option."

"I really think I should go," I say, more than a little freaked out.

"No."

"No?" I parrot back.

"No. You're not going anywhere."

"Are you saying I'm a prisoner here?"

"No. You're not a prisoner, you're mine."

SIX

GRANGER

I am fucking this up so badly.

She can't leave, I can't let her leave. I won't let her leave but I sound like a fucking crazy person and other than fucking her into unconsciousness, I don't really have any idea what to do to convince her to want to stay.

Leaving her alone isn't an option, now I know what her pussy tastes like, now I've seen her face when she's coming from an orgasm I've given her, I'm completely addicted, so much more than I was just from knowing she's mine. I'll never be able to let her go and I don't know how I explain that to her without making her run from me.

For a minute, when she decided to let me touch her, when she pushed her cunt up into my hands, offering herself to me, I thought she was starting to understand, but I can see in her eyes that she has no idea how all in I am. It barely makes any sense to me, so why would she understand?

My dick is so hard it feels like it has its own pulse. I know I'm going to be in pain until I spread her legs and take what's mine, but I can't fuck her until she understands that giving herself to me that way is cementing herself as my property, my woman for the rest of our lives.

Shit, I sound fucking nuts to myself. Is this how Beau and Huck felt? This crazy, possessive need to own their woman like she was property? My mama was one of the strongest, most independent, fierce women I've ever known, if this is how daddy felt about her, did she give herself over to his ownership or did they spend their lives fighting about how he thought she belonged to him and she disagreed.

I don't want that.

I want Alice to be completely mine in this seriously old fashioned, me man, you woman way that I have never considered attractive until today. I want her to need me for everything. I want to be the person she goes to for every need, thought and desire. I want her dependent on me, but not in a fucked-up way. More because it already feels like she's the reason I breathe, and I need to not be in this alone.

Her eyes are wide and kind of horrified as I slowly pull away from her, no longer pinning her with my body, but close enough I can stop her if she tries to make a run for it. I denied she's my prisoner, but honestly, I don't hate the idea. I could lock the door to this room and refuse to let her out until she gives herself to me.

"Fuck," I mutter, not realizing I've spoken the word aloud.

"What? Realized how much of a psychopath you sound right now?" she says, her voice still a little raspy and rough.

"I'm not sorry," I shrug. "I know I'm coming on strong and throwing a lot at you, especially because we only met today, but have you never felt that something was instantly right the moment you found it?"

She shakes her head, even as her eyes tell me she wished she had. "All I've ever known was things that felt instantly wrong."

That confession irks at something inside of me and I want to comfort her, to be her safe place. Unable to resist, I pull her off the bed and cradle her in my arms, sitting her ass against my hard dick as I position her in my lap.

"Tell me you feel nothing for me?" I challenge her.

"I don't know you."

"So it should be easy to tell me you feel nothing. I'm a stranger."

"I feel nothing," she says, lying, badly.

"Don't lie to me, Alice, never fucking lie."

"This is ridiculous."

"Tell me you feel nothing."

"I don't have to tell you anything. In a couple of days when I'm gone, you won't even remember my name," she says with a self-deprecating laugh.

"I won't ever forget you, because I don't think I could let you leave even if you begged me," I confess on a whisper against her ear.

She says something that sounds like, "I wish that were true," but it's so quiet that I can't be sure I heard her correctly as she sighs tiredly and confusingly relaxes into my hold, her body sagging into my chest. "I promise you everything you think you feel for me now will be completely gone in a matter of days."

"If you feel nothing for me, why do you sound so sad when you say that?" I ask.

"I'm not sad, I just know it's the truth." I wish I could say she was lying again, but even if I don't agree with her, it's obvious she believes what she's saying is the truth.

"Let me prove you wrong," I growl.

"What?"

"Spend the weekend with me. In my bed, in my arms,

be mine, let me prove how good it'll be to belong to me."

"Then after the weekend you'll take me back to town and we'll agree to never see each other again," she says simply, like it'd be that easy for me to let her walk away.

"No. I can't agree to that. How about you agree to be mine and if after the weekend you decide that isn't what you want, we can talk about it. Then, if you really want to leave I'll take you to town." I say, silently adding that I'll take her to town, then throw her back over my shoulder and bring her right back home again.

She's quiet and thoughtful for a minute, and for a second I think she's going to refuse, but then she nods decisively. "Okay, but you have to promise that when all these feelings you think you have go away, you'll tell me, you won't drag things out for the whole weekend once you realize it was all just a weird brain fart."

"I promise I'll tell you," I say with a smirk. Does she really think I'm making up what I feel for her? If this was just about sex I could be balls deep in her by now, but I stopped myself because when I fuck her for the first time, I plan to claim her. Despite what she imagines is going to happen, I won't be giving her up on Monday morning, I'll be sliding a ring on her finger and putting a baby in her belly.

Gripping her chin with my fingers, I tip her head back and lean in until my lips are a hair's breadth from hers, then I wait until she closes the distance between us and kisses me. From now on I won't wait for her to come to me, but for this kiss, her offering, her surrender is her sealing herself to me. This first kiss was binding, and now I have three days to show her why I'm keeping her and why she'll want to be kept.

For the next hour we make out like teenagers, and my dick hurts so much I think I may actually have to go to the ER for the worst case of blue balls in the history of man. She keeps pushing her tits into me, grinding her ass against me like she's daring me to touch her, but I manage to hold myself back. If I start touching her now, I know I won't be able to stop and I at least want to feed her before I devour her.

A knock at my door forces me to pull away from her mouth and she whines, disgruntled that we're not kissing anymore.

"Dinner's ready," someone shouts.

"Come on, honey, let's go eat."

"I'm not hungry," she pants, grabbing my face and trying to pull me back in for another kiss.

"You can feel how hard my dick is, you know how much I don't want to stop, but we need to eat and then we need to move your stuff from the guest room into here. Then I promise I'll spend the rest of the night showing you what it feels like to belong to me."

Her lips part and heat fills her cheeks as if she's embarrassed, even though I've already had my mouth on her pussy and my fingers buried deep inside of her.

"You're too fucking cute, I love this pink in your cheeks." I laugh. "Come on." Lifting her from my lap, I hold onto her until she's steady on her feet, loving that just making out has got her so off balance.

"I'm…" she trails off, obviously trying to say something.

"What's up, honey?"

"Do you think they heard us?"

"Yeah," I nod.

"I'm just gonna hide in the guest room," she groans, covering her face with her hands.

"Honey, do you know how often we listen to Cora or Bonnie screaming? Almost daily, no one will say a thing to you. They know you're mine so they'll have been expecting it."

"What do you mean, they know I'm yours?" she asks, her brow arched and a hint of defiance that it's incredibly sexy creeping into her demeanor.

"Exactly what I said. You're mine, I knew it the moment I saw you, and they all knew it the moment I bought you home. We don't have women here unless they're our women," I explain succinctly.

"Look—" she starts.

"No," I snarl, closing the distance between us and

slamming my lips to her, silencing her and dominating her in one action. I'm done listening to her argue and tell me I'm imagining my feelings for her. "I know this is quick and overwhelming and honestly a little crazy, but you agreed to give me this weekend, so the next time you question that you're mine I'm gonna pull down your panties and spank your ass. You got me?"

"You want to hurt me?" she asks cautiously.

"Never, if I spank you, it'll be to remind you that you're mine and that I won't put up with you constantly questioning me."

"Have you ever read fifty shades or seen the movie?" she laughs.

"I'm not a fucking dom, Alice, I don't have a play room or a spanking fetish, I've never spanked a woman in my life. I'm a Barnett, and when it comes to the women that belong to us we tend to turn into cavemen. I'm not gonna apologize for it, or try to change myself," I tell her honestly. "Now, let's go eat with my family, and then I'm gonna strip you naked and fuck you until you forget your own name and all you can remember is that you're mine."

Before she has time to argue, I take her hand and pull her forward, opening my bedroom door and leading her into the living room. All eyes turn to us for a moment and I see Beau barely hiding a smile before he turns his attention back to his wife, whispering something into her ear that has her twisting around to throw herself into his arms.

It's been nearly eight months since Beau came home and realized he was obsessed with Bonnie Williams and knew she was his. She didn't make it easy on him, but within weeks they'd realized they were perfect for each other. They've been married for nearly five months now, and the love they feel for each other is so palpable it almost feels like being around my parents when I was growing up.

When our mama died, we all died a little too and even though none of us ever wanted to leave this house, I think we all felt the loss of the love she was filled with. Now we have Bonnie and Cora here, this place is becoming a home again and now I have Alice, I'm starting to understand why my brothers are as whipped as they are.

It's been less than a day and I'd already do anything for her, imagine how I'll feel in a month, a year, ten years.

Her fingers tighten on mine, and I love that just this tiny gesture makes me feel like she wants my support when she's feeling apprehensive. I need that from her, and that's not something I knew about myself until I saw her.

"Food's done, come sit down," Penn calls, so instead of heading for the couch like I'd planned, I turn and go to the dining table, pulling out a chair for Alice and holding it for her while she sits. Taking the seat next to hers, I lay my hand on her thigh and shuffle my chair toward hers, wanting to crowd her, hell, I'd have her on my lap if I didn't think she'd freak out. I don't know how I know, but if I give her a chance to think about this thing between us, she'll run. So many things she's said have been red flags, like her expecting me to get bored of her before the end of the weekend and her insistence that I'm making up my need for her in my head.

I don't know her well enough yet to be able to make her understand how sure I am of this thing between us, so until I do I'll keep her close, preferably within touching distance until she's as sure as I am that I'm just as much hers as she is mine.

When Penn places an empty plate in front of her, she immediately drops her gaze, like a child hoping if she can't see him, he somehow won't be able to see her. It's a strange thing for a beautiful, adult woman to do and I feel my brow furrow as I try to understand why her body language has suddenly become so closed off.

"Miss Alice, that RV of yours is definitely a classic," Bay laughs, taking the salad forks and dropping a portion onto his plate.

"My dad bought it when I was a kid, it's probably done well to last this long," Alice says, barely above a whisper.

"I've got a contact out in Arizona who thinks he might

have an engine for it, he's gonna have a look and let me know," Penn says, taking the serving dish full of ribs from Cody and putting some onto his plate.

"Okay, thanks," Alice says, not elaborating or trying to get any more details.

Penn's brow furrows as he looks from her and the way she's blatantly trying not to engage in a conversation, then to me. I shrug minutely, not wanting her to see me.

Beau passes me the salad and I put some on my plate, then add some to hers as well, before I pass it off to Cora who is sitting next to Alice. I do the same when the ribs, then the baked potatoes come to me, automatically serving her as well as myself without really giving it too much thought.

The conversation goes on around us, but Alice doesn't try to get involved, giving one word answers when she's asked a direct question, but not asking anything or entering into discussion with anyone, even though my whole family tries to include her.

"You okay?" I ask, when dinner is finished and Penn is collecting the plates as Cody grabs the pies he made earlier for dessert.

"Yes, thanks," she answers quietly.

For some reason, her dismissive answer pisses me off and I grab her chin in my fingers and lift her face up, forcing her to actually look at me, rather than hide from me by acting like the table is the most interesting thing she's ever seen. "Look at me when you speak to me," I growl quietly, not wanting to make a scene but needing her to mind what I'm saying.

Her eyes blink slowly, her brow furrowing like she can tell I'm mad but she has no idea why. "I'm fine. Are you okay?"

"You've barely said two words the whole way through dinner, and you're staring at the table like it's about to give you the winning lottery tickets. What's going on?"

Her eyes dart around the table and I'm glad that if they can hear us, my family are at least pretending like they can't. "Nothing, I'm just minding my own business. Your family are being polite and I appreciate that, but I'm a stranger in your home."

"My family want to get to know you."

"Why?" she asks, like she honestly doesn't know the answer.

"Because you're mine, you're going to be family."

"Look—"

Just like before, I cut her off by kissing her, not giving a fuck that we're at the dining table or that they might be watching. "Mine," I say, as I reluctantly pull away from her mouth.

When she sighs, I'm not sure if it's lust, or relief or tension that she's exhaling, but she relaxes into my hand that's cupping the back of her neck, not trying to get away from me.

"I know they're overwhelming, but I know you'll like them if you just give them a chance," I whisper, pressing my lips to her ear.

"Okay," she breathes.

Three perfect, golden crusted pies appear on the table in front of us, along with a huge bowl full of fluffy whipped cream.

"Peach, cherry and custard, I am the motherfucking god of pie," Cody announces loudly, his hands raised above his head in triumph.

"Well, me and the baby are sorted, I don't know what the rest of you are having," Cora laughs as she pulls the entire custard pie in front of her and immediately digs in, not even bothering to cut a slice.

"Not the peach, Peaches?" Huck asks her.

"Not today, today is all about custard pie," Cora says through a mouthful of desert.

Laughter fills the air as Cora shovels pie into her mouth, rubbing at her round pregnant belly and humming appreciatively. Huck moves his fork to take a bite and Cora slaps his hand away, glaring at him evilly. "Mine," she snarls.

"If you're mine and that pie's yours, it makes it mine too," Huck laughs, leaning in to stab his fork into the dish again, only for Cora to attempt to stab him with her fork this time.

"Listen, asshole, you got me pregnant and now I'm fat, I need to pee constantly and I haven't seen my pussy in almost a month. This pie is mine, and if you have even an ounce of sense in that neanderthal head of yours, you'll stop trying to steal mine and my baby's happy."

Bonnie laughs so hard her face goes red, and she almost chokes on her own piece of pie she's taken while everyone's attention has been on Cora.

When I glance at Alice, her wide eyes are moving between Cora, Huck and Bonnie as if she can't look away but doesn't know who to look at first.

"Cora," Huck says, a warning in his tone.

"Huck," she says back, with just as much warning in her own voice.

"They love each other, I swear they do," Bay says with a laugh to Alice.

My girl nods, but she doesn't look at all convinced.

"Do you have any siblings?" Teddy asks Alice, his voice soft and surprisingly gentle as if he doesn't want to spook her.

"Just one sister," my girl tells him, and it looks like she's having to physically force the words out. For the first time, I realize that's how she was at lunch too, like it's an effort to have a conversation. I wonder if maybe there's a reason she doesn't like to speak? Although she had no issue telling me I was imagining how I feel about her.

"Older or younger?" My attention is split between my girl and my baby brother as he coaxes a response from her.

"She's older than me."

"How many years?"

"Five," Alice says, and if I'm reading her right, talking about her sister seems to make her sad.

"Oh, that's the same as between me and Granger," Teddy smiles.

Alice tries to smile, but her attempt seems a little brittle. "She enlisted in the Army straight out of high school."

"Do you get to see her much?"

"No, she has her own life and I move around a lot..." Alice trails off as if that explains why she doesn't see her sibling. For a minute my chest tightens, I hated being away from Rockhead Point and all my brothers while I was at college, I came home for every holiday and moved back as soon as I graduated. I think the longest I've gone without seeing my family is three or four months, and reading between the lines I get the impression she hasn't seen her sister in at least five years, maybe longer.

My hands move without thought, curling around her waist to pull her back to my chest, holding her as close to me as I can get without taking her out of her chair and putting her into my lap. She stiffens for a minute, but then she surprises me by not pulling away from my touch, she even relaxes a little, letting some of her weight fall into me.

"Do you work at the garage too?" she asks Teddy, actually engaging for the first time.

"No, I work with Beau and Huck up on the mountain. Beau owns a logging company."

"Beau started his company, then Bay started the garage and Cody owns his own building contracting firm too. I have my furniture business. Huck and Teddy work with Beau, and Penn works at the garage," I explain.

"They keep trying to get us to give up our jobs and work for one of the family businesses, but I work at the coffee shop in town and at my daddy's ranch in my spare time, and Cora basically runs her mom's clothing store," Bonnie says, sticking her tongue out at her husband when she mentions not working for a Barnett business.

"You don't want to work for your husband?" Alice asks.

"Hell no," Bonnie says vehemently. "Christ, he has enough control issues with me at the coffee shop. If I worked with him, he'd be a nightmare," she laughs, pressing a kiss to Beau's cheek to soften her words.

"Baby girl, you know it's only a matter of time till I

convince you to give up working completely. No space, no distance," Beau says to his wife, pulling her onto his lap and nipping at her neck with a playful growl.

"See what I have to put up with," Bonnie giggles. "Alice, I'd tell you to make a run for it but they're all cavemen in this family and Granger would only chase after you."

Alice squirms uncomfortably in her seat and I glare at Bonnie who isn't paying me an ounce of attention, as Beau whispers something into her ear that makes her cheeks turn pink.

"Jesus, if you pair are planning to have another spanking session tonight you need to go do it at your dad's, I can't listen to you screaming then begging for more again," Cora says straight-faced, her fork still in the now half gone custard pie.

"Cora," Bonnie snaps.

"Don't Cora me," Cora says, shaking her head. "We all hear you, I can't wait until the contractors fit the soundproofing."

"As if we don't all hear you guys," Bonnie cries. "Harder Huck, I'm pregnant not breakable," Bonnie says in a very when harry-met-sallyesque way.

Cora giggles, then Bonnie starts too and suddenly the girls are laughing as they high five across the table, then lift their glasses in toast. "To big axes and men who know how to swing them," Cora says.

"Alice, you're gonna want to get in on this," Bonnie prompts, and both girls wait until Alice reluctantly lifts her glass and clinks it against the other women's at the table, while the rest of us stare on in part amusement and part horror.

Maybe suggesting Alice talk to the girls to help her understand the Barnett men might not be such a good idea.

SEVEN

ALICE

I think they seriously just called each other out for having very loud sex in the house they share with a lot of other people, then high-fived in support of the other having great sex, then made a kind of weirdly inappropriate toast about their men having big dicks and being good in bed and insisted I be involved.

These women are crazy.

This whole family seems crazy. Granger has apparently decided I'm his, because he *knew* the minute he saw me. Apparently that's just the way it happens for these guys and his family seem to just think that's totally okay, because they all seem to think it makes perfect sense that

I'm here, that I'm now part of a couple with Granger, a guy I met for the first time today.

The craziest thing is that I think I actually kind of agreed to be with Granger, at least for the rest of the weekend. I definitely made out with him like I was a freshman doing seventy-seven minutes in heaven on his bed, after I let him give me not one, but two orgasms with his fingers and mouth.

I have a plan for my life. I don't get involved. I don't attempt to make friends. I don't engage. Ever. For the last five years this plan has worked perfectly. I've moved around with the seasons, I have zero attachments that feel obligated to like me. I haven't gotten hurt or been judged by anyone for being clingy and pathetic.

My life is simple and pain free, just how I like it. Yet in the span of a day, everything has been thrown into chaos and I think it might be all my own fault.

Granger places a piece of cherry pie and a huge scoop full of whipped cream onto my plate while I accept a beer from one of his brothers, the one who is so close to Cora I wouldn't be surprise to find out he's half sitting on her chair.

As I eat, I watch with almost morbid curiosity as this family interact with each other. They're nothing like my family, not even back in the good days before Serenity left me behind so she could get on with her own life and be happy.

There's a playfulness between them, even the girls, that's odd. I think I was about ten the last time I sat down to dinner with my mom, her boyfriend of the moment, my sister and me, and the meal wasn't homecooked, it was probably microwaved Hungryman dinners in front of the tv. We certainly didn't sit and talk, or laugh, or tease one another.

For a moment as I watch them, I wonder if it's this family or my family that are the odd ones out. Is this how normal families work, and mine was just always disconnected because of me? Or are the Barnett's the strange ones, and normal families avoid conversation and each other in almost equal parts?

Granger wants me to engage, but I feel like I'm watching a nature show as I eat my pie and observe the Barnett's in their natural environment. When I'm finished, and Cora has somehow managed to consume an entire custard pie without sharing even a single bite with Huck or anyone else, everyone moves at once. The guys clear the table as Bonnie appears at one of my shoulders and Cora at the other. They coax me away from the table and sit me between them on the couch before I'm even aware of what's happening and I just go with it, too overwhelmed by all these crazy people to even argue or attempt to flee.

"Okay, so we have some time while the guys clean

up," Bonnie says quietly. "Are you okay? Has Granger gone full blown caveman? Do you need an escape plan?"

"I…"

"We know what they're like," Cora says conspiratorially. "We've both dealt with the crazy, so we just want to know he's not doing anything too insane. Like kidnapping you, or anything."

"Is kidnapping likely?" I ask cautiously.

"No… well probably not. I mean Huck sort of kidnapped me, but only after we were already together and I was pregnant," Cora says, waving her confession away because apparently kidnapping really is an option with this family.

"Ignore her," Bonnie says, pushing Cora in the shoulder and scowling at her. "Beau never tried to kidnap me, that's a Huck thing not a Barnett thing."

"Beau just turned up one day and refused to leave, so much better," Cora rolls her eyes.

"Okay I wasn't that freaked out, but now I think I might need that escape route," I tell the women.

Sighing, Bonnie takes a long sip of her beer. "We're doing a really shitty job of explaining things. The guys aren't dangerous crazy, they're just crazy intense. I one hundred percent promise you that Granger will never, ever physically hurt you. He might smother you with caveman attention and affection, there's every chance he'll drive you to absolute distraction, but he'll never intentionally hurt you."

"Look, I'm not sure what you think is going on here, but I'm only staying for the weekend, and only because my RV is out of action and you guys have this festival thing in town. Granger seems like a nice guy, but I'm not looking for a boyfriend."

"That kiss he planted on you didn't seem like something you do to someone who is leaving in a couple of days," Cora smirks.

"It's just a bit of fun while I'm in town. Granger explained the whole obsession at first sight thing, but I'll tell you, like I told him, I'm not his anything. Maybe with you pair it worked out, but I'm not the girl guys see forever with. Maybe his girl was standing behind me, or passing in a car when he glanced my way and that's why he's gotten all mixed up. But I don't do permanent, I don't do commitment, and I definitely don't do some fabled happy ever after. Honestly, saying yes to this weekend was a stretch for me and I'm already anticipating he'll be ready to pretend he's never met me by tomorrow night," I tell them both.

Jaws slack, they both stare at me, then simultaneously burst into laughter.

Rolling my eyes at their amusement, I make to stand up only to have them clamp down on me, one on each arm. "We're sorry," Bonnie laughs. "It's just that we know what they're like and we know that there is no way Granger's going to let you go. You might think he's joking, or mistaken about you being his, but he believes it down to his core. Beau had been coming into the coffee shop I work in every morning and night for a year and he barely spoke to me, then one day he told me I was his and kissed the hell out of me. After that he wouldn't leave me alone, he turned up at my house, invited himself to dinner, literally carried me to where ever he wanted me over his shoulder when I refused to do what he wanted and sexed me into submission. I tried to fight it, I denied my feelings for him, denied his feelings for me. I even went out on a date with another guy, but he was so single mindedly sure that I was his it was futile to fight him."

"Huck decided I needed someone to look after me after I got a little drunk on a girls' night out. He literally let himself into my apartment and then refused to leave. Then he made it his mission to give me so many orgasms that I was in a cum drunk haze as he fucked me until he got me pregnant," Cora says, her lips pursed, her eyebrow arched.

"Wow," I whisper. "Do you guys need some help? I'm sure there's agencies to get women out of these kinds of situations," I tell them quietly, surreptitiously glancing around to check none of the guys are listening to us.

Both women smile widely at me. "I have a shotgun that I'm really good at using, if I didn't want to be here, I wouldn't," Bonnie says softly. "Beau might be intense, he might be over the top, jealous and protective. But I love him and he's mine as much as I'm his."

"Yeah, and my brother's the deputy sheriff," Cora giggles. "Huck is not allowed near my birth control ever again, but I don't work without him, him and our baby are my world." Her hands cradle her pregnant belly and she smiles happily.

"Look, I know you guys think you need to be nice to me but you really don't. I know who I am and I'm aware of my issues, and Granger will see he was wrong about me, probably much quicker than I'd like. Deep down, I know I shouldn't take advantage of him and allow us to be physical, but it's been a long time for me and he's hot, so I'm going to enjoy it while it lasts and then on Monday, I'll leave."

A mix of confusion and sadness crosses the women's faces and I can see that they're planning their next arguments, so I stand, smiling. "Thanks for the chat, it's been a long day so I'm gonna go to bed."

I walk away before they can say anything, not meeting anyone's eyes as I escape into the guest room, happy to be alone when I close the door behind me. There isn't a lock, but I wish there was and for a moment I consider grabbing my bag and climbing out the window. If I wasn't in the middle of nowhere half way up a mountain in Montana in the winter, I probably would. But I know wandering around in the dark when I have no idea how long it would take me to walk back to my RV and no way of leaving even if I could get to it, isn't a good idea.

The desire to call my sister and ask her to fix this hits me so fast and hard it takes my breath away. I haven't allowed myself to think of her as my savior since the day she left, and I won't let a man and his very consuming family push me back down that painful path either.

Saying yes to this weekend with Granger was a mistake, I'm already too involved with him and I need to stop this train careening downhill before I end up smashed to pieces at the bottom.

The door pushes open and Granger strides in without bothering to knock or wait for my permission to enter.

"Alice, honey, you okay?"

"I'm tired, I'm going to go to sleep."

"Grab your stuff and we can go to my room."

"No, I changed my mind, I know this is your house, but I think you should go."

"No," he says, ignoring my words as he marches toward me, closing the distance between us in an instance.

"You can't just say no," I tell him, backing away and refusing to look at him, because somehow I know I'll weaken if I look into his eyes.

"What's happened? What did the girls say to you?" he demands, his tone harsher than I've heard from him before, my panties dampening at how sexy he is when he's bossy and growling.

"Nothing, they're just all on board with this mystical insta-lust thing you think you feel for me."

"There's nothing mystical about it, Alice. I'm not some fucking idiot, I know who you are."

"That's the thing, Granger, you don't know me and I don't know you, because we met today." I roll my eyes and turn away from him.

His hands wrap around my waist and I'm spun around to face him. I look up before I can remind myself not to, and immediately get lost in the intensity and need in his eyes. I should be stronger than this, I've got five years of immunity to people, but a day with him and all of my defenses have shattered to smithereens around his feet, that's how affected I am by him.

"You've had your say, now it's time for you to shut the hell up and listen to me for a minute."

Swallowing thickly, I part my lips to speak, but he covers my mouth with his hand, literally silencing me. "I said it's time for you to listen to me, you understand? Nod if you get me."

I nod and he slowly lifts his palm, cupping my jaw

instead, holding me still beneath his touch. "I have never claimed a woman in my life. I've fucked, I've enjoyed, but I've never claimed, never even been tempted until you."

His hold on my face softens a little, and he runs the pad of his thumb over my cheek as he smiles down at me. "I'm thirty-five years old, I'm a man, not some pup with a hard dick, full of false promises and a big game with no follow through. When I say you're mine, it's because you are. When I tell you I'm gonna fill you with my dick and own every fucking inch of you, it's because I'm going to and you're gonna beg for it. When I say I know you, it's because I do. I know who you are on the most basic level where a man fundamentally knows his woman by sight and sense and smell. I might not know the everyday stuff like what you like on your pancakes, or if you're a morning person, but what I know about you is much more important because it's instinctual, going all the way back to when humans were nothing more than caveman. I know you, because you belong to me, and unless you can look me in the face and tell me with complete honesty that you don't feel the same way, I'm gonna take you to my room, strip you naked and make you mine in the most primal way a man can claim a woman."

Waiting expectantly, his eyes pierce me, daring me to argue, to lie to him, because somehow, we both know there's no way I could tell him with sincerity that I don't understand what he's saying on some level, but I still need to do something. "This is a mistake."

"Nothing about us could ever be a mistake," he croons, his eyes softening.

"We shouldn't do this, it'll only end up with pain," I warn, hating how sad I sound.

"Honey, tonight's gonna end with you screaming my name while I pound your cunt full of my cum. Any pain I give you, you're gonna have to beg for, but by the time you wake up in the morning, you're never going to question how well I know you again."

Releasing my face, his hands go to my hips again and he lifts me, encouraging me to wrap my legs around his waist and my arms around his neck. He doesn't give me a moment to question him before he's moving, carrying me out of the guest room and into his own, where he lowers me to the floor and begins to kiss me as his fingers find the hem of my shirt, peeling it up and over my head, only releasing my lips when he drags the fabric off me and drops it to the floor. His mouth finds mine again and somehow, he undresses me without ever stopping kissing me until I'm naked, cool air coating my bare nipples and pussy.

Finally pulling his lips from mine, he separates us as he looks down at me, taking me in, while I squirm beneath his appraising gaze.

"Undress me," he orders.

Tentatively, I reach out and wrap my fingers around the hem of his shirt, slowly pulling it upwards, revealing his firm abs and torso, a smattering of dark hair covers the top of his chest and moves down to his happy trail. His arms are thick, tight with muscle and there's a tattoo covering his right pec, a beautiful tree with the roots stretching out wider than the branches. It's gorgeous and I lift my hand and stroke my fingers across it, while Granger watches me with heat filled eyes.

"Take off my pants," he rasps, his voice losing its cadence, nothing more than need and want now.

My hands feel unsteady as I feed the button of his jeans through the hole then slowly pull down the zipper, gasping when his dick pops free, bursting out of the tight confines of his pants as I start to push them down over his butt and hips until they pool on the floor at his feet.

Stepping out of my own pants that I hadn't realized were around my feet, I bend down and push off his shoes and socks as he steps free, and then we're both naked, strangers bought together by his unrelenting belief that somehow we're meant for each other. If I was a different person, I'd stop him. If I was better, I'd warn him I'm toxic, that I'm a drain, but I want to be wanted by him. For once I want someone to fight for me, and since I met him he's done that. He's taken all my objections and squashed them, he's refused to let me distance myself, he's bought me into his home, into his family and told me that I'm his.

It's been so long since I've been wanted, and right now this man wants me and I'm not strong enough to resist.

EIGHT

GRANGER

She's standing in front of me naked, willing and giving herself to me. She's perfect, and when I reach for her, I know I'll never be able to give her up. Her skin's warm, despite her nipples being pebbled as I hold her against my chest. Cradling her jaw in my palm, I lead her lips to mine, claiming her mouth the moment she's close enough. She doesn't resist, it's like now she's made the decision to do this, all of her reservations and fight has gone and in its place is this giving innocence that has my inner caveman screaming with the need to consume her.

Tentative hands find my chest and she explores my skin, her fingers brushing over the tattoo on my chest like she thinks she'll be able to feel the bark of the tree as if it were real. I reach out and cup her breast, it's the perfect handful, perky with a tight, high nipple that's begging to be sucked.

Unable to resist I lean down and pull the tip into my mouth, sucking hard to see how she reacts. Her head falls back and she moans, long and low, so I run my teeth over the taut peak, almost groaning myself when the hint of pain has her shuddering with delight.

Releasing her breast, I slide my hands beneath her butt and lift her from the ground. Her legs immediately wrap around my hips and my dick finds her pussy, eager to slide into her heat. If this wasn't the first time I'd taken her, I'd feed her onto my cock, slam her back against the wall and fuck her like this with her clinging to me, her moans against my ear. But not this time. This time I want her in my bed, spread out like an offering, where I can touch and lick and devour all of her.

Carrying her to the bed, I put my knee on the mattress and crawl onto it, not letting her go as I lower her to the comforter, immediately caging her in with my elbows on either side of her head.

"Mine," I whisper as I kiss her, pushing my tongue into her mouth as she tightens her legs around my waist, not letting me go. I already know what her cunt tastes like, so I keep my lips on hers and instead push my hand between us, my fingers easily sliding into her soaking sex.

She's tight, but I don't feel any resistance, and at twenty-three I'd be surprised if she was still a virgin. Scissoring my fingers, I push them deeper, searching for her g-spot, wanting to make her come before I take her for the first time.

I don't release her mouth, fucking her cunt with my fingers as I own her mouth with my tongue. Her hands cling to me, her fingernails digging into my shoulders as her hips grind and she rides my hand, chasing down an orgasm, until I feel her muscles clench, then a gasping moan vibrates against my mouth and tremors wrack her body.

Not giving her time to think, I pull my fingers free and guide my cock to her entrance, releasing her mouth so I can watch her expression as I slide into her for the first time. Despite stretching her with my fingers, she's so tight I worry for a moment that I won't fit. After I slide in an inch, I pull out, coating the head of my cock with her arousal, then push in again, sliding in a little further with each thrust.

Her eyes are molten, her lips kiss swollen, her chest heaving as she pants and lifts her hips a little higher off the bed, opening herself up to allow my dick to fill her completely.

"You okay?" I ask, when each rise and fall of her breath

is accompanied by a tiny gasp.

She nods. "You're big."

"I fit perfect, your cunt's clinging to me, I can barely move," I rasp, pressing a kiss to the side of her mouth, then her neck as I tentatively roll my hips, half thrusting, half grinding, giving her body time to adjust.

"Oh god," she moans, her eyes falling closed as she arches her neck, tipping her head back.

"God's got nothing to do with it, Alice, you're mine now, all mine, and it'll be me making you scream."

Her eyes widen as I pull back and slam forward, taking her and owning her in a single movement. Gripping me tighter, her hips move with me, pushing back against each thrust, willing me to go harder and deeper. Her moans become pants, then mewling gasps as her pussy ripples, gripping and tightening as she gets closer and closer to release.

"Granger, I'm so close."

"Come for me, honey, come on my dick, I want to feel it," I coax, pinching her nipple between my finger and thumb, hoping the edge of pain will tip her into orgasm. When she comes, it's the most free I've ever seen her. Her lips part on a silent scream, her eyes locked with mine as if she doesn't want to look away. Her pussy grips my dick so hard she squeezes the cum out of me and I spill inside of her, feeling this sense of proprietary rightness filling her cunt with my cum.

My own orgasm lasts almost as long as hers and when we both come down, I collapse against her, our bodies damp with excursion. Running my fingers through the length of her hair, I stay quiet, not willing to interrupt this moment by speaking. Despite her total surrender to me, I know she'll fight this, but I warned her I'd own her the moment I fucked her and I meant it. She's mine now and I'm keeping her, no matter what she thinks.

"Granger."

"Shhh, I don't want to argue, so just don't. Right now, I just want to enjoy this."

"Okay," she whispers, relaxing beneath me.

Lifting up, I keep her held to me, rolling us to the side, keeping my softening dick still inside her as I pull her head down to rest on my chest. She stiffens, as if she's unsure what to do now the sex part is over, but after a moment she melts into me, her hand resting over my heart.

I press my lips against her hair, feeling something inside my chest settle. I've never felt like this, I'm not an asshole who's got his pants on before the sweat's even dry, but I've never felt the need to cuddle a woman like I do now with Alice.

Everything with her feels different, but I suppose that makes sense given that she's mine and not just a random fuck to scratch an itch. I like her in my bed, I want here all the time, but I don't know how to make that happen. I can delay her leaving, get my brothers to tell her repairs are taking longer than expected, but it's only a matter of time before her RV is fixed or she buys a new one and then she's going to leave. Letting her go isn't an option, neither is leaving with her. My business is here, my family and roots and life are here. If she had a home, a place she lives with things and ties and stuff, I'd follow her there in a heartbeat, but I can't help thinking that her moving around, living in a tiny old RV is more about her running away from something, rather than her enjoying the nomadic existence she's created for herself.

Her breathing slows and eventually she goes lax in my arms, sleep pulling her under, my dick still semi-hard and inside her. I want to take her again, to roll her to her belly and fuck her from behind, to lift her on top and watch her ride me, but I won't, not yet anyway. I need her to trust me, to want to be here, to believe all the things I know to be true about us are real, and that won't happen if I treat her like my personal sex slave, even though that sounds about perfect to me right now.

Maybe she'd be into that too, then I could keep her locked in a beautiful cage where her leaving isn't an option.

No, what the fuck is wrong with me? I'm thinking about locking my woman up so she can't leave, that's fucked up on a level I've never dipped to before, not even in my most depraved fantasies. No, I need to make her want me, need me, then the thought of leaving would become as abhorrent to her as it is to me.

I didn't use a condom, and I didn't ask her about birth control, I know Huck tricked Cora into getting pregnant, but I won't do that. Not that I'll be upset if she is, in fact I'd be elated if my kid was taking root in her womb right now. But I don't want our future to be based on an accidental baby, I want her to be unequivocally mine when I breed her, I want her to want it.

Stroking my fingers through her long blonde hair, I try to decide what I should do. I've never tried to make a woman fall in love with me, but that's what I need Alice to do. I need to her to slip off the edge into obsession, I need her to need me for everything, to want me in every aspect of her life, and I only have a weekend to do it.

***

It's still dark when I wake up and find she's rolled away from me, her back to my front, her ass pressed up against my dick as she sleeps with her hands tucked beneath her cheek. Dipping my head down, I press a kiss against her shoulder, then slide my knee between her legs, opening her up to me, as I position my dick against her sex from behind. She's asleep, but I don't care, I need inside of her right now.

She's wet and I slide right in, her body still ready for me after the sex we had only a few hours ago. Curling my arm around her waist, I drag her ass and hips back and slowly start to fuck her in long, dragging thrusts.

My mouth rests against her shoulder, kissing and nipping at her creamy exposed skin as I drive myself into her body so slowly it's like I'm torturing myself. She wakes up slowly, her body emerging from her dreams quicker than her brain.

"You feel perfect," I whisper against her neck when her eyelids begin to flutter.

"Granger," she says raggedly, her voice full of sleep and the pleasure she's woken up to.

"I couldn't resist, your cunt's like a siren call, singing to me, begging me to fuck it, to own it and fill it," I groan, moving faster now, fucking her deeper as she arches into me, her arm reaching back and latching onto my bicep.

"Oh god," she pants, clutching at the sheet beneath her.

"I want you to come, honey, come for me."

"I can't, I'm close, but I can't."

My hand slides down from her waist and I find her clit, rubbing and pinching as I fuck her without restraint, leaning over her and tilting her ass further onto my cock.

Her moans only make me fuck her harder, dragging her back onto my dick with each thrust as my other hand works at the clit until she comes on a garbled cry, my name falling from her lips as I fill her once, twice more, then come inside of her, filling her again as she shudders around me.

My teeth find her shoulder, and I bite down as the last stream of cum pulses from my cock, exhaling a shuddering breath against her skin. "Perfect."

I feel her nod, but she doesn't speak as our breathing slowly evens out and the sun starts to rise in the sky. "This is how every day should start," I smile.

"I'm okay with that," she giggles shakily, as her muscles begin to relax and her back melts back against mine.

Pulling her against me as close as I can get, I close my eyes and fall back asleep with my woman held tightly in my arms.

***

The next time I wake up, Alice is exactly where she was when I fell asleep, her breathing slow and even, her hair a tangled mess across the pillow. It's Saturday morning, so all of us are off work except for the girls who regularly work weekends, but the house sounds quiet and still. I'm not ready for real life to encroach on this moment. I didn't know I was waiting for Alice, but now she's here it's obvious how hollow my life was without her.

This sense of certainty is the part I wasn't expecting.

Until I saw my brothers fall, I didn't believe in my dad's proclamation that he knew in an instance mom was his. It took Beau over a year and another guy to know Bonnie was his, even though he'd been watching over her before he even realized and laid claim, but for Huck, he says he knew the moment he saw Cora, even though he fought it to start off with.

With Alice I just know, even though I can't explain how I know. I guess I never expected it to happen to me, but now it has I'm not sure how I lived in a world without her for so long. Just thinking about being without Alice feels desolate, there's no me without her now and no matter how startling that revelation seems, I'm not alarmed, because everything about her settles me. She's the other half of my soul and now she's here, I'm complete.

NINE

ALICE

I'm warm and comfy and… there's a person in bed with me!

Blinking my eyes open, it takes me a second to remember I'm not in the lumpy fold out bed in my RV, but in Granger's bed, in his room, in his house. We had sex last night, and again at some point either super late last night or super early this morning. We had sex and afterwards he pulled me in and cuddled me until we both fell asleep. I've never done that before. In fact, there's a list of firsts I've done with Granger.

First time receiving oral, first time being cuddled by a guy, first time sleeping in the same bed with a guy, first time having sex from behind, first time falling asleep with a guy's dick still inside of me. First time waking up, not once but twice in a guy's arms.

I'm not sure if it's all the firsts, or the fact that I've liked them all that's making me freak out a little. The urge to sneak out is waring with my desire to stay exactly where I am and enjoy this while it lasts. Maybe it'll all be over when he wakes up, and if it is I don't want to have wasted a moment of being wanted, or being held like I'm special.

Last night I planned to tell him no, to arm myself against anything he did to persuade me, but instead, I crumbled and gave in so fast it's almost a little pathetic to remember how easily he won me over.

"Morning honey."

"Morning," I whisper, tense now I know he's awake and probably on the verge of kicking me out.

"Are you sore?"

My pussy clenches without thought and a low pang of pain twists up from the inside out. Another first. "A little."

"Fuck, I want you so bad, but I won't take you again if you're already sore," Granger says, with what sounds like genuine regret in his voice.

"You want me again?"

"I don't think I'll ever stop wanting you. I've never felt anything like the way it feels when I'm inside of you."

My lips clamp shut, because what do you even say to

that?

"I can feel you freaking out, but you shouldn't. You're mine, Alice, you'd be so much happier if you just accepted that and relaxed," he laughs, actually laughs.

Pulling free of his hold, I try to climb out of the bed, but his grip on me tightens as he stops me. "Where do you think you're going?"

"To pee," I say, even though it's mainly an excuse to get some breathing space from him.

His hold gradually loosens and I'm free to move, dragging the comforter with me, so I don't have to make the run for the bathroom naked.

His laugh follows me as I stumble away from the bed and close the bathroom door behind me, pissed that yet again there's no lock in here.

Avoiding the mirror, I sink down onto the toilet, resting my head in my hands. What the hell am I going to do? Staying is impossible, but he's not behaving the way he should be. By now he should be desperate for me to go away, not practically holding me hostage so I don't run. I don't know how to deal with this.

Flushing the toilet, I turn on the tap to wash my hands when the bathroom door opens and Granger strolls in, completely, unashamedly naked, his dick hard and bouncing as he walks. "I'm almost done," I tell him.

"That's okay, I'm gonna run us a bath."

"I can shower once you're done."

"You could, but we're gonna take a bath together, honey," he smiles.

"Err, I've… no, that's okay," I mumble, stumbling over my words.

"I wasn't asking. We *are* gonna take a bath together, so why don't you go put the comforter on the bed, then stop hiding from me and get your ass back in here."

Slack jawed at how bossy he's being, I do what he says, even though I'm really not sure why. I read books and watched films with alpha men, but I've never encountered one in real life before. Is that what Granger is? He seems to enjoy telling me what's going to happen and what I'm going to do.

I don't hate it.

I've been alone and in charge of my own decisions and actions since I left home, really since Serenity left, so it's actually nice to let someone else take the reins for a minute, but even if I like it, I shouldn't let him take control, especially when he has all these ideas about me belonging to him.

Dumping the comforter on the bed, I search the floor for my clothes, planning on getting dressed and retreating back to the guest room to have a shower and try to find somewhere else to stay, but before I get a chance to even locate them Granger appears in the bathroom doorway, his arms crossed across his tempting chest as he arches an eyebrow at me.

"Going somewhere, honey?"

"No," I lie.

Stalking to me, he drops his head and scoops me off the floor and over his shoulder in the blink of an eye. "Didn't I warn you not to lie to me," he scolds, smacking his palm against my ass cheek.

I squeal in shock. He just spanked me. He just spanked me on my ass like I was a little kid. He just spanked me and I didn't hate it. He spanks me again on the other cheek and this time instead of squealing, a tiny moan escapes from my lips.

His shoulder shakes with amusement beneath my stomach and I clamp my lips shut, stopping any more embarrassing noises from escaping.

"Oh honey, I heard that little whimper and it wasn't because your ass is on fire, it's because your pussy was clenching and I barely tapped you."

He lowers me to the floor, making sure as much of me as possible touches him on the way down, until I'm on my feet in front of him, his arm loosely wrapped around my back. "I'd rather shower on my own."

"Stop lying, you're terrible at it, your face is too expressive and you wince every time bullshit comes from your lips. Now you can either tell me why you don't want to take a soak in my tub with me, or not, your choice. I'd rather you be honest. I've always been honest with you and you keep lying to me."

Blinking slowly, I pointedly look away from his expectant gaze and sigh. "I've… I've never taken a bath with someone else before."

"Good," he says, a smug smile on his face as he lifts me off the floor and lowers me into the water. Following me in, he pulls me down to sit between his parted thighs. "I want to steal all of your firsts from now on."

Bathing with him is weird. The water is nice and it's the first time I've had the luxury of anything but a communal shower stall at a campsite in years, but I can't relax with his still hard dick pressing into my back.

"How are you still hard?" I blurt, wishing I could swallow the words back down.

"Because you're naked."

"Surely you've been around naked women before."

"I have, but knowing you're *my* woman has my dick harder than it's ever been. I want to be inside of you again, but I don't want to hurt you, so I'm hard and I can't see that changing unless you want to try anal? I can't wait to take your ass, but that doesn't feel like a day two activity."

My muscles all tense as one and I jump forward a full foot, before he grabs me and drags me back to him, laughing. "Don't worry, honey, I won't try to get into your ass today."

I want him to say ever, anal is a total no-go for me, not that I plan to be around long enough for him to get ideas.

"I swear you think so loud you might as well have speech bubbles over your head. Calm down, we'll need to build up to me fucking that sweet ass of yours, I promise not to just try and shove my dick in it," he says, clearly amused.

"No, no building up, you keep that monster away from my butt."

Chuckling, he wraps his arm around my waist and drags me back into his body, leaning down to press a kiss against my shoulder.

"Your ass is safe… for now. Talk to me instead."

"I don't know what to say."

"I don't care. Tell me about you, I want to know all the boring everyday things."

"Like what?" I ask, suddenly more uncomfortable than I was at us just being naked together.

"Coffee or tea?"

"Coffee but I don't need it to live like some people."

"Cats or dogs."

"Dogs, cats are only apposable thumbs away from taking over the world."

I feel his laughter vibrate from beneath me. "Not a cat person then?"

"No."

"Action movie or chick flick?"

"Comedy."

"Night in or night out?"

"In, I don't really enjoy going out."

"Good, me neither," he says sweetly, cupping water in his hands and scooping it over my breasts.

He continues firing questions at me quickly, always nonsensical things that don't really delve too deep into anything beyond cursory thoughts.

"Country music or rock n roll?"

"Both."

"McDonalds or Burger King?"

"White Castle."

"Stay or go?"

"Stay," I answer, then immediately slap my hand across my mouth in an attempt to swallow back down my far too telling answer.

I can't want to stay.

I don't want to stay.

Only I do.

Until I met Granger and he showered me with all this attention and niceness, I was always planning what I'm doing and where I'm going next. My life is all about the next town, the next job, the next group of people to avoid. This is the first time in five years where the thought of staying somewhere is even remotely appealing.

"Good," he growls, turning my head and claiming my lips in an almost punishing kiss.

I open my mouth to object, but his tongue invades and I'm lost to the sensation of his kiss, of his tongue caressing mine, of his hand gently holding my chin, of his grip keeping me grounded and centered… even though it's him that's setting me adrift.

"Mine," he rasps as he pulls back until he can stare into my eyes.

"No," I try to argue, but the single word is barely more than a rasp.

"Yes." The tone of his voice leaves no room for arguments and I fall silent, feeling a little chastised and somehow sad that I might have upset him.

His arm releases me and I freeze, waiting for his reaction. Maybe this is the moment where he realizes I'm not worth the hassle. But instead, he grabs a wash cloth, coats it in soap and starts to bathe me.

Another first.

He starts with one arm, coating my skin in the thick, creamy lather, then moves across my shoulder, across my chest to my other arm. He pays particular attention to my breasts and pussy, teasing me with the cloth, but never breaching the entrance of my sex. Once I'm covered, he uses the cloth to wash all the suds away, until I'm panting and squirming against every stroke of the rough cloth across my sensitized skin.

Next, he washes and conditions my hair, massaging my scalp, neck and shoulders as he cares for me in a way I've never even dreamt of before. When he lifts me from the tub, I feel boneless and pampered. Brick by brick he's pulling down my defenses and I feel unequipped to fight back, to protect myself.

"Wrap your legs around me," he orders softly, wrapping me in a towel as he carries me into the bedroom and slowly lowers me to the bed. "I need to taste you again, honey."

I don't protest, I couldn't even if I wanted to, because I'm a heady mix of relaxed and wanton and I think he might be the only person who can help.

Crawling between my legs, he pushes my knees apart, spreading my thighs wide and displaying my sex for him. "Such a pretty pussy," he murmurs, leaning forward and pressing his nose against me. "You smell so sweet, and you're leaking, dripping for me already."

The first lick of his tongue makes me arch off the bed and gasp with pleasure, the second and third have my eyes rolling back in my head and my hands find his head, holding him to me, silently begging him not to stop.

After that, I lose myself to the sensation as he licks and sucks and nips at my folds, clit and mound. I'm nothing more than a ball of sensation as he pushes me through first one, then two orgasms as he tells me how perfect my pussy is, how tight and sweet and wet I am.

"I've got to fuck you, honey, I can't wait, I need you too much," he drawls, grabbing my hips and flipping me onto my stomach. Firm hands lift my pelvis, until I'm on my hands and knees, then he pushes my shoulders back down, so my cheek is pressed against the comforter, my pussy and ass up in the air for him.

"Fuck," he growls as he positions his dick at my entrance and pushes inside, filling me in one hard thrust. "Mine. My pussy, my woman, you're mine, Alice," he says through gritted teeth as he holds me in place and fucks me with a punishing brutality I've not experienced with him until now.

He warned me he was going to claim me and that's what this is, claiming. This isn't fucking, or making love, this is territorial branding and I love it. I meet him thrust for brutal thrust, slamming my ass back against his dick and claim him just as emphatically as he's taking me.

I can feel his fingers digging into my hips and I know there'll be bruises there, but I don't care. Until I met this man, sex was something I'd done that had been disappointing and dissatisfying. But with Granger it's so different I'm not even sure it's the same act. This man fucks me with his whole body, his mind, his presence.

When he touches me, I feel it from the top of my head to the bottom of my toes and even if this is the last time it ever happens, I'll remember every detail for the rest of my life.

An orgasm splinters through me and I scream his name. "Granger, harder, fuck me harder."

He does as I ask, slamming into me, each thrust jolting me forward as his hold on me stops me from moving. "Again, I need you to come again before I do," he says, his voice barely human.

When he smacks his palm against my ass, I come, the light behind my eyes turning white as pleasure so blinding I never could have dreamed it explodes within me. I'm only partially aware of him following me over the edge or his roar of completion as he comes, fucking me through his orgasm, until we're both done, wrung dry, and we collapse to the bed beneath us.

TEN

GRANGER

Fuck. I didn't plan to fuck her this morning, I definitely didn't plan on taking her like a madman from behind. Today I wanted to be gentle, to worship her and show her how good I can be to her, how much of a princess she'll be when she's with me. Instead, I completely lost control and took her like an animal claiming its mate.

But the thing is, she is my mate. My mate, my woman, mine, and every time she denies it just makes me want to prove it to her, to force her to accept that she belongs to me now. My dick's still rock hard and buried inside of her, even though I've filled her with my cum. We still haven't discussed that I haven't been using condoms when I've fucked her, and that each time I've enjoyed coating her cunt in my cum. I don't know if she's on birth control, and even though it's totally irresponsible to be happy that I might have got a woman I met yesterday pregnant, I just can't bring myself to care.

Rolling us to the side, I band my arm around her waist and pull her back into my front. "You okay?"

"Yeah," she says, her voice a little raspy from all the screaming.

"Not gonna lie, honey, I didn't intend to get rough with you, but I fucking loved it."

"Me too."

Her butt wiggles back on me and my dick twitches still inside of her, soaked with a mixture of my cum and hers. "We need to get cleaned up again."

"Do I get to shower on my own?"

"No," I laugh.

"Then I'm good here."

"Me too," I say against her neck, rolling my hips as I slowly start to fuck her again.

***

It's after noon by the time I finally let her out of our bed. She wanted to shower alone, but I refused, climbing in after her, not allowing her any time to change her mind about me and being here with me. I don't know everything about Alice yet, but it's obvious that given a chance to think too hard, she'll run and I'll have to start convincing her all over again.

She protested when I insisted on washing her again, but I can tell she loves the way I'm doting on her. I love it too. When we're both clean again I hold out a towel for her, waiting for her to step into it before I dry her skin, then reluctantly leave her naked in our room, while I go and get her things from the guest room.

Unpacking her meagre belongings, I place them into the dresser next to mine, then pick out an outfit for her and help her dress. Alice is a complex enigma of a woman. She's fiercely independent until I take over and take care for her, then she effortlessly slips into the role of submissive and allows me to provide everything for her.

Until her, I had no idea how much I needed my woman to need me. But with Alice I want to give her everything she'll ever need to make her happy. I don't want her to be able to be happy without me, because I know I won't ever be happy without her.

Taking her hand, I lead her into the kitchen and lift her up onto the counter. Bonnie is humming happily with her earbuds in as she buzzes around, baking something that smells amazing. She smiles happily at Alice and me when she spots us, but she doesn't stop working as she adds something to the bowl in front of her.

"What do you want to eat, honey? Breakfast or lunch."

"I don't mind," Alice says.

When it's just the two of us, she's louder, more vocal and demonstrative, but now, like last night, when we're in a bigger space with more people she seems to withdraw into herself. For a moment I contemplate asking her about it, but something stops me. I don't want to ruin this progress we've made, so for now I'll stop prying and just enjoy her.

"How about bacon and cheddar bagels with mushrooms and peppers?"

"That sounds great. What shall I do to help?"

"Nothing, you just sit your sexy little butt there and watch your man cook for you."

Her cheeks pink and I'm not sure what I've said that's embarrassed her, but I love the way she blushes. "Honey, you look sexy as fuck sitting there, my dick's still hard, I want you again," I say quietly so no one else can hear.

Her cheeks turn an even deeper shade of pink and I can't help but chuckle. I enjoy teasing her and watching her reactions, but I give her a reprieve and start on our lunch.

"Anyone else want bagels?" I shout. There's a chorus of yeses and suddenly I'm cooking for ten. As my siblings fill the kitchen and dining area, I notice Alice becomes even more withdrawn, her face dropping, her chin tucking into her chest as if she's trying to make herself as small and unnoticeable as possible.

The urge to go and demand to know what's the matter is almost overwhelming, but I get the feeling I'll learn more about her by watching than I will by asking her a direct question, so I keep half an eye on her while I quickly fry off bacon and veggies, toast bagels and grate sharp cheddar.

Almost all of my family make an effort to speak to Alice, asking her questions, playfully teasing her and generally attempting to break the ice that's so thick it's practically opaque. But despite all their efforts, my woman thwarts every attempt at friendship they offer her.

She did the same last night until I asked her to try, and then when she did speak it was like it was almost painfully against her nature. I wonder if perhaps she was bullied in high school, but she's too beautiful to have been a target and I would have thought she'd have been popular, or at least chased by every horny teenager.

Obviously she's shy, but this seems like more of a choice not to be friendly rather than an introverted disposition.

When Teddy jumps up and positions himself next to her on the counter, I find myself tensing for her dismissal, but instead she quietly replies to everything he asks. My baby brother has always had a soft way of speaking to people that others sometimes assume is weakness, instead it's this innate awareness of how to deal with people. He's soft when he needs to be, forceful when he has to, and a down-right asshole when he chooses. But as I watch him pull a reluctant smile from my woman's lips, I'm grateful to him.

I hadn't realized how tense I was, until I start to relax, but I still can't stop myself from checking on her as I finish off our lunches. Plating up the bagels, I grab mine and Alice's and head toward her. Teddy smiles at her and jumps down from the counter.

"Come here, honey," I say, encouraging her to shuffle toward the edge so I can lift her down.

"I can get down on my own," she says coyly.

"And I can lift you." Raising my brows, I dare her to argue, but she just sighs, a slight smile twitching at the corners of her lip, as she wraps her arms around my neck and lets me lift her down. Reluctantly, I let her go once her feet are on the floor, but I wish she'd let me carry her about like Bonnie does with Beau. Until today I've always thought it was a bit odd that Beau likes to carry her like a child, but now I have a whole new appreciation for having my woman wrapped around me like a baby monkey.

"What's everyone want to drink?" Penn asks.

"What do you want?" I ask Alice.

"Water or soda would be great," she tells me quietly.

"What soda do we have," I call to Penn.

"Coke and Sprite," he calls back.

I look to Alice and she wrinkles her nose adorably "Water's fine."

"Water for me and Alice," I tell Penn, urging her forward and toward the couch. She moves, but I can see her glancing toward our room almost wistfully. I'm not against the idea of us hiding naked in my bed all weekend, but if I'm going to convince her to stay here with me, I need her to get used to my family.

"Are we going to the opening ceremony tonight?" Bonnie says, brushing flour from her pants as she drops down into Beau's lap and takes the plate from his hand.

"I have a date," Penn says.

"I'll come for an hour, then Bay and I have plans," Cody announces.

"Who's your date with? Don't tell me you've picked back up with Roxanne again?" Beau snarls angrily.

"No," Penn scowls. "Not that it's any of your fucking business, but I'm taking Mariana Cole out."

"Mariana who works at the surplus store?" Cora asks.

"Yeah."

"Oh, wow, I always thought she was into girls," Cora shrugs.

"She is, but she's into guys too, I'm not sure if she's bi or bi-curious but we're gonna find out," Penn laughs.

When I glance at Alice, her eyes are a little wide, but

apart from that she shows no reaction at all. I don't know if this disinterestedness is an act or if she really doesn't care, but I'm desperate to know, to understand.

"You want to go to the opening ceremony for the festival tonight? You never answered yesterday about if I could take you out on a date, but I think I might know a way to convince you to say yes now," I tease, leaning in and pressing a gentle kiss to her shoulder.

I haven't spoken too loudly, but I also want my family to hear me, just in case Alice tries to argue and refuse. I've fucked her more than once, I've eaten her pussy and sucked on her tits, I don't think a date is too much to ask.

"Sure," she says with zero enthusiasm.

The urge to pull her to me, to demand she explain how she went from smiles and giggling in our room thirty minutes ago, to one-word answers and borderline ignoring everyone around her now swells inside of me. But I don't, instead I hold it in and eat my food, hating how awkward and tense the room feels as my brothers and sisters try hard not to look at each other or Alice.

The oven pings and Bonnie jumps up from Beau's lap, darting into the kitchen and pulling three trays of delicious smelling muffins from the oven, placing them on the counter. "These need to cool for a minute, then I'm going to run them over to the ranch. Beau, you gonna come with me?"

"Sure, baby girl," he says. "I'll go change my pants, no doubt we'll end up doing something over there."

"Granger, Alice, you fancy a walk? I know my dad wanted to talk to you about seeing if you could fix his kitchen table for him, the old one has started to crack right down the middle."

"Sure, we'll come," I answer without asking Alice. "We'll go get ready."

Bonnie nods and I stand, holding out my hand for Alice to take. She places hers in mine, easier than I expected and I help her up, taking her plate from her and loading it into the dishwasher on the way to our bedroom.

Once we're both inside, I close the door behind her and cross to my dresser and pull open the drawer. "You need to bundle up, it's colder this far up the mountain and the forecast says we should be getting snow any day."

"Okay."

Her voice is barely above a whisper, but I don't turn and look at her, needing to think about what I'm going to say, rather than just bursting out and demanding to know why she's sweet with me, but glacial with the rest of my family.

Pulling out a sweater and my winter coat, I step aside and motion for her to find whatever clothes she wants to wear. I could step back and give her some space, but I don't want her to have the room to create mental

148

distance between us, so I stay where I am, inches from her shoulder, close enough that I can see her chest rising and falling with each breath.

"Friends or family?" I ask, continuing the game from earlier.

"Neither."

"Why?"

"I don't like to be tied down," she answers, but it's a lie.

"Why don't I believe you?" I ask, crowding her against the dresser, my chest pressed against her back.

"I..." she trails off, as if she's never had anyone question her bullshit lies before.

"Do you need to borrow a sweater? Yours doesn't look like it's gonna keep you warm." Plucking at the thin fleece sweater, I don't bother waiting for her answer as I pull out one of my thick, knit fisherman sweaters I wear in my workshop in the winter and drop it over her head.

The sweater swamps her much smaller frame, but I like seeing her in my clothes, so I curl my arm around her waist and turn her to face me. "I'm taking you out tonight, the opening ceremony is cheesy, but the town goes all out with carnival rides and food stalls, it'll be fun."

"Okay," she says sweetly, all the disinterest from earlier gone as a soft, almost earnestly excited expression crosses her face.

Even more confused, I lean down and kiss her, needing to know if I'm imagining her hot and cold behavior. When she kisses me back eagerly, I'm none the wiser about her strange mood swings, but I enjoy her giving herself to me so freely and take control of the kiss, cupping the back of her neck and deepening our embrace.

After a long moment, I reluctantly pull away from her perfect mouth, nipping at her full bottom lip before I drag myself away. "Come on, Bonnie and Beau will be waiting." I hear her sigh, and again have to hold back a myriad of questions. I need the answers, but they can wait for the moment.

When we get into the living room, I help her into her jacket, zipping it up before pulling my own on, then sliding my feet into my boots, while she pulls hers on. Bonnie has a platter covered with a blue and white checked cloth, but steam is escaping through the fabric from the heat of the muffins.

"Muffin?" Beau asks, holding out one in each hand.

"Banana-pecan?" I ask hopefully.

"Blueberry," Bonnie answers.

I take them both and pass one to Alice, while Beau pulls another from somewhere and starts to eat, as he opens the front door. We all file out, ignoring the golf cart we usually use to move between Bonnie's daddy's ranch and our place, and instead head to the new road we had built not long after Bonnie moved in.

"Where are we going?" Alice asks quietly.

"Bonnie's family's ranch is the next property over, when she moved in, we had a road built straight across the middle so it was easier for her to get home and for her daddy to get to her," I tell her.

"I work on the ranch in my spare time and my dad usually comes for dinner a few times a week," Bonnie says, not arguing when Beau takes the platter of muffins from her, holding one in each hand.

"What do your parents do?" Bonnie asks Alice.

"I don't see my dad, but my mom travels with my step-dad, she's never really worked, she's just always mooched off whoever her boyfriend or husband was at the time," Alice says a little bitterly, but it's still the most she's spoken about her family since we met.

"And your sister is in the Army?"

"Yeah, she joined straight out of high school."

"Does she have a specialism?" Bonnie asks.

"I don't know, I haven't seen her since she left for basic training," Alice says, her voice breaking a little.

"Me and my brother aren't close. My parents had him when they were young and me when they were much older, we haven't gotten on since my mama passed away," Bonnie says, sadness lacing her tone.

"Did you get on before that?" Alice asks, amazing

me that she's asking a question rather than ending the conversation as soon as possible.

"Yeah, I guess so, he's so much older than me, so he was married and moved out before I was born, but I love his wife and they did stuff with me when I was little. He thinks because our daddy is older that he has to take responsibility for me, but I haven't been a kid in a really long time. He's resentful of me, but I don't really understand why," Bonnie tells her, and I realize it's the first time I've heard her talk about her relationship with her brother. I knew it was strained, that they weren't sure if he would come to their wedding, but hearing her talk about it now, I can see how much it upsets her.

"My sister took care of me when we were kids. Dad was out of the picture and our mom was always more interested in whichever boyfriend or husband she was with at the time to pay much attention to her kids. Serenity was basically my mom, even though she's only five years older than me. I guess I never understood how much that ruined her childhood until she left as soon as she graduated high school. I'm glad she's happy and living her own life now."

My throat thickens with emotion as I listen to Alice talk about her sister and the way she grew up. Her sister basically raised her, then she just left and from what I can piece together from the little Alice has told me, she hasn't seen her since. Maybe that explains a little about why she's resistant to form attachments? Or maybe I'm over thinking this and Alice just doesn't like people, I don't know. Either way, it's nice to know a little bit more about the woman I'm falling for.

"You're not close with your mama?" Bonnie asks.

"No, I was close to my Gram Gram, we lived with her and Pops for a while when my dad first left, but they've both passed now."

"I'm sorry, it's hard losing the people you love," Bonnie says knowingly.

"Yeah, it is. My pops went first, then Gram Gram died of a broken heart, she couldn't live without him. We lived on the other side of the country at the time and didn't get to go to the funeral," Alice tells her as I stay silent, not wanting to speak and interrupt my woman happily and opening conversing around me for the first time.

Bonnie's dad's house comes into view and the conversation ends. I wish I could push the house further away, I've learned more about Alice in the last few minutes than I've managed to pry from her before now, and I want to know more. I want to know everything.

Everyone we pass waves and greets Bonnie and Beau as we walk down past the house and to the large bunkhouse behind the barns. All the single ranch hands live on-site in the bunkhouse, while the married ones live in the small houses closer to the main entrance. Hal takes care of his staff, which is probably why some of them have worked here for decades.

Bonnie leaves the larger of the two trays in the bunkhouse kitchen, then carries the smaller tray around to her dad's office. "Hey daddy," she calls as she pushes into the small untidy room.

"Hey sweetheart," he says. "Beau, Granger."

"Hi Hal, I'd like you to meet Alice Lowe," I say, curling my arm around Alice's waist possessively.

Hal's brows lift in surprise, but he just smiles, pushes out of his seat and crosses the room to us. "It's a pleasure to meet you, Alice."

"Nice to meet you too, Sir."

"Call me Hal."

"Hal," Alice says quietly.

"Well, what can I do for you all?" Hal asks.

"I baked, thought you'd want a muffin before I take the rest out to the guys."

"Oh, banana-pecan?"

"Blueberry," Bonnie sighs, rolling her eyes.

Hal shrugs. "Still good." He reaches out and plucks a muffin from the tray.

"I'll go take these ones out to the barn, it's break time," Bonnie says, leaving the office with Beau following on behind.

"Why don't you take Miss Alice out to the back pasture, Cornflower just had her foal," Hal suggests.

"Bonnie said you wanted me to see about your table?"

Hal waves me off. "It's survived thirty years, it'll survive a few more days, I'll have one of the guys bring it down to the workshop."

I nod. "Come on," I say, linking my fingers through Alice's and pulling her from the office. She doesn't argue, just lets me pull her along behind me until we're outside again and I release her hand, curling my arm around her shoulders and pulling her close to me.

The pasture where the mare and foal are grazing is hidden behind the bunk house. Since Bonnie and Beau got together, we've pitched in a few times when Hal's needed extra help, so I know my way around pretty well.

"Oh, she's beautiful," Alice gasps, pulling away from my hold to rush to the post and rail fencing that surrounds the small paddock Cornflower and her pure white foal are grazing on.

Her hands are wrapped around the top rail, her body leaning forward as she watches the beautiful chestnut horse and her baby. Unable to resist, I move behind her, pressing my front against her back and caging her in with my arms resting on the rail on either side of hers.

She stiffens and I lean in and press a soft kiss against the side of her neck, scrapping my teeth over the same spot a moment later. A fine tremor shudders through her body and I kiss her again, immediately replacing my lips with my teeth.

Her lips part, but she doesn't make a noise. Lifting one of my arms from the fence, I wrap it around her waist, pushing my hand under her jacket and toying with the waistband of her jeans.

My lips continue kissing, then nipping at her neck and she silently arches into my touch. I know I shouldn't, we could be seen, but I ease my fingers into her pants and under her panties, sliding down until I'm cupping her sex, the heat of her pussy seeping into my skin.

ELEVEN

ALICE

His fingers slowly part my folds until he's toying with my entrance, teasing me, dipping the tip of a single finger into me before pulling back. We're out in the open, anyone could see, but I don't seem to be able to muster up enough good sense to care.

"Your pussy is greedy for my fingers isn't it, honey?"

His voice is as sweet and smooth as good whiskey and instead of pushing him away, I part my legs, silently pleading with him to touch me.

"Such a good girl," he coos against my neck, the slight hint of pain every time he scraps his teeth over the skin he's just kissed, driving me a little crazier with each touch.

A single finger slides inside of me and I gasp, closing my eyes and thanking every God that's up there that my pants are stretchy enough that he can move.

"Is all this wetness for me? Is your greedy pussy weeping for my fingers. Do you need more?"

I can't speak. I can't ask him to bend me over this fence and fuck me, even though that's exactly what I want.

A second finger enters me, pumping in and out of my sex in slow, shallow thrusts that only make me want more.

"So wet, your sticky juices are coating my hand. I think you need more, I think you want me to fuck you with my hand, I think you want to ride my fingers like they were my dick."

A choked sound escapes my throat and I feel his lips smile against my neck. "Such a dirty girl. Say please."

"Please," I pant.

A third finger slides into my core and I push up onto my tiptoes as he stretches me, filling me, fucking me with his fingers.

"I want you to come for me, Alice. I want to feel your pussy gush onto my hand," he orders, his voice feral and rough, all of the calm authority I've gotten used to gone and replaced with barely restrained need.

The heel of his hand presses against my clit as he fingers me, fast and hard and I come on a cry, burying my face into my shoulder as I desperately try to muffle the sounds of my orgasm. My body is still shuddering with release when his fingers are ripped out of me and he's grabbing me around the waist and carrying me away from the field and into a barn.

Opening a stable door, he marches inside, unceremoniously drops me to the floor, and bends me at the waist as he drags my jeans and panties down. His feet kick my legs apart, and I barely have time to lift my hands and brace my arms against the wall before his dick is slamming into me. He's fucking me hard, the sound of his flesh slapping against mine filling the empty space.

"Mine, this cunt is mine," he growls, his hands holding my hips as he forces me back to meet every single one of his brutal thrusts, dragging me onto his cock as he fills me.

I orgasm spontaneously without warning and his damp hand covers my lips. He forces two fingers into my mouth and I taste my own arousal.

"Suck them, clean your cum off my fingers," he demands, and I do as he says, completely unable to defy him. I suck and lick while he fucks another orgasm from me with no finesse, just brutal force that completely overwhelms me, until I feel like I belong to him, just like he keeps telling me I do.

With one last thrust, he slams into me as deep as

he can go and growls, low and long, his cock twitching inside of me. Sliding his fingers from between my lips, he gathers my hair into his fist and pulls me back, turning my head so he can press a kiss to my mouth.

"I like the taste of your pussy on your lips," he smiles, kissing me again, filling my mouth with his tongue.

I'm too lost, too overwhelmed with shock and need and pleasure to respond. The fumbling touches of the couple of boys I've had sex with before now, were nothing like the confident, sure way Granger takes me. Were my back seat disappointment's the exception or the rule? Is sex normally like what's happening between me and Granger? Is that why people are always doing it, or looking for it? Have I been blinded by my unfortunate experiences? Instead of avoiding sex, if it's always like this should I have been indulging instead?

"God, honey, the way you feel," Granger says, pulling his hips back and slowly pushing into me again. "I want to live in this pussy, I'd die a fucking happy man."

"Is it always like this?" I force out.

"No."

"No?"

"Never, I've never felt anything like this before. Mine, you're mine, that's why it's this perfect, why it's this intense, this desperate."

Tensing, I try to ignore his words, even though I'm

starting to believe him. If this isn't how it normally feels, if sex isn't normally like this, then is this weird fate thing he keeps talking about real? Or is he just pushing his fantasies onto me in an attempt to make me fall for his pretty words?

I don't know. All I do know is that for the first time in a very long time, instead of wanting to run, I want to stay.

I'm not sure how long we stay there, both of us only naked from the waist down, my hands braced against the wooden stall wall, his fist wrapped around my hair. But when he slowly slides his dick from inside of me, curls his arm around my waist and slowly pulls me up until my back is pressed against his, my limbs feel stiff.

"I want you again already," he growls, his voice sounding like a confession. Turning me in his arms, he cups my face with one hand and stares down intently into my eyes. "I want to see you on your knees with my cock between your lips. I want to fuck you in every position, beneath me, riding me, bent over. I don't want there to be an inch of you I haven't touched, licked, kissed. I want to own all of you, your mouth, your pussy, your tight ass. I'm obsessed and it's been two days, this is more than fate, it's madness and I can't wait to slip into oblivion with you."

His words and the way he's looking at me stuns me to silence, even though I have a thousand things to say. That

I want him too, that I feel the madness, but that I can't, that I won't, that I shouldn't embrace it. But I don't say anything, and instead when he leans down and kisses me, I kiss him back.

"Was I too rough? Did I hurt you?" His fingers find my soaked, dripping sex and he carefully slides a single finger into me.

"No."

"We haven't used condoms, I don't plan to either, I won't have anything between us. I'm clean, I wouldn't ever put you at risk like that."

"I'm clean too."

He nods and smiles, his finger slowly pumping into me. I wait for him to ask me about birth control, but he doesn't and that bugs me. I could be pregnant, he should be worried.

"I have the birth control implant fitted."

The smile on his face wavers a bit, as if... is he disappointed?

"Can you take me again? I can't get enough of you," he laughs, leaning forward and capturing my lips with his.

I part my lips to tell him yes, that somehow, he's made me as needy as him, but then the barn doors open and male voices fill the air. In seconds he's pulled my panties and jeans back up and tucked his dick away, but he doesn't turn to leave, instead he backs me up to the wall

I was braced against earlier. "Open," he orders, tapping at my lower lip with his finger tip.

I part my lips as if he's moving me around with strings and he slides his fingers back into my mouth. "Suck."

Closing my lips around him, I suck.

"My cum and yours, how do we taste?" he smiles, dragging his fingers from my mouth and pushing them into his own. "Fucking delicious."

More voices fill the barn. "Come on, let's go take a nap before we go to the festival tonight, I want you naked and in my arms."

Shellshocked and with no real desire to resist, I let him pull me under his arm and sneak me out the small door we came in through without anyone in the barn ever noticing we're there, then he spends the rest of the walk back to his house, telling me all the dirty, delicious things he wants to do to me.

"Go get naked, honey, I'll grabs us some drinks and snacks and I'll be there in a minute," he says, tapping my butt playfully as we enter his house.

"Nice walk?" one of his brothers asks.

"Yes thanks, one of the horses has had a foal," I answer, and it's like all of a sudden, the world of lust and sex and orgasms he's surrounded us in shatters around me and I fall to earth with a thump. I don't know how Granger's managed to wrap me up in this pretend world he's created, but until this moment I didn't realize how much I was falling for it, how ingratiated I'd allowed myself to become with the fantasy he's created for us.

I'm not the girl who gets the guy. I'm not the girl who inherits a huge family that love and support me. I'm not the girl who gets a home and security.

No.

I move around, living alone so that my poison doesn't affect those around me. I never get close to anyone so I'm not tempted to allow myself to turn into the needy, pathetic woman who becomes a burden to anyone who offers me even an ounce of niceness. I'm the girl who alienates people who try to be friendly, because within hours of meeting me they see me for who I really am.

No.

It doesn't matter how pretty a picture Granger paints for me, none of this imaginary future he's created can ever come true, because he might be the white knight, but I'm not the damsel in distress. I'm the crone, the poisoned apple, the dagger. I'm the one who sucks the joy and life of those around her.

I can't and won't do that to Granger.

I'm fairly sure someone speaks to me, but I don't answer. I need to get away, to hide while I rebuild the walls Granger's managed to knock down. Pushing open the door to his bedroom, I wish I could take my stuff back to the guest room, but if I do, I know he'll just come and fetch me. I promised him this weekend, and I know he won't let me back out, even if I tell him the truth about who I am.

Spotting my duffel bag, I move toward it, open it and pull out my cell and charger. I try to remember to keep the battery alive, but because I don't really use it, I tend to forget to check how much charge it has, and so most the time it's dead. Today I'm in luck and it still has ten percent. Plugging the charger in, I put it on charge and then sit on the bed and pull up google. It doesn't take me long to find a list of local RV's for sale and I slowly start to sift through the ads.

I work a lot and my life style is pretty cheap so I have over fifty thousand dollars saved in my bank. I'd rather not spend it all on a new RV but right now, I'd spend every penny if it means I can get away from here and the promise of a future that can never happen, no matter how much I might want it to.

The door opens and Granger walks in, his arms laden with bottles of water, beer and snacks. "I thought I told you to get naked, you've got far too many clothes on."

"I'm not really tired, I should go hang out in the guest room," I suggest, hoping he'll say yes.

"Where you are, is where I want to be and would you look at that, you're on my bed," he says playfully, placing his bounty on the dresser and slowly stalking me onto the bed.

"You don't need these," he says, pulling first one boot off then the second. "Or this," he smiles, taking my cell, glancing at the RV's on the screen with a frown, then placing it on the bedside cabinet before pulling my jacket, then the sweater he gave me off. "These are definitely in the way," he smirks, peeling my jeans down and off. "And this needs to go." My shirt is dragged over my head, leaving me in just my bra and panties. "Much better." He smiles, leaning back to assess me. "Oh no," he mock gasps, unclasping my bra with one deft twist of his fingers. "Your bra popped, might as well take it off."

His warm finger easily slides it down my arms, leaving goosebumps in its wake, then he rubs a knuckle over the front of my panties. "These are wet," he says seriously. "I don't want my pussy to get cold, let's take these off." Then I'm naked, while he's fully dressed and all of my resolve from only minutes before, all those affirmations of why I need to leave, why this can't happen, just fade away and try as I might, I can't think of a single good reason why I would ever want to leave this man.

"Come snuggle with me," Granger orders, shedding his own clothes and dumping them in a pile on the floor until he's naked, his dick hard again.

"How are you still hard?"

"You," he says simply. "My dick knows you're his and he wants to be inside of you."

"We've already had sex twice today."

"I know, but there's still your mouth and your ass."

"My ass is out of the question," I gasp, appalled.

"Nothing on you is out of the question, honey. My dick is gonna be in your ass, not today, but soon."

I shake my head, but he just smiles. "Let's play a game."

"What game?"

"Lie down, on your stomach."

"Tell me what game first."

"I'm gonna make you come."

"You've already made me come, how is that a game."

"I'm gonna make you come by fingering your tight virgin ass."

"No," I shriek, backing away.

"If you run, I'll chase, then it'll be my dick in your ass, not my finger," he warns with a chuckle.

"You're not putting anything in my ass, that's non-negotiable."

"Wanna bet?" he smirks.

"No. I don't even want to talk about it."

"If you let me play with your ass and show you how much you're gonna love my dick fucking it, I'll pay for your RV to be repaired no matter how much the repairs cost."

My mouth falls open and I stare at him. "No."

"Honey, I promise, I'm gonna have you seeing stars and begging for me to fill your tight hole with my big dick, and you'll get your RV repaired for free. It's win, win."

"I won't like it. Asses aren't for that," I say, shaking my head.

"If you don't like it, I'll never bring it up again." His finger draws a cross over his heart as he pouts.

He's closed the distance between us without me noticing, and he curls his arm around my waist holding me to him tightly. "Got you," he whispers against my ear, his warm breath making me shudder.

"I…"

"Don't think, just let me take over and I promise I'll make you feel so fucking good. All you have to do is lie down and let me take control." Turning me in his arms, he urges me toward the bed. "Crawl on, lie with your cheek on the pillow."

I move, climbing onto the bed, placing my knee on the comforter. Why am I doing this? Is it because secretly the anal scenes I've read in my books have turned me on, or is it because the idea of giving up control to him is just too tempting to resist? I've been in charge of everything for the last five years and since he barged his way into my life yesterday, I'd forgotten what it's like to have someone take care of me.

He wants control and the truth is, I want to give it to him. I want to throw it at him and let him be in charge and not just of the sex, but everything. But I can't. It's too much and no one, not even Granger, should be expected to take on my burden. So this is the last time, I'll give him this, maybe enjoy it, then I'll take back my life and walk away, because he's too perfect for someone as toxic as me.

"Good girl," he praises, and I feel the bed dip behind me as he follows, maneuvering me into the position he wants, my knees bent beneath me, my sex and ass open and on display for him. "I promise I'll get to your ass in a minute, but I need a taste of your pussy first."

His tongue enters me as he fucks and licks and eats me until I'm squirming, swaying my ass from side to side, chanting his name and begging for something that I can't even define. "You taste like you belong to me, Alice, it's the sweetest taste in the fucking world."

His mouth leaves me for a minute and the mattress moves, then a drawer opens before he's back, his lips finding my ass cheek, pressing a kiss then a nip to first one cheek then the next. A soft, teasing finger finds my clit, circling it, pinching it slightly, then backing off and dipping inside of me for a moment before moving back to my clit and starting the cycle all over again. Need distracts me until I hear the clicking of a bottle and feel the heat of his tongue, not on my sex, but instead on my ass.

Gasping in shock, I clench my ass cheeks together and instinctively move away from his touch. His finger leaves my clit, grabbing my hip and pulling me back to him. "Stay still, let me play."

TWELVE

GRANGER

Her ass cheeks clench tight as she fights against the hold I have on her hips. I'm tempted to spank her again because she definitely likes that, but she's so freaked out by the ass play I don't want to scare her off. Instead, I lean forward and sink my teeth into the fleshy globe of her ass and bite down. She shrieks, but I use her distraction to press my lubed up finger against her tightly puckered rosebud and start to circle.

She immediately freezes and I have to stifle a smile at her reaction. I want to fuck her ass, I want to watch my dick sink into her tight hole and know I own her completely, so I need to make sure she enjoys this. Now she's still,

I release her hip and move my hand back to her cunt, finding her clit with my thumb while I slide a finger back into her soaked sex.

I've never come inside a woman before, but tasting both my release and her own arousal on her cunt is fucking intoxicating, and I know this won't be the last time I eat her out after I've finished claiming her. With my thumb on her clit and my finger slowly fucking her pussy, she starts to relax and I slowly, gently start to play with her ass.

The tight ring of muscles is a dark pink and the urge to rim her again takes over, so I lean in and press my tongue against her. She tenses for a moment and I press down on her clit, distracting her until she relaxes again. Pulling back, I circle her ass with my finger, not putting any pressure on her hole, just teasing her with the sensation. Her breathing increases and I smile, pressing a little more insistently over her opening with each pass while I decrease the pressure on her clit.

My fingers are coated in lube, so I run a second finger over her hole, then push lightly against her, not forcing my way inside, but giving her a chance to get used to the way it feels.

"That feels..." she pants.

"Such a pretty little asshole, honey, so tight, I can't wait to watch it stretch around my dick." Pushing a little harder, the tip of my finger breaches her and I twist it around, coating the lube all inside of her as I slowly push my finger into her ass.

"Oh fuck. Oh fuck," she chants.

"That's it, let me in, let me take care of you while I fuck this tight little ass with my fingers." I've never been much for dirty talk, but with Alice, it's like I know I need to coax her with my words as much as my touch. If I give her a chance to retreat, she will.

She was barely alone for five minutes when we got back home earlier, and she'd already begun to hide back behind those walls of hers and started looking at RV sales. I won't let her do that, and if that means I can't allow her an ounce of breathing space, then that's what I'll do.

Her breathing becomes ragged as I push my finger further into her, slowly retreating then sliding back in until it's in her to the second knuckle and she's unknowingly arching back into me, asking for more.

Leaning down I tongue her clit, teasing her as I slowly start to work my finger in and out of her. She tenses at first and I increase my attention on her clit, distracting her while I get her used to having her ass stretched around my finger. Slowly pumping into her ass, I release my hold on her hip and slide a finger into her pussy. She's so wet that no matter how she may try to deny it, it's obvious she's turned on by the ass play.

"Oh god," she says, her words muffled from where

her face is buried in the pillows.

Smiling, I drag my finger out of her ass, loving the moan of disappointment that falls from her lips. Coating my fingers in even more lube, I add a second finger and push them both against her tight hole, sinking my teeth into her flesh as her muscles relax and she allows me entrance.

"It burns." Her hips move from side to side in a half-hearted attempt to get away, but then she pushes back onto my hand, moaning wantonly as both fingers slide into her. "Oh god, it feels so…"

"So what, honey?"

"So wrong," she pants.

"Nothing about me being inside of you could ever be wrong," I snarl, keeping up the pressure on her ass as my fingers slide all the way inside of her.

"Oh fuck, oh god."

The words sound torn from her, but there's no denying she's enjoying having her ass fucked. "Do you want more?" I taunt.

"Move, I need you to move."

"Do you want me to fuck your tight ass with my fingers?"

She's silent for a minute and I hold my breath, even as her hips move, her pussy clenching and unclenching around the single unsatisfying finger I still have buried inside of her.

"Please."

"Please what?"

"Move your fingers."

"Ask me to fuck your ass, honey, beg me."

"Fuck my ass, Granger, please, please."

My eyes go hooded as I do what she begging for. Slowly I drag my fingers almost all the way out of her, scissoring and twisting as I do, coating her forbidden passage as I go. Then when only the tips of my fingers remain, I slowly force my way all the way back inside of her again. Again and again I move slowly, dragging out her pleasure even as she tries to take over, to force me harder, faster into her as she grinds her hips.

"I'm so close," she pants.

"Do you want to come?"

"Yes, god yes."

Her ass relaxes completely, even as her pussy clenches and I start to increase my pace, until I'm fucking her ass with earnest and she's pushing back on me with every thrust. Pulling my finger from her pussy I slide it through her sopping folds until I find her clit, stroking it once, twice, never giving her enough friction to come, just overwhelming her with sensation. I curl my fingers inside of her and she detonates, her ass clenching around me so tightly I can barely move them as I fuck her through her orgasm until she slumps to the side, her body wrung out and exhausted.

"How. That. Oh god," she rambles deliriously.

"I think I win," I laugh, curling my body behind her, pushing my leg between hers and wrapping my arm across her waist.

Her body is lax and I can tell she's on the verge of sleep. If I didn't have to clean her up, I wouldn't move, but I force myself away from her and head to the bathroom. Washing my hands, I soak a washcloth with warm water then head back to her. She tenses as I clean the lube from her ass and pussy, enjoying the way she's allowing me to take care of her. Throwing the cloth toward the hamper, I peel back the covers and then drag her beneath them, pulling her into my body again and loving the way she seems to fit so perfectly.

"You cleaned me up. I could have taken care of it."

"I like taking care of you. I want to look after you, no fucking clue why, I've never felt like this before," I confess.

"I can look after myself." Her body tenses completely and I wonder why being cared for is such an issue for her.

"We're all capable of looking after ourselves, Alice, but that doesn't mean we have to choose to. You're mine and I take that fucking seriously. Too seriously if I'm honest. From the moment I saw you leaning up against your RV, I've had this desire to take away everything that could harm you, hurt you or make you sad. I want to give you the fucking world, I want to do every little thing for you."

"That's because you're a nice person." She sighs wearily.

"If you were anyone but you maybe. But this need I have isn't generous." Inhaling deeply, I prepare myself for the confession that may make her want to run twice as far and twice as quickly. "With you, all I feel is selfish. I want to own you, to keep you. I want you to need me the way I need you. But more than that, I want you to be dependent on me. I want your happiness, your pleasure, your joy to all be linked to me."

I wait for her to pull away from me, to tell me I'm sick, that I'm a freak, a psycho because that's how I feel. But the hatred, the fear and repulsion never comes.

"Be careful what you wish for," she whispers shakily.

"Having you, all of you, every single bit, is more than a wish come true, you're a compulsion that I don't plan to fight." I pause. "I don't think I could let you go now even if I tried."

Neither of us speaks, but she doesn't try to pull away, or maybe my hold on her is just so tight she can't move even if she wants to. Confessing that to her has shed a weight from my shoulders, but I know how I'm feeling about her isn't normal. I've never wanted to control a woman; I've never cared enough to even make regular plans. But Alice isn't just any woman, she's mine.

"My sister left because I relied on her so much, she was more like a mom than a sibling."

Alice's voice feels loud in the silence of the room, but her words shock me. She's volunteering information about herself and I don't want to miss out on the chance to learn something about her.

Releasing my death grip around her waist, I move, then roll her to face me, holding her again, only now I can see her as she speaks.

"I thought you lived with your mom?"

"We did. After we left our grandparents house, we moved to Florida to live with my mom's new boyfriend who was a long-distance truck driver. She was worried he'd stray while he was on the road, so most of the time she went with him."

"Who looked after you?"

"No one. We stayed in the trailer he lived in and Serenity took care of us."

"How old were you?" I ask cautiously.

"I was eight, Serenity was thirteen."

"No one ever reported it to the authorities? Two kids living alone in a trailer?" I can feel my anger rising, fury at two small kids being left to fend for themselves while their mother chased after a guy.

"There was an old lady who lived in the trailer near ours, she figured out pretty quickly we were alone, so she kept an eye on us. But the trailer park we lived in, we weren't the only kids who looked after themselves."

"How long did you live in Florida for?"

"Not that long, Mom moved from guy to guy and we went too. Most of them she'd met on the road somewhere or other. Truck drivers, sales reps, the kind of guys who spend more time away from home than not. She married Bob when I was thirteen, Serenity was eighteen and in her senior year of high school."

"What's he like?"

"Who, Bob? He's okay. He loves my mom, doesn't cheat on her, or hit her. He never wanted kids of his own, so he was glad that we were teenagers and self-sufficient when we moved in."

"You said your sister went into the army as soon as she graduated high school, so that must have been right after your mom married this guy?" The jigsaw pieces of her life that I've managed to glean so far all start to fit together with just this little bit of information she's told me so far. I hate her mom already, what parent leaves her kids to go chase after a guy? Is this why Alice is so against being here, why she's fighting to not get involved with my family?

"She left four months after they got married. I

179

understand why she had to leave. I wasn't her child, but she was basically my mom. She booked my dentists appointments, made my lunch, bought my clothes, cut my hair. She took care of me and I let her, because she'd always done it and I had no idea how awful that must have been for her."

The guilt in her voice is so evident I want to kiss her to stop her from talking about something that causes her so much pain. But I need to know, I need to know what's caused all her walls and how I can destroy them completely. "I'm sure she didn't think it was awful."

"She did. I ruined her life. I took away her childhood and I didn't even realize. She was my fixer, I laid all my problems at her feet and just expected her to take care of them. I was so selfish, so thoughtless, I never even considered that she had her own life and her own problems. I took advantage of her and the things she did for me and I don't blame her for running from me at the first chance she had."

"You were a child."

"So was she. I took advantage of the sweet, giving, caring person my sister is and I'll never forgive myself for it. When she left, I took a long hard look at myself and my life and I realized I didn't just take advantage of my sister, but I did it to everyone around me. I'm toxic. I infect everyone who gets too close to me. I use them, I take advantage, I suck the life out of people because that's just who I am. I know you think I'm this fated person that's meant to be yours, but I'm not, and even if I was, I'll only end up doing to you what I do to everyone else. I'll drag all the good out of you until you can't stand to be around me. I Know who I am and I won't do to you what I did to my sister, I won't sit back and watch while all the want you feel for me drains to nothing but hatred and resentment."

My mouth falls open and I stare at her in shock. Surely she doesn't really think that about herself. She can't really believe she's toxic. "Alice."

"Please don't try to convince me I'm wrong. I'm not. I live my life in a certain way so I don't ever have to see anyone else look at me the way my sister looked at me when she told me she was leaving. Even after the short time I've known you I can see you're a good person, I won't infect you with my poison."

"Honey, there's nothing poisonous about you."

Shaking her head, she tries to pull away from me, but I hold on tightly.

"You listen to me. I know we only met yesterday but it only took me a moment to know you were mine. You are it for me, I'll never find anyone else and I can guarantee you fate wouldn't send me someone who was a bad person, or who would hurt me or my family."

"You don't know me," she argues.

"You're right, I don't. So tell me. Tell me how you'll hurt me." Cupping her cheek, I force her chin up, daring her to look away.

"I'm needy, I'll drive you insane with my constant insecurities."

"I already told you I want you to need me. If I had my way, I'd make it so you can't breathe without me."

"I'm clingy. I won't want to be alone, to be independent."

"Be clingy. Move in with me, marry me. I'll do that all now happily. I don't want you away from me ever again. You can come to work with me, we don't ever have to be apart."

"I'll lay all my shit at your door; I'll need you to take care of me and all my problems."

"Give them all to me. I want them, I'll take your problems, issues, idiosyncrasies, I'll take them all, just give me you in return."

Shaking her head, she closes her eyes. "You'll hate me."

"Impossible," I instantly reply. "It's been two days and I'm already head of over fucking heels in love with you. There's nothing you could do to ever make me hate you."

Her shocked inhale makes me pause for a blink of an eye, remembering that I just confessed how caught up in her I am, that I already feel like my world makes no sense without her, that I love her, even though it's ridiculous and impetuous and insane, but I don't care.

Alice wants to run, even though I know she really wants to stay, all of her reasons are just excuses, but I'll do whatever she needs me to do to keep her. I'll dress her, pay for her, love her, touch her, fuck her, overwhelm her. I'll be her lover, captor, controller, I'll take away every choice if she needs me to and I'll do it happily, because she's my life now and I won't, can't let her go.

Her body's as stiff as a board and I feel the moment that she decides to bolt. Rolling her beneath me I trap her to the mattress, resting my weight on her, stopping her from moving. "Tell me what you need and I'll do it."

"No. No, you need to let me go."

"I can't, so tell me what you need. Show me the worst and I'll prove that I want it all."

Her head shakes from side to side, so I reach out and trap her cheeks with my palms. "Tell me. We have tonight, then the next two days, show me how needy, how clingy, how much you'll need me. If by Monday night it's too much, I promise I'll tell you, I'll help you leave and I won't follow."

"You promise?"

"I promise *if* I can't handle you, I'll let you go, but if I can, you have to promise to stay, to take the job with Beau if that's what you want, or just spend every day with me. But you have to promise to stay."

"I—"

I can sense her hesitation so I interrupt her, not giving her a moment to come up with an argument. "Feel this." Parting her legs, I push my dick into her, impaling her until I'm fully seated inside of her, her legs stretched wide around my hips. "You're mine, tell me you feel it too, I know you do."

"I—"

"Tell me." Pulling out, I slam forward, fucking her roughly, too roughly. "Tell me."

"I'm…"

Dragging my dick almost all the way out of her, I slam home again. "Tell me," I demand.

"I'm yours," she cries, as her pussy clenches around my dick and she comes on a garbled cry.

I try to hold myself back, to drag this out, force her to confess she belongs to me over and over, but her orgasm triggers my own and my body takes over, fucking her ruthlessly until I come, filling her with my release, biting my lip so I don't tell her that I hope it takes root, that I hope I breed her.

"Granger."

I love hearing my name on her lips, even when she sounds as small and as unsure as she does now. Siding out of her, I roll us to the side, keeping her close to me.

"Yeah, honey?"

"Please don't hate me."

"Never," I assure her, pulling her closer as sleep drags me under.

THIRTEEN

ALICE

The sound of someone knocking at the door pulls me from sleep just as Granger climbs out of bed and silently pads to answer it. Opening it a crack, he shields the bed and me from whoever's at the door, speaking quietly, before closing it again and turning back to face me.

"Hey honey, sorry, didn't mean to wake you up." Crossing the room, he sits down next to me on the bed, leans down and kisses me. The moment his lips touch mine, I relax. How can he affect me like this? I know he said he wanted my worst, but he can't really mean it, no one wants a mess of a twenty something girlfriend who becomes annoyingly dependent.

"What's the matter?"

"I just…" I trail off, unsure what to say.

"Tell me, I want to know all your thoughts, all of them, not just the things you think I want to hear," he says, his expression serious.

"What we talked about before."

"About you showing me how bad you think you are so I can prove that I can handle it," he says succinctly.

"Yeah, that was… That was, I shouldn't have said anything." Heat is pooling in my cheeks and I drop my gaze, too embarrassed to look him in the eye.

His thumb hooks under my chin, forcing my face up, waiting for me to look at him. "I'm glad you told me, I want all of your fears, all of your insecurities. I've got big shoulders, I can take them so you don't have to."

I try to shake my head, but his hold on my chin tightens to just shy of painful, keeping me still. "Tell me what you need me to do. I can take complete control if you want, fuck if I don't think I might like that." His smirk is sin itself and my body trembles.

"Complete control?"

"I can dress you, feed you, fuck you. I can make you my willing pet, never more than an arm's length away."

His voice is seductive, but there's a hint of amusement that makes me feel like he's making fun of me. "I'm not a child," I snap, pushing his hand away, but only making his grip firm until I'm frozen beneath him.

"I know you're not a child, you're a beautiful independent woman, but even the strongest of people can enjoy giving up control."

"Is..." I pause. "Is that what you like, for your girlfriends to give up control?"

"It's not something I've ever dabbled with before, but then I've never really had anyone I cared about enough to want to be in control. Everything's different with you, I'm different with you."

"I don't understand," I whisper.

"Neither do I," he confesses. "You make me feel out of control, so maybe exerting some of that on you will balance things out."

"You'll get sick of me."

"I doubt it. You think you're needy and clingy, but you feel too far away right now and my hands are on you."

A giggle escapes my lips and have to bite my lip to fight the smile that tries to fall free.

"How bout we lay down some ground rules, so we both know where we are," he suggests, lifting me up from the bed like I weigh nothing and placing me back down in his lap.

"Rules?" I furrow my brow.

"Yeah, nothing over the top, just simple things. I want

you with me all the time, but I'm not a fucking psycho, I know that's not always gonna be possible, so when we're not together if I ring you, you answer, if you ring me, I answer, no questions."

I nod, not wanting to tell him that if I'd called and he didn't answer I'd drive myself crazy thinking he hated me and was ignoring me. "I can do that."

"If I text, I expect a reply within five minutes and the same for me, you text I'll reply."

"Okay."

"You're in my bed every night, no excuses."

"Until Monday," I say, reminding him that we have a time limit on this.

"No, permanently. I said if I couldn't handle you at your worst I'd let you know by Monday night, but if I can, you stay, permanently."

"I—"

"That's non-fucking-negotiable, honey. Unless you've got a husband and a brood of kids waiting for you somewhere, then the only reason I can see that you're fighting this thing between us is because you have these fucked up ideas that you're toxic. Well I'm gonna prove that you're wrong, that you're my fucking elixir, not my poison, and I don't want you to go into this counting down till Monday. I want you to plan to stay, to want to stay."

God, I wish it was as simple as just saying yes, but it's not. He thinks I'm exaggerating, he thinks I'm just a normal woman with a few issues, he has no idea. I'm obsessive, compulsive, a fucking nightmare and when he finally looks at me the way everyone eventually looks at me, it'll devastate me. But I want to play pretend with him, even if it's only for a couple of days, so I humor him and nod, even though I'm sealing both of our fates and the pain that will follow.

"What else do you need from me?"

His expression is so earnest that instead of answering, I just lean forward and kiss him. It's the first time I've initiated anything between us and the familiar doubts fill my head just as he takes over, devouring me and vanquishing all thoughts but one, that he's mine, at least for the moment.

"God, you have no idea how much I want to fuck you again, but I don't want to hurt you and you've got to be sore, I've barely kept my dick out of you since we met," he says, tearing himself from my lips and resting his forehead against mine, his arms still holding me tight. "Talk. We need to talk." His words sound like he's warning himself, more than me. "So tell me how bad you think you'll get."

"It's not. I'm not." I swallow, wondering how I can explain this. "I'm not crazy, I'm not gonna go Norman Bates and be wielding a knife in the shower. I just. I'm insecure, but like a million times more than a normal person. I'll assume you hate me, so I'll either overcompensate by harassing you, or I'll withdraw and not speak because I'll think I should just stay quiet. I'll wear a shirt, then assume I look like a frump, or a slut, then I'll obsess over it and either ask you a thousand times if I look okay, or worry that you hate it. I'm too much. I know I am."

"So how about I look through your stuff and pick you something to wear," he says with a shrug, like the solution is obvious.

"It's not just clothes, it's everything. Have I eaten too much, too little, am I too blonde, not blonde enough? Am I strong enough, weak enough, assertive, submissive, loud, quiet?" Fuck, I can't believe I just spewed all that at him. Clamping my mouth shut I squeeze my eyes closed and will time to go backward so I can erase this entire conversation.

"Honey."

Inhaling slowly, I ignore his voice.

"Alice, look at me."

If I can just block him out, I won't have to see the look in his eyes, the one that says I'm a fucking mess and he doesn't want to deal with me anymore.

"Alice, look at me now."

The order in his words has my eyes snapping up and finding his, that aren't hard like I expect them to be, but soft and full of warmth. "I can't make you more secure overnight; I wish I could, and in time, I promise I'll do whatever it takes to make you feel like you can trust yourself and this thing between us. In the meantime, when you start to worry, just ask."

"Just ask," I cough incredulous.

"Just ask. That can be one of your rules. You start to overthink, then you ask me about whatever thought is spinning in your head at a million miles an hour."

"I can't."

"Why not?" he asks simply.

"Because."

"Because you think I won't answer? Or because you think I'll lie. Would it make you feel better if complete honesty is one of my rules?"

I think for a minute and yes it would, but how can I believe he'd tell me the truth even if he promises me complete honesty.

"What are you thinking right now? I can hear your brain spinning."

"You don't want to know what goes on inside my head," I say with a self-deprecating smile.

"Another rule for you is that you have to answer my questions when I ask them. As much as I wish I could read your mind, I can't, so you have to be honest too."

Stiffening my shoulders, I glare at him. "Fine. I was

wondering how I can be sure you'd tell me the truth."

I'm not expecting it when he smirks down at me. "Have I lied to you so far?"

"I..." I faulter, not sure how to deal with his calm attitude. Don't guys get defensive when you question their honesty? Shouldn't he be attacking, not calm and just... waiting.

"I asked you a question, honey."

"I don't know if you've been honest."

"I wish I could prove it, but you're not a mind reader either, so you're just gonna have a little faith. You have to be in this too, Alice."

I nod, unable to speak past the huge lump of fear and worry and hope that's lodged in my throat.

"Good girl," he praises, turning my face and claiming my lips in a heated kiss that has me wanting to climb into his lap and curl up like a kitten. "Now shower, before I forget about all my good intentions not to slide into that wet pussy of yours again."

Slapping my ass, he lifts me out of his lap, lowering my feet to the floor before following me up, taking my hand and leading me to the bathroom. I don't argue when he turns on the shower, then pulls me with him under the spray, taking over and caring for my body like it's the most natural thing in the world for him to do. By the time he's done, I feel pampered and cared for and wanted. It's a heady feeling.

Instead of letting me walk, he carries me to the bed, sitting me down on the edge as he chooses clothes for both of us. The adult who walked away from her family so she didn't have to burden them with her toxicity rises up inside of me, telling me I shouldn't be doing this, that I shouldn't hurt him, that I shouldn't allow this to happen. But the lonely little girl who longs to be wanted somehow wins, because this feeling he's managed to create inside of me is almost overwhelming. I want to be wanted. I want him to want me and so I'll take all he can give me; I'll bask in his care and attention.

Pulling a clean bra and panties from the dresser drawer where he put my stuff alongside his own, Granger returns to me, crouching down at my feet. Pressing a kiss to the front of one foot, he guides my panties up my legs, pressing a soft kiss against my mound as he pulls the fabric over my butt and into position.

His palms curl around my ass and he buries his nose in my slit over the soft cotton, pressing his face into my pussy. "You smell like mine. If it wouldn't drive me insane to know you were bare, I wouldn't let you wear panties. I like the idea of your jeans rubbing over your wet pussy all night."

"Granger," I gasp, when he pulls the front of my panties down and pushing his tongue between my folds.

"Just a quick taste, honey, then I promise I'll be good." His tongue strokes over my clit quickly, then he pulls my panties back into place and stands. "I like you naked too much, it feels wrong putting clothes on you." His pout is adorable.

"I can't be naked all the time," I giggle.

"When you come to work with me, you can. No one but us goes in in my workshop, you can be my reward for working hard, my naked little prize. I suppose in public I'll have to let you wear clothes." Holding up my bra, his brow furrows and he stares at it for a moment, then at me. "Gonna be honest here, honey, and say I have no idea how to put this on you, I've only ever taken them off in the past."

Reaching out, I try to take the bra from him, but he snatches it back. "No, I want to do it, you just need to tell me how."

Blushing, I talk him through it and moments later, my bra is in place and fastened while Granger plays with my nipples. "Fuck, Alice, I can't get enough."

"Stop touching me then."

"Never," he mock gasps, palming both my breasts in his huge hands and pulls me to him, my back flush against his front.

A giggle bursts from my lips, and I smile wider than I can ever remember smiling. He spins me in his arms, and when I look up at him, he's smiling too. "I like you like this, without the shadows in your eyes."

When his lips touch mine, I sigh into him, wondering if this is all a dream, or if by some odd twist of fate it's all actually real.

The rest of my clothes go on quicker and soon I'm dressed in tight jeans, a pink knit sweater and my boots. My hair is wet and still up in the towel Granger wrapped around it when we came out the shower. "Where's your hair dryer?"

"I don't have one, I usually just let it air dry."

Granger's dressed in a few moments, and somehow he looks even sexier with his hair rumpled with water, wearing jeans with rips at the knees and a flannel shirt. "Come on," he says, offering me a hand to take.

I take it and he leads us out into the living room. When he spots Cora he winks at me, then says, "Cora, can you blow dry Alice's hair? It's too cold for her to go out with wet hair."

"Sure," Cora beams. "Bonnie does the most gorgeous braids if you want to get it out of your face for the night."

I tense, hating that all of my ease and happiness from only moments ago has evaporated. As if sensing my change in mood, Granger's arm curls around my waist and he pulls me back into him, his lips moving to my ear.

"I don't want you to go out with wet hair. Cora is my

sister and she'll be your sister soon too. She loves to play with Bonnie's hair and she wants to get to know you. Please give her a chance and do this because I want you to."

My gut reaction is to pull away, to deny his words and curl back into my protective ball where I'm an island barricaded against hurt, but his grip on me tightens and his lips press against my neck. "I want you to try, for me, please."

It's the please that gets me. "I'll try."

"Good girl," he whispers, pressing a heated kiss against the pulse point in my neck.

"Alice, come sit over here," Cora calls, and I reluctantly leave Granger's embrace and make my way to where his sister is grinning gleefully.

Cora chatters almost constantly, even while the hair dryer is on and I can barely hear a word she says. I try my best to engage, but my self-conditioning to just stay quiet and not get involved is so ingrained in me now that I forget and stay silent, until Granger catches my eye, mouthing the word 'please' at me. The words I speak sound foreign coming from my mouth, but I force them out anyway, answering each question with more than a one-word answer. By the time my hair is dry and so smooth it feels almost weightless, I'm exhausted.

When Granger appears in front of me, his smile soft

and sweet, I sigh past my malaise and lean into his touch when he palms my cheek. "You want Bonnie to braid it, or have you had enough?" His voice is so quiet for only me to hear.

"It's fine loose."

He nods knowingly and I'm grateful that somehow my man understands me already even after such a short amount of time. My man. When did I start thinking about him as mine? Before I have a chance to process the thought, the living room is full of Barnett's and I'm too overwhelmed to think.

"Lets roll, beers to drink, funnel cake to eat and ladies to make swoon," one of the brothers, Penn I think, announces.

"Come on, honey, let's go," Granger smiles, pushing up to his feet and grabbing my hand to urge me to follow. I hadn't noticed my jacket, but he carefully turns me, helping me into it, before turning me again and zipping it closed, pulling my hair from the collar. "Do you have a hat? It's gonna be cold tonight, you need gloves too."

"I'll be fine," I try to assure him.

"No you won't. Where are they?"

"My hat is in my RV, my gloves are in here," I say pulling them from my pockets.

"Stay here," he orders and marches off to his bedroom, returning a minute later with a grey knit beanie. Pulling it onto my head, he positions it into place, then takes my gloves from me and slides them onto my hands.

For a moment, I wonder if his family will think it's odd for him to be looking after me like this, but when I glance around I notice that Huck is on his knees, kissing Cora's pregnant belly while he helps her slide her feet into fur lined boots and Beau is teasing Bonnie who looks so tiny against his enormous frame.

Is this what these brothers do? They find *their* woman and then dote on her with love and affection? I'd assumed this was just Granger pandering to me, doing and saying whatever he had to, to get me to stay, but could I be wrong? Is this care and attention a family trait and Granger is just giving me what I need?

"Ask me," Granger says, his warm fingers turning my face away from his family to look at him, his brow furrowed.

"What?"

"I can hear you thinking, don't break the rules so early on or I'll have to think of a way to punish you. So ask me whatever you need to ask to slow that brain of yours."

How does he know? How could he possibly know what I'm thinking? "Do they do for Cora and Bonnie what you want to do for me? Are you guys only attracted to broken, messed up women?"

His smile is blinding. "No, honey. We're jealous, protective, obsessed, maybe a little crazy, but we don't seek out women that need our brand of insanity. In fact, Bonnie ran so hard from Beau once he tried to claim her, she even tried dating someone else and threatening him with a shotgun. I'm not sorry that you need me though. Cora's so independent that Huck had to knock her up to find a place in her life. I'm glad you're softer, because I need you to need me, it turns me on to be the one to help and care for you."

Grabbing my hand, he discreetly places it over the hard bulge in his jeans. "You're always hard." I roll my eyes.

"Taking care of you, being the one to slow your busy mind, watching your eyes settle when they land on me, that's got me harder than I've ever been in my entire life. The more you need me, the hotter that gets me."

His words are a confession, even as he smiles while he says them to me and I can't help but smile back. Maybe me being needy and pathetic isn't so bad if it's his kink? His lips silence my thoughts and I lose myself in his kiss, on the way his fingers tug at my hair, the hint of pain keeping me present and in the moment.

When he pulls away and I open my eyes, we're alone in the living room. I had no idea everyone else had left. "Come on," he chuckles, dropping his arm over my shoulder and pulling me outside.

The small town of Rockhead Point has been

transformed into a winter wonderland. Booths, food stalls and carnival rides fill the town square and there are people everywhere. Twinkly lights seem to cover every tree, streetlamp and anything else they could be twined around and it's beautiful.

Bay pulls the huge SUV in front of the garage and we all pile out. For some reason I expect everyone to stay together like some weird, Montana brady bunch, but Penn, Bay, Cody and Teddy wave the rest of us goodbye and disappear into the crowd, and then it's just the couples left as we head into the crowded festival.

"Drinks, food or rides first?" Granger asks.

"Rides," I say, barely able to hold back my enthusiasm, even as I try to hide it from him. Does he even like carnival rides? Do I sound like a kid? Surely he wouldn't have suggested the rides as an option if he didn't enjoy them.

Granger pulls me to a stop, waving his family away as he drags me out of the flow of people, pinning me against a store front. "Tell me."

Shaking my head, I try to pull away from him, but his grip tightens until I'm completely restrained in his arms, unable to run, to hide from him and his ability to read my mind. "It's nothing."

"We're not moving from this spot until you tell me," he says sternly.

"It's stupid."

"You're breaking the rules again, honey. I wonder what I can do to enforce them? Maybe my fingers in your pussy, or your ass with no release would be an incentive to talk to me. I can't soothe those doubts if you don't open your pretty little mouth."

Closing my eyes, I block him out.

"Open your eyes, Alice."

My eyes snap open, shocked by the angry tone of his voice. This is the first time I've heard him sound angry, and the idea that it's aimed at me makes me want to tell him every thought I've ever had rather than feel his displeasure. "I was worried you were only offering to go on the rides for me, that you didn't actually want to and would think I was childish for enjoying them," I blurt.

His expression instantly softens, his tense muscles relaxing around me as his hold on me relaxes and instead of a restraint his arms become and embrace. "I love carnival rides. When I was a kid, I'd save all my chore money for when the county fair came to town, then I'd buy enough tickets to ride every ride three times."

I find myself smiling at the memory with him, my anxiety assuaged with his confession.

"Thank you for telling me, honey. I think I should reward you for talking to me, I know this is hard for you."

"You basically had to force it from me," I admit, hating that I'm this way.

"But you told me and you let me fix it, I felt the moment you felt better, when you relaxed and leaned into me. I bet if I was to slide my fingers through your folds, you'd be wet for me, I think you get hot when I look after you. I think you need to rely on me to solve all your problems, just as much as I want to solve them. That's why you're mine, because we're perfect for each other."

FOURTEEN

GRANGER

Her pupils dilate and her breathing quickens as I stare down at her. She might think she's hiding, but every single one of her emotions is written across her face. In moments like this when her guard is down, she's so easy to read. She wants to be cared for, coddled, protected and I'm so fucking glad; because now that her barrier of stoic indifference is gone, she's just a scared, needy woman who longs to be loved.

I love Bonnie for her fight and Cora for her sassy independence, but I knew my woman would be different. I didn't know until I saw Alice that I need to be needed, and she needs me.

My dick actually gets harder every time I think about how the ravaged look in her eyes calms when I hold her close, when I take the time to settle her anxious thoughts. I think she thought I'd run a mile when she told me she's needy, clingy and dependent, but all it did was make my cock swell, and my need to claim her in every way possible surged to life even more persistently than before.

I know she didn't take it seriously when I said I'm going to keep her, to marry her, but I wasn't joking. The courthouse is open first thing Tuesday morning and by lunch, I plan to have my ring on her finger and have her last name changed to Barnett. She's a flight risk, so I'm going to tie her to me in every way legally possible as quickly as I can, and I'll do whatever it takes to make that happen.

Curling my arm around her shoulder, I pull her back into the stream of people moving around the festival, leaning down to whisper into her ear as we walk. "Do you want your reward with my tongue, my fingers or my dick?"

Her breathing stutters and I smile into her neck. "I don't want to make you any more sore than you already are, so maybe I should eat you, lick you clean, then get you all wet again, so I can taste you all over again. Maybe I should lick and suck on your nipples until your pussy is creaming for me, I haven't had enough time to play with your tits yet. I don't want to neglect them."

When she stumbles, I tighten my hold on her, keeping her upright. "Are your panties soaked yet, honey? I'm gonna check when we get on the ghost train, I'm gonna finger your wet pussy in the dark and you'll have till the ride finishes to come all over my hand."

"Granger," she whines, her voice breathy.

Smiling, I chuckle. "Come on, honey, let's go ride some rides."

Two hours later, we've ridden nearly every ride and she's come on my fingers twice. After the second time, I made her lick my fingers clean and almost came in my fucking jeans. "Food and a drink, a man cannot live on your taste alone," I announce, dragging her away from the tilt-a-whirl and toward the food stalls.

"Can we have hotdogs?" she asks sweetly.

"Of course, then funnel cakes."

Her nose wrinkles. "Funnel cakes are gross."

Clutching my jacket over my heart I turn to her with an outraged expression. "Take that back, funnel cakes are the king of the carnival foods."

"They're too sweet, if I'm getting cavities then I want to do it with cotton candy." She laughs and I realize I'm becoming a little obsessed with making her smile and laugh like this. The way she looks now is so different from the closed off stranger I met yesterday; I need to keep her carefree and grinning like this for the rest of our lives.

"Cotton candy is the brainless cousin of the carnival desert. Funnel cakes are the king, cronuts, hand pies and ice cream the royal court, then cotton candy and snow cones are the poor relatives," I say decisively.

"No, cotton candy is the queen, funnel cakes are the court jester," she laughs, shrieking when I dig my fingers into her side and tickle her.

We wait in the line for the hotdog vendor and I hold her close, wanting everyone in town to see us together. Rockhead Point is a small place, so word will spread fast that I'm here with Alice and I want it to. I don't have any regular hook ups here in town, but I'm happy for the news that I'm taken to spread through to anyone who was hoping to land a Barnett for a husband.

"What do you want on your dog?" I ask her.

"Everything, is there any other way to get it?"

"Nope, there isn't." When we get to the front of the line, I order us each a hotdog, handing the guy the money as he passes me the food.

"I can pay," Alice says.

"So can I," I tell her, with a stern authority that I'm hoping warns her to stop talking.

"Granger."

"Honey, you're my woman, I pay, that's it, no arguments, nothing to talk about." Pressing a bruising kiss to her lips, I pull back and hand her a hotdog, warning her with a look not to push me on this.

Her eyes widen and that stubborn streak that's held her back from engaging with people for years flashes rebelliously in her eyes, but I grab her chin with my free hand and lean down into her. "My woman, I pay," I say again, and after a moment she nods.

As we eat, I drag her over to the bar tent that's been set up outside Barney's bar. "What do you want to drink? There's beer, or alcoholic hot chocolate and hot cider."

"Oh, alcoholic hot cider sounds yummy."

Ordering a beer for me and a hot cider for her, I finish the last bite of my hotdog, just as Barney hands me our drinks.

"Here you go, Granger."

"Thanks Barney, this is my girl, Alice, she's new to town."

"Hello Alice, welcome to Rockhead Point," Barney says, pushing his hand out for her to shake.

"Nice to meet you," she says shyly.

The caveman inside of me rears his ugly head at introducing her as mine, so for the next hour I wave to every neighbor, friend and acquaintance and tell every single one of them that the beautiful woman at my side is mine. She stops tensing after about the tenth time and by the time it's late and the festival is starting to wind down, she's rolling her eyes, more than aware of the game I'm playing.

"Is there anyone you haven't told I'm yours?" she snarks.

"Don't worry, if there is, I'll track 'em down." I wink. My cell beeps and I pull it from my pocket and look down at the message from Beau who's driving tonight.

Beau

Bonnie and Cora are ready to go.
You coming?

Glancing up at Alice, I take in the pink of her cheeks from the cool night air, the way my hat sits too big for her head, her blonde hair flowing just past her shoulders. "You ready to go? Or do you want to go get another drink?"

"I'm ready if you are."

Me

We're coming, see you in five.

I take her hand and she doesn't try to pull free, instead she happily walks beside me as we make our way back to the garage where the SUV is parked.

"I should check on my RV," she says, when she spots it parked up at the side of the building.

"The engine's fucked, honey, it's not going anywhere. You want to grab the rest of your stuff? We can get it now, or come back down for it tomorrow."

"I've got my clothes, what else do I need?" she asks, her brow furrowed like she's genuinely unsure of the answer.

"Everything else, I want you to feel at home in our room till our wing is finished, then you can decorate it however you want."

"Why would I decorate your home?" she asks slowly.

"Because it's gonna be our home."

She shakes her head slowly, but I yank her into my chest, startling her as I stare down at her intently. "Yes, honey, *our* home where we live together." Her lips part to argue, but I don't want to hear the same protests I heard the other day from her lips. Ducking down, I put my shoulder into her stomach and scoop her into the air, her head dangling down my back. Reaching up, I slap my hand against her ass hard, then march toward the car, opening the back door and depositing her inside, before following her in.

"Did you seriously just throw me over your shoulder like a barbarian?" she gasps, a hint of outrage in her eyes.

"I sure as fuck did."

"Get used to it, Alice, Beau still does it all the time when he can't win an argument," Bonnie laughs.

"I spank your ass to make you behave too," Beau growls quietly, but still loud enough that I hear.

"I like it too much for it to be a punishment," Bonnie

says, leaning across the front seats and pressing a kiss to Beau's mouth.

The car starts to move and I lean across my girl, grabbing her seatbelt and fixing it in place as she stares slightly open mouthed at my indiscreet brother and his equally enthusiastic young wife. "Their marriage is a little unusual, but it works for them," I say with a smile, draping my arm across the back of Alice's shoulders and pulling her into me.

"He spanks her?" she whispers.

"Because it's a huge turn on for both of them. He'd never hurt her," I assure her.

"Do you…" She pauses, turning wide eyes at me. "Do you want to do that to me?"

"It's not something I've ever thought about, but we can try it if you want. Your ass would look fucking hot all pink from a spanking then coated in my cum."

Her eyes somehow widen even further and I stifle a chuckle. "You like that idea?"

"No," she says too quickly.

"Don't lie, Alice, never fucking lie to me," I hiss.

"I don't…"

"I'd rather hear the truth, even if you don't think I'll like it, even if it's embarrassing, I don't care, I'll take it over a lie."

She swallows thickly, then nods.

The drive home is quiet, Cora falls asleep on Huck's shoulder and Bonnie and Beau whisper between themselves in the front seat. All my attention is on the quiet, stoic woman at my side. I saw another side of her tonight, the playful, funny woman who is ensnaring my heart more and more at every turn.

Her confession earlier seems to have lightened her a little, but I know that one conversation won't break through years' worth of barriers. I'll get there eventually though, I have to. When the car pulls to a stop outside the house, I unclip her seatbelt, open the door and step out, before reaching in and offering my hand to help her out. She takes it after a moment's reluctance, and the second she's out of the car I lift her into my arms, carrying her bridle style into the house and toward our bedroom.

I've enjoyed showing her off tonight, but now I want her to myself. My woman, in my arms in our bed. This is the start of forever with her and if this is how I'll feel in a year, and ten years, I can't wait for every day for the rest of my life.

Silently, I lower her to the floor and start to strip her clothes, pulling off her hat and gloves, jacket, boots, then shirt, pants and underwear until she's naked in front of me, her expression soft, like she can feel my need just to be close to her.

I strip quickly, pulling her into my chest, loving the

way her naked skin feels against mine. Lifting her, I carry her to the bed, pulling the covers back before climbing in and covering us both over again.

"I'm so fucking glad you're here. I didn't realize a part of me was missing, until I saw you."

She tenses for a moment, then relaxes, melting into my chest as I hold her in my arms. My woman, my love, my world.

***

The sun seems brighter, the air sweeter when I open my eyes and find Alice asleep on my chest, her blond hair spread over me like a halo. My dick is rock hard, but I ignore it, in favor of simply staring down at her.

There're a hundred dirty, filthy things I could do to her right now, but nothing feels more urgent than just enjoying this moment. I want to fuck her, claim her, watch her eyes roll as she comes around my dick. But all of that is secondary to this sense of ownership I feel having her pressed against me, vulnerable and naked in my arms.

Alice is mine and I dare anyone to try and take her from me. I'm counting down the moments till I can put a ring on her finger and legally bind her to me, but in the meantime maybe keeping her naked and in our bed might be the most sensible option.

She stirs and I still, stroking my fingers through her hair as she slowly wakes up, blinking sleepily up at me.

"Morning beautiful."

"Hey," she says, her voice raspy and filled with sleep. "What time is it?

"I don't know, sun's up, so not too early."

"Oh." Lifting her head from my chest, she starts to move and I clamp my hand down onto her ass and hold her in place.

"Where you going?"

"To pee." She blushes.

Giving her ass a quick squeeze, I let her go, watching as she debates taking the covers with her. "No point trying to hide, I've seen and licked almost all of you." I chuckle.

Her blush deepens but she heeds my words and makes a dash for the bathroom, still naked. Shuffling up the bed a little, I prop my back against the pillows and keep my eyes fixed on the door, waiting for her to come out.

The toilet flushes, then water starts to run and a minute later the door opens and she emerges. "Come here, honey," I call, crooking my finger and beckoning her to me.

Somewhat awkwardly, she rushes toward me, diving under the covers to hide her body. "Don't get shy now. I got a seat right here for you," I say, pushing the covers back and patting my thighs.

"Shouldn't we get up?"

"Why?" I ask, raising my brows in questions.

"Because…" she trails off, unsure what to say to win an argument she was never going to win.

"I don't have to work today and you go where I go, so no. I can't think of a single more important thing we have to do than you bringing your beautiful self here and sitting in my lap."

Slowly she emerges from beneath the comforter, straddling my legs and sitting tentatively on my thighs. Grabbing her legs, I yank her further up so her pussy is mere inches from my hard dick that's resting against my stomach waiting for his call to arms.

Her expression startles for a moment, then she settles and looks up at me from beneath thick dark lashes. Reaching out, I stroke a finger over her nipple, watching as it pebbles beneath my touch. Pinching lightly, I move to the other, giving it the same treatment until her dark pink nipples are hard and begging for my touch.

Leaning back against the pillows, I watch her.

"What are you doing?" she asks unsurely.

"I'm taking a minute to remember how much of a lucky bastard I am that you're mine."

"I'm definitely no prize, trust me."

"You're the greatest prize in the entire fucking world, honey, never fucking forget it and if I ever do, make sure you fucking remind me. I'll never fucking deserve you, but

I swear I'll spend the rest of our lives trying to prove to you that I do."

FIFTEEN

ALICE

As his words sink under my skin, I realize that he's starting to make me believe all of this is true. That everything he's said, promised, talked about could all be real.

Could it?

Since Serenity left, I've spent my time feeling like I understand why I repel people, why they all inevitably hate me and reject me. But in two short days, Granger is making me question everything I thought I knew.

Is it possible that he's the exception to the rule? Is he the one person who can tolerate me, who's immune to my poison? Only his family don't seem sick of me yet either.

Bonnie and Cora have been nothing but sweet to me, his brothers kind and nice.

Is it this house? This legacy that Granger seems to believe in so wholeheartedly. If I'm his, does that somehow counteract how the rest of the world sees me?

We've had sex so many times in the last two days I've lost count. My body is sore and well used, but the moment he touches me I want him again, no matter how much my vagina protests. He's sparked a sexual awakening I never thought was possible. In the years it's been since the last time I had sex, I'd assumed I was A-sexual because there hasn't been a single occasion where I was remotely attracted to anyone. But Granger is the exception to the rule, he's the exception to all my rules.

Granger's hand cups my butt cheek, pulling away to slap it, leaving a sharp, not unpleasant heat in its wake. "I want to spank this ass, then fuck you from behind and come all over your pink, hot cheeks," he growls, spanking me again. "I never thought that would turn me on, but it really fucking does."

"I," I splutter.

His laugh is warm and full of amusement. "You're making me want to do all kinds of fucked up things to you, honey."

"I don't know how I feel about you spanking me."

"If you hate it, we'll stop."

"Now?" The word comes out on a high-pitched shriek.

"No honey, not now. I know you're sore, I'll try to keep my dick to myself until tonight."

His cell phone beeps and he squeezes my butt cheek as he leans over and grabs it from the bedside table. Tapping at the screen, he smiles then taps some more, before his cell makes a swooshing noise and he starts tapping again.

"Who is it?" I ask, then hate myself for asking. It's not my place to question who's texting him, if it is a text.

"My brothers, we have a group chat," he says easily, like me wanting to pry into his personal messages isn't a problem.

His cell swooshes again, then again and I try to roll away but he holds me to him, looking down at me with a quizzical glance. "What's the matter?"

"Nothing," I lie. "I'm just gonna start the tub, I'm sticky." Maybe he won't hear the lie if it's blended with some truth.

"I can do it. You stay in bed."

"No, I need to pee too," I say, rolling away from him to avoid his penetrating gaze.

I'm half way to the bathroom door when his growling rumble stops me. "Alice."

I don't want to turn around and look at him. I'm sure he'll see the insecurity filling my eyes and I don't want that. I don't want to be toxic and pathetic to him.

"Look at me, honey."

His voice is softer, but I can still hear the steel in his tone, and I slowly spin around with an exhale. I'm naked, and until this moment I hadn't even noticed, but I do now, when I feel his eyes rake over my skin with a predatory gleam.

"You need to see my cell?"

"No," I say, shaking my head quickly.

"I don't want lies and secrets between us. I've got nothing to hide, for you I'm an open book and I'm hoping that eventually you'll offer me the same. I'm texting with my brothers, that's all."

"It's none of my business."

"I'm yours as much as you're mine, so it's completely your business."

Squeezing my eyes shut, I shake my head. "I don't want to be like this. I'll ruin everything, I always do." I'm pathetic. The realization hits me like a freight train and I wilt beneath the truth. Two days, that's all it took for me to become a needy, pathetic mess.

His fingers wrap around my arms firmly as he pulls me to him, pressing my cheek against his warm, firm chest. "I won't let you ruin us," he purrs into my hair. "We all have our shit, honey, this is yours. Wanna know mine?"

I nod, not lifting my face from where it's pressed into

him.

"You make me feel."

His confession surprises me. So far, Granger is by far the most openly communicative person I've ever met.

"What do you mean?"

"Before you, I enjoyed women, but they were never mine. They came and went, I came and went, no commitment, no feelings, just simple. With you I want to own you, possess you, consume you. I don't think I could let you go even if you begged." His words are little more than rasps, but I hear them clearly.

"Do you like it?" I ask, suddenly compelled to know if he enjoys feeling this way about me.

"I fucking love it. Everything about this obsession I have for you feels right. You think you're the toxic one, but I'm gonna drive you crazy. I'm jealous just thinking about someone other than me looking at you, I want to lock you in this room and never let you go. You're mine and I'm not sure if that will make you trust me or drive you away but I can't help myself, I couldn't stop feeling this way even if I tried."

Shocked, I lift my face from his chest and look up into his stormy eyes, wondering if his gaze will be full of lies or sincerity. Nothing but open, lust filled honesty looks back at me.

"You wanna read my messages, search through my

cell, share a fucking toothbrush, I'm happy to do it, because I'm sure as shit gonna wanna know who's texting you. I'm gonna want to know where you are, who you're with and what you're doing. You think you're toxic, then I'm gonna feel like a nuclear explosion."

A giggle rises up my throat, bubbling out before I have a chance to swallow it back down again.

"Oh, you think that's funny?" He smiles.

I nod.

"You think me being insane for you is funny?"

I nod again.

His fingers find my sides and he tickles me. I shriek, wiggling away, but he grabs onto me tighter, torturing my sides as his fingers tickle up and down my ribs until I'm laughing and panting and dancing around in his hold, his hard dick pushed into my stomach. "Go pee, before I bend you over and fuck you," he growls with a laugh, turning me in the direction of the bathroom and slapping me on the ass as he pushes me gently away.

We bathe together and he pushes my hands away when I reach for the body wash, telling me he hates the idea of even me touching what belongs to him. Then he cleans every inch of my skin, then shampoos and conditions my hair before finally wrapping me in a white fluffy towel and carrying me back to the bed. The care and attention he's showing me is addictive, he's spoiling me with affection and I love it.

"I need to get Cora to show me how to blow dry your hair," he announces after her passes me some underwear, a pair of my soft lounge pants and one of his huge hoodies.

"Why?"

"Because I want to be able to do it for you."

"Why?" I snicker

"I want to look after you."

"So that means blow drying my hair?"

"Obsessed," he says with a smirk and a crazy gleam in his eyes.

Smiling, far more pleased than I should be, I shake my head at him and get dressed, sniffing his hoodie as I pull it over my head, enjoying the way his scent surrounds me.

"Come on, woman, I need to feed you," he announces. "Jump on."

Turning around he motions for me to jump on his back and with a girlish giggle, I do, wrapping my arms around his neck and my legs around his hips. Then I let him carry me barefoot from his bedroom and out into the living room, so consumed by this man that I completely forget about the nine other occupants of the house.

For some reason, I expect them to all come to a screeching stop and turn and stare at us, but instead they don't even lift their heads from what they're doing.

Granger carries me over to the kitchen, depositing me on the counter. There're two plates covered over with silver foil and Granger grabs them, lifting the foil and examining what's beneath. "You good with waffles or you want something different?"

"Waffles sounds good."

His smile is breathtaking when he looks up at me, and I feel all the air being sucked from my lungs as I take in how beautiful this man truly is. Dark ruffled hair, warm brown eyes that seem to see inside of me to the very core of my being. High, regal cheekbones and full lips. He's perfect and if he wasn't looking at me like I hung the moon, I'd probably feel too insignificant to be in his notice. But he is looking at me, he's staring at me and smiling, and suddenly this feels okay and right and real.

Leaning in, Granger presses a soft kiss to my lips before he pulls away and moves around the kitchen, warming up our waffles, pouring me both coffee and juice before he comes back to me, lifting me from the counter and lowering me onto one of the bar stools that sit beside a breakfast bar.

"Do you want them drowning in syrup or drizzled?" he asks.

"Drowning, but I can do it."

"Drowning it is." Ignoring my protests, he liberally coats my waffles in syrup, doing the same to his own, then he cuts off a piece, skewering it with his fork and lifting it to my lips. I take it, chewing and swallowing as he takes a piece for himself, then cuts another for me, feeding me, like it's the most normal thing in the world for a man to feed a full-grown woman.

"Let me take care of you," he whispers when the protests in my head grow too loud to keep at bay. I don't know if I have an external tell that warned him I was getting anxious, or maybe he really is as in sync with me as he seems to believe he is, but his words do exactly what he intended and I calm down, my mind clearing as he feeds us alternating bites, until I'm stuffed.

He finishes all of his own and what's left on my plate and even lets me load the plates into the dishwasher, only growling at me once that I should let him do it. "Go get a jacket and we can drive down into town and box up the rest of your stuff from your RV."

"Do we need to do that now?" I protest, not wanting to go deal with my RV and the decision I need to make about what I'll do when it's fixed.

"You wanna stay here and I can go do it?" he offers.

"I just don't see the point of me emptying it, I don't need anything but my clothes at the minute."

Granger's expression darkens. "I want your stuff here, in our room."

"Why is it so important that my nik-naks are here?"

"Because this is where you live now, so you need to have your shit here," he snarls, practically spitting the words out. "You can either come with me to get your stuff, or I can go and get it on my own. Your choice, but either way, your shit is moving in here today."

His anger is so unlike the Granger I've seen so far, I almost step back, but even though I barely know him, I know he'd never hurt me.

"Granger."

"Alice, don't start. We agreed you'd throw your worst at me and so far, I've seen nothing I can't happily cope with for the rest of our fucking lives. I want you here, I need you here. I need to know you're not half way out the door planning to run the moment I turn my back. Give me one good reason why we can't go get your stuff and move it in here?"

I try to think of one, or at least something other than the obvious *we've only known each other for three days* but absolutely nothing comes to mind, and for a moment I flounder, my lips parted to argue, but with nothing to say.

"Exactly," Granger says triumphantly. "Go get your boots and a jacket on and we'll get going."

Thirty minutes later, I'm sitting in the passenger seat of Granger's car, Teddy and Bay following behind us in a big truck to 'haul my stuff' back up to the house. I tried telling them I doubt I have even a box full of possessions, but they're determined that *everything* be moved today.

The large hand on my thigh squeezes and I look up at the man beside me. "You freaking out?"

"A little. Don't you think this is all a bit too soon?"

"No. I'd have bought all your shit with you on Friday if I could have convinced you to pack that as well as your clothes."

"You're insane," I scoff, rolling my eyes at him.

"Obsessed," he says, smirking lustfully at me.

My tension rises as we enter the small town, like the mountains have acted as a buffer from real life, but now we're here, reality has slipped back in. Granger pulls into the garage, and Bay and Teddy park next to us, climbing out the truck and rolling up their sleeves as if they've forgotten I live in an RV not a mansion.

"I'll grab the keys from the office," Bay says, unlocking the front door of the garage and disappearing inside.

"Honey, you wanna get in and start sorting, then you can pass stuff back and I'll pack it into a box?" Granger says, taking my hand.

"Nah, I can just box it up as I sort."

"Okay, then just let me know once you've filled a box and we'll start loading it into the truck."

"Sure," I laugh.

His brows furrow, but I just smile, taking the huge

cardboard box Teddy has built for me and making my way toward my RV as Bay appears with the keys. Taking them from him, I unlock the door and the familiar smell of damp and the peach air fresheners I keep hung throughout the small space hits me.

A wave of what feels a lot like melancholy washes over me and for the first time, I see how narrow my life has been for the last five years. Living in an RV doesn't allow for clutter, but there's not a single personal item out on display. The sides, cupboards and tiny shelves are empty and when I climb inside, I already know that if I leave Rockhead Point I'll struggle to survive in the bubble of self-imposed isolation I've lived in since I left Missouri.

Dragging the box in behind me, I place it on the floor and it fills all of the available floor space. There's no way I can move around it, so I drop it to the ground outside and start to lift up the seats to where the only personal stuff I have resides. Taking out a small box, I lift the lid and glance down at the handful of photos and mementos inside. My sister's smiling face stares back at me and I quickly close the lid, not wanting to deal with the rush of emotions that comes with anything to do with her and what I did to her.

Placing the small box into the bigger box, I sort through each storage area one at a time, methodically moving from one side of the RV to the other, pulling out everything I want to keep. Turns out there's less than I thought and by the time I'm done, the cardboard box is barely halfway full.

"I'm done," I announce, climbing out of the RV and finding Bay and Teddy leaning against the truck, both studying their cell phones.

"Need another box?" Teddy asks.

"No, I'm done, that's it." I look from side to side, wondering where Granger is. "Where's Granger?" A sense of panic starts to rise up inside of me as my eyes frantically look from side to side, searching for his familiar face. When I don't see him, my breaths become erratic, my chest feeling tight.

"He went to get donuts," Bay says, pushing his cell into his pocket and peering around me. "Where's the rest of your stuff?"

"That's it." I motion to the half full box. Placing my hand against my chest as I struggle to breathe, my ribs actually hurt as the air surrounding us seems to evaporate and my eyesight narrows, black appearing at the sides of my vision.

"Granger is gonna be pissed if you don't bring everything," Teddy says, a hint of warning in his soft voice. "Hey, are you okay?"

I don't reply, I don't have enough air in my lungs to form words. He left me, he told me to pack my belongings and then he left me. Is this it? Has he had enough of me now? He's not here and that must mean that he doesn't want me anymore. I should unpack, but I can't move, my head getting fuzzy as it gets harder and harder to breathe.

"Alice." Someone's calling my name, but I can't see them, darkness invading my sight. I'm alone again. Two days was all I got with him, two days of him not hating me. It was blissful, but it was probably longer than I deserved and now he's left me, and I can't even blame him. But I also can't breathe without him, he told me he wanted my problems, that I could rely on him, then he left. It's a cruel trick, but I can't really hate him for it, I'd leave me too.

"Alice." There's someone in front of me, but it's not Granger, because he's gone. "Breathe, Alice, deep breaths, follow me, breathe in and then out."

I can hear more voices, snippets of conversation as I wheeze, all of the air almost gone from my burning lungs.

"Panic attack."

"Teddy's trying."

"Get back here."

Then there's a thudding and suddenly I'm surrounded by him, his scent, his familiar touch. Granger.

"Alice," he snaps, his voice harsh, but clear. "Breathe. Listen to me. Breathe."

The order in his voice filters through the darkness and I do as he says, dragging in a painful, shallow breath, then another, my vision slowly clearing as he comes into focus.

"Good girl, and another in and out, slow and steady. Come back to me, honey."

With each breath, his voice becomes a little clearer, louder, the feel of his arms around me, his palm pressed against my chest, feeling the slow, jagged rise and fall of my breaths.

"She okay?" someone asks.

"Yeah," Granger tells them. "Just give us a minute, okay."

The fear and panic that had overwhelmed me starts to recede and I realize I'm in his lap, on the cold floor. "Alice."

Turning my head toward his voice, I look at him and find his jaw tense, his eyes wide.

"Thank fuck," he snarls, palming my cheek and pulling me to him, resting his forehead against mine. "Are you okay?"

"You were gone," I whisper.

His face pales. "I went to get coffee and donuts."

"I thought you'd left me."

A wildness fills his expression, not solely angry, more feral and intense. "Never. Never."

"I'm sorry." Tears fill my eyes and I look away, feeling stupid and hating that I'm being so needy.

"No, I should have told you I was going to get food.

I'm sorry, baby."

"You went for coffee and I lost my shit, no wonder people don't stick around."

"This is on me. My fault. I should have told you, but you have to have some faith that I'm not just going to abandon you. New rule, we tell the other person where we're going, even if it's just for coffee," he says, his voice hard and unyielding.

I nod, still feeling like an idiot. "I can get up."

"No. Sit your ass down and just keep breathing, in and out, in and out."

I do as he says, but it's still ten minutes later before he finally lets me pull myself out of his lap and stand up.

"You okay?" Teddy asks, concern lacing his voice.

I nod.

"Panic attack?"

I shrug, because honestly, I don't really know, whatever it was I've never experienced it before, but then it's been years since I've allowed myself to care about anything except where I was driving to next.

"She's okay now," Granger assures them, his arm protectively around me. "Let's finish packing."

"That's it," I say, nodding to the box on the floor.

"I want all your stuff, honey."

"That is everything. I live in an RV, did you really think I was hiding a sixty inch tv and a hot tub in there?"

I taunt, trying bravado to hide how stupid I feel over my meltdown.

"But there's not even half a box. Everyone has stuff," Bay says, gesturing to the RV again.

"That's it," I shrug.

I look up to find Teddy staring at me curiously and I immediately look away from him.

"That's everything?" Granger asks, turning me to face him, looking at me intently, searching for a lie.

"That's everything. All that's left is kitchen stuff which I really don't need, most of it is old and came from thrift shops and dollar stores."

"That's everything?" Granger, Bay and Teddy say in almost perfect unison.

I shrug, uncomfortably, wishing I'd told him to just come pack this stuff up on his own.

"The moment our wing is finished, we're going shopping, I'm gonna buy you everything you didn't know you wanted," Granger snarls.

"I don't need a lot of stuff."

"I don't care, Alice; I want to give you everything." His lips smash against mine and I let him claim me, sensing how fervent his need is, even if I don't really understand it.

The tension in the air dilutes and I hear his brothers chuckle and move around as Granger reluctantly pulls away from my lips.

"Well fuck, it took us nearly the whole damn weekend just to move Cora's clothes. Alice, you're my new favourite sister," Bay laughs, scooping the single box from the floor and loading it into the backseat of the truck just as the first snowflake falls from the sky.

A blush fills my cheeks at Bay's words. Sister? He called me his favourite sister, does that mean they all think I'm a permanent fixture now? Did Granger tell him to say that? Or was it a joke? Surely it had to be a joke, it's been three days, no one can possibly believe that this thing between Granger and I could be that serious already.

But Granger does, and truthfully, he's kind of got me believing it too, so maybe to him and this family it's perfectly normal to move a woman in and informally adopt her. I snigger lightly to myself at that thought, avoiding Granger's quizzical expression and pushing down the surge of hope that maybe it is all possible and real and true. Because I want it to be.

Taking my hands, Granger pulls me to my feet, glancing at the empty RV behind me and scowling slightly, before his expression neutrals and he smiles down at me. "Keys."

After handing him the small bunch of keys, he closes the door, and as he locks it, a sense of finality settles over me. It's like a part of my life has ended and although there's a hint of lingering sadness, I'm not as upset about leaving behind my fortress of solitude as I always assumed I would be. This run down, ancient, damp RV has been my home, my safe place for five years, but with Granger holding my hand and leading me toward something new, maybe it's time to put the RV in my past.

Opening my car door for me, he waits while I climb in, then leans over and plugs my seatbelt in for me, his rough fingers sliding along my jaw before he pulls away and closes me in his car. He settles into the driver's seat and we pull away from the garage, leaving my RV behind without even a backward glance.

SIXTEEN

GRANGER

To say I'm not sad to drive away from that fucking sad, depressing RV would be an understatement. One box, one fucking box. Apart from a small duffel of clothes, my woman has one box of possessions to her name. The idea infuriates me and if I didn't want to get her home and as isolated from town as I can, I'd be taking her shopping and showering her with stuff.

She was genuine when she said she didn't need much, but I don't fucking care, I want to give her the world. Exploring a new life with Alice is enlightening, I'm a fairly simple guy, I buy myself what I need, I'm not the type of person who needs fripperies and nik-naks. Though, seeing everything she has in that pathetic half-filled box, has shown me an urge to fill our lives with every kind of random shit that no one needs, but that fill a vapid want for a fleeting moment or two.

This woman, *my woman*, deserves the finest of everything.

She didn't look back when we drove away from the garage and my heart is still racing from fear that she might truly be happy living as a nomad, but the fact that she chose to look at me, instead of the life I was taking her away from fills me with a joy I've never felt before.

I sound like an asshole in my head, even thinking this bullshit, but that's what she does to me. She's turned me into a sappy caveman, not exactly two words you usually put together, I want to growl and possess her, while telling her what she means to me, how much I love her already, how excited I am to plan a life with her.

The car ride back home is quiet, but it's not stilted silence, more a peaceful lull. It's Sunday, only three short days since I met her, yet the ring box in my pants pocket still feels like the most natural next step for us. As much as I wanted her to officially move in with me today, I had another motive for going into town. Bay has a fuck buddies arrangement with Wendy-Ann, whose family own Hutchinsons, the local jewelers, and at his request she had trays of engagement rings out waiting for me to pick one when I left Alice under the guise of getting coffee and donuts.

Bay laughed his ass off when I asked him to give Wendy-Ann a call, but he still slapped me on the back and said he was excited to get a new sister. That's why our family works, that's why we all enjoy living together even though we're grown ass men, far too old to be living at home. It's because we are more than just brothers, we're each other's best friends and when your best friend meets the woman of his dreams you don't tell them it's too soon, you don't tell them they're rushing, you just slap them on the back and tell them you're happy for them.

I thought picking a ring for Alice would be hard, but it wasn't. When I got to the jewelers, she'd pulled out all the trays of traditional diamond rings, then a single tray of more unusual rings with rubies, emeralds and colored diamonds. The moment I laid eyes on the princess cut yellow diamond, surrounded by smaller white diamonds, I knew it was the one. The yellow is the exactly color of Alice's hair and I can't wait to slide it onto her finger and know she's completely mine.

I've had to take a guess at her size because she doesn't wear any jewelry I could take to compare, but we can get it sized once she says yes. And she will say yes, no isn't even an option. I wasn't lying when I told her I was obsessed, I am, completely, obsessively, obsessed.

She thinks her anxious behaviors will drive me away, but she's got no fucking clue the lengths I'll go to make her stay. Huck lost his shit and kidnapped Cora when she tried to leave him, but when I think about Alice trying to run, kidnapping seems like child's play in comparison to the things I'd do to keep her.

Exhaling slowly, I push away the anger that always follows thoughts about her leaving me and turn to the woman beside me. Her face is serene, her full pouty lips curled up, her eyes clouded with peace. She's not trying to look away, or at her feet, her gaze is straight ahead, her head held high and the urge to pull over and fuck her over the hood of my car almost has me stopping. Except it's snowing and my brothers are in the truck behind us.

"I want to fuck you so much right now."

Her lips tug up into a smile. "You do?"

"So bad. My dick is aching for your tight, wet little pussy."

"Such a sweet talker," she smiles.

"Nothing sweeter than my cock filling you up, your cream dripping down my length, your fingers clinging to the smooth metal of my hood where I've got you bent over, your nipples rubbing against the paint."

Her teeth drag across her bottom lip, biting down on it as her hands move restlessly over the fabric of her pants. She changed out of the soft lounge pants I picked for her earlier and into tight fitted jeans before we left the house, and I want to take a bite out of her ass every time she moves.

"I'd fuck you till you were on the verge of coming, then I'd eat you and play with your ass until you come all over my face, then I'd slam my cock back into you and fuck you until you scream my name and I fill your cunt with my cum."

She shudders, actually shudders, and I can't help but reach over and shove my hands between her thighs, cupping her hot pussy over the fabric of her jeans.

"Are you wet for me, honey?"

"Yes," she stutters, planting her hands against the seat, lifting her ass off the leather and pushing herself into my palm.

"You want my fingers in your pussy?"

"Yes," she rasps.

"You want me to fuck your wet cunt until you come all over my hand?"

"Oh god, please."

"Has anyone else ever made you feel like this?" I rasp, trying to keep my eyes on the road even though I want to put all my attention on her.

"No."

"No one ever will, only me."

"Only you," she pants.

Undoing the button on her jeans, I push my hand beneath the fabric, cupping her hot pussy over her panties, feeling the wetness waiting for me. "You'll never leave me, will you?"

Her breath hitches and her eyes close as she tips her head back and presses it against the back of the seat.

Finding her clit beneath the fabric, I rub in slow, mocking circles that I know won't give her enough friction to come, only tease her until she's writhing. "I'll never let you go."

"Please," she begs.

"Are you going to try to run?"

"No." her voice is more rasp than anything and I smile to myself, pushing my thumb beneath the wet fabric of her panties and rubbing the pad up and down her wet folds.

Her moan is pure pleasure and want, and I have to fight the urge to take my hand off the wheel completely and stroke my dick while I play with her pussy. "Tell me you'll never leave me, and I'll make you come."

"I'll..."

My thumb finds her clit, pushing back the hood and fully exposing the sensitive bundle of nerves.

"Oh fuck." Her hips lift even higher and I deliberately move the pad of my thumb away from her clit, circling it without touching to drive her mad.

"Promise me you'll never run from me, that you're mine."

"I promise, I'm yours."

"Mine," I growl as I find her clit, rubbing hard until her breathing turns ragged and she mewls as her muscles tense, then shake as she comes, gasping my name. "Oh fuck, Granger."

I play with her until we pull up in front of the house and slow to a stop, then I pull my hand free of her jeans and lick her arousal from my fingers while she stares at me with wild abandon. "You taste like perfection, honey."

Her cheeks turn pink and I laugh, dirty talk and playing with her pussy while I drive doesn't embarrass her, but licking my fingers clean and telling her she tastes amazing pushes her over the edge. "Come on, let's go unpack your box of stuff then we can decide what we want to do tonight."

Slightly dazed, she waits until I open her door, taking my hand when I offer it and letting me help her from the car. Her legs seem a little wobbly so I curl my arm possessively around her shoulders and lead her to the house while she nervously pulls her top down to cover her unfastened jeans.

Bay and Teddy meet us at the door with her single solitary box and we walk inside together. "I can take that," Alice says when she comes to her senses a little.

"That's okay, sis, considering what we were expecting to move today I can carry this all the way to your room," Bay teases playfully.

Alice's cheeks turn pink again, but unlike when I embarrass her, her gaze drops to her feet and her shoulders hunch. My expression darkens as I glare at my brother, who looks genuinely regretful when he notices her reaction.

"Sis, I'm just teasing," he tries to explain.

"It's fine," she says tersely, in that monotone voice that I haven't heard at all in the last couple of days. "I'm gonna go use the bathroom." Her gaze never lifts as she takes the box from a shocked looking Bay and heads to our room, her whole body curling in on itself in a way that makes me want to find her mom, her sister and everyone who's ever rejected her and beat the living shit out of them.

I wait until the bedroom door shuts behind her, before I turn my stony glare on my brother. "What the fuck!" I explode. "She already had a fucking panic attack; you couldn't just leave her alone."

"I was just teasing," Bay exclaims.

"Did you see her reaction? I already caused her to nearly fucking pass out and now you do this. You can't tease her like that, it's taken me three fucking days to get her to relax and now it's all just fucked." I know I'm being irrational, this isn't Bay's fault but I can't hide the fear that all the work I've done to get her to trust me, to see a future here with me might have just been destroyed, that one stupid error in judgement from me and a stupid comment that shouldn't have had an impact might ruin everything.

"I was just teasing, I didn't..." Bay's voice is regretful and shocked. "What did I say?"

"She has..." I pause, wondering if I'm betraying her by telling him anything. "She has..." Sighing, I rub my hand over my forehead. "She has anxiety and some serious abandonment issues. She legit told me that she's a toxic person and that I shouldn't be around her because she's poison to anyone who comes in contact with her. Today when I left, she thought I'd gotten sick of her and wasn't coming back."

Bay's mouth falls open and he glances toward my closed bedroom door and my woman who hopefully isn't packing her shit right now.

"That sweet little thing thinks she's a toxic person?"

"Among other things, yeah."

"Fuck, so why did she react so badly to my teasing?!"

"Honestly I have no fucking clue, I need to go check on her, make sure she's breathing and not throwing her stuff out the window."

"She's that much of a flight risk? You can't keep her a

prisoner if she wants to leave."

"Can't I?" I say indignantly. "She's mine and she's not going anywhere." Turning, I stomp away from my brother, opening my bedroom door and tensing for what I might find inside.

Instead of her packing her bags, she's sitting on the edge of her bed, her head lowered and staring at her hands that are twisted together in her lap. She looks young and sad and tired. Closing the distance between us, I crouch down in front of her and place my hand over hers.

"You okay, honey?"

She nods her head.

"I thought we agreed, no lying was one of your rules. So wanna try that again? You okay?"

This time she shakes her head, but she doesn't look at me and that pisses me off. "New rule," I snap, tipping her chin up and forcing her to make eye contact. "When we talk to each other, we look at each other."

Her eyes are hooded and full of sadness. I prefer the dazed, post orgasm look she had when we got out of the car, but even though I'd like to keep her cum drunk, it's not a realistic full time option. "Bay was only teasing you."

"I know," she says quietly.

"Tell me what you're thinking. I know you've got some

bad shit swirling around in that head of yours, so time to put all of it on me and let me deal with it for you."

"I can't—"

"Alice," I interrupt. "This is what we agreed, that you'd tell me when you're feeling anxious. I want your problems, I need them, so tell me." It's not a suggestion, but an order and as I watch my stern words settle over her, her shoulders relax a little.

"I'm pathetic and weak, and now you and your brothers all know."

"How are you pathetic?"

"I had a panic attack when you left for five minutes. I live in an RV, I have a bag of clothes and half a box of stuff to my name. They're going to think I'm using you."

I laugh, I can't fucking help it. "That's what you're worried about."

"It's not funny, Granger."

"I'm not laughing at you, I'm laughing with relief, I thought you were going to run."

"Why?"

"Because I hurt you today and because I'm so obsessed with you, I'm ready to kick my brother's ass for upsetting you."

"No," she cries. "Don't, he'll hate me, he probably already hates me. Oh my god, they'll all think I'm a freak that they have to walk on eggshells around. It's been three days and they already think I'm a gold digging princess who's using you for your money. I invaded their home and now I'm acting like I'm so sensitive and prickly they can't even speak to me. This is why I don't engage, because people hate me, because I'm a freak."

Her words come faster and faster as she berates herself, what my family think of her, how they hate her already, how they'll want her to stay away from me. How she's so pathetic she literally couldn't breathe thinking I'd left. Fuck, is this what it's like in her head? This constant stream of negative thoughts. Is this how it's felt to be her since her sister up and left?

A sudden and compelling sense of hatred for her mom and sister swell inside of me. Who would Alice be if she hadn't been neglected by her mom and deserted by her sister?

"Honey, stop," I say, more forcefully than I intended. She stops talking immediately, her huge doe eyes full of unshed tears.

"My family could never think badly of you, because you are sweet and nice and adorable, but more than that, you're mine and if you'd never spoken a word or done nothing but curse and shout at them, they'd still love you simply because I do."

A single tear rolls down her cheek and I reach out and catch it with my thumb. "Don't cry, honey, it makes me feel fucking ragey seeing tears in your eyes."

"I thought maybe you and this place would be the exception."

"What do you mean?"

"It's been three days and you don't hate me yet."

"Of course I don't hate you."

"I'm a mess."

"My mess and I love you, Alice."

"You can't, I'm unlovable, look at everything I've done today, all the trouble I've caused."

Anger ignites within me and instead of comforting her and reassuring her, I grab her hips, flip her to her stomach and smack her ass as hard as I can.

She shrieks, but I don't care as I spank her a second time, then a third. I don't hold back, lashing all of my fear and anger and frustration through my palm and into her ass. "I never want to hear you fucking say you're unlovable again. Ever. That shit stops right here, right now, or I'll tan your fucking ass until it's bright red and you finally hear what I'm saying. I am in love with you, Alice Lowe, have been since the moment I set eyes on you and I won't let you or anyone else lessen that."

Flipping her over, I climb on top of her, caging her in with my arms on either side of her head. "Say it. Say I am loveable."

Her eyes are wide and full of shock.

"Do I need to spank your ass a few more times to make you hear me?"

She shakes her head.

"Then say it.

"I'm loveable." The words are barely audible, but she said them and over time I'll convince her to truly believe them.

"Again."

"I'm loveable."

"Now fucking kiss me."

Shellshocked, she lifts her head off the comforter and presses her lips to mine. I take over immediately, forcing my tongue between her lips and plundering her mouth until her hands are clawing at my shoulders, pulling me closer. "I wanna fuck you so bad right now," I say into her mouth.

"Yes," she nods.

"No, honey, you're sore, I'll take you later."

"Now," she pants into my mouth.

"Later," I chuckle. "For now, lots of making out, then tonight I'm taking you on that date I tried to get you to agree to the day we met."

She stills, then pulls her lips from mine, blinking up at me. "A date?"

"Yes, honey, a date. Dinner, a movie."

"I don't have anything to wear for a date."

"I don't care what you wear, naked is my favourite on you, so whatever clothes you have on, I'm only gonna wanna take off," I chuckle, pressing a kiss to her earlobe then nipping it playfully with my teeth.

"I'm serious, Granger, I can't go on a date in jeans and a fleece."

"I love your jeans, they're so tight they make your ass look fucking edible."

"Granger," she whines, and the sound is so fucking adorably unfamiliar from her that I can't stop the smile from filling my face. Ten minutes ago, she was calling herself names, stressing over her insecurities and convinced my family hate her, and now she's a sweet little kitten worried about what she's going to wear, all soft and gorgeous.

"Cora can help you find an outfit, her and her mom own a clothing store down in town."

"I don't have a car here."

"I can take you."

"We just got back from town, I don't want you to have to drive all the way down there again," she says worriedly.

"It's fine, Huck would have gone to pick her up at the end of her shift anyway, we'll just bring her home with us instead. I don't care what you wear tonight, honey, but I want you to be comfortable and happy, it's a trip into town, not to Mexico."

"I could..." she trails off, then visibly swallows. "I

could ask Huck if he wouldn't mind taking me with him, that way you don't have to drive."

"No," I snap immediately. "If you go, I take you."

"But—"

"No fucking buts, Alice, you had a fucking panic attack when I left earlier, no way am I risking you getting upset and me not being there to help you, I'm not letting you out of my sight." My words and tone are harsh, but she visibly relaxes at my vehement honesty.

"Okay."

"No arguments?"

She shakes her head. "I forgot how nice it is to have someone care about you."

A lump forms in my throat and I force down the bile that tries to surge forward. I love this woman, she's mine now to protect and care for and I fucking hate that she's been alone for so long, feeling she was unlovable, unworthy, poisonous. All of these feelings she has go back to her fucking mother and her fucking sister.

I need her whole and healthy and as much as I know that giving her all my love will help her, she needs to understand nothing shy of cheating on me will ever make me walk away. Her stuff is in my house, now I need my ring on her finger, to give her my last name and to put a baby in her belly. I'll surround her with so much love and happiness she never has to question it again.

We spend the rest of afternoon making out like teenagers, dry humping over our clothes, winding one another up without either of us getting the relief we both need. When I tear myself away from her, I escape to the bathroom, grab my dick and fuck my hand in short desperate strokes, spilling my cum all over my fingers and into the toilet beneath me as I pant, lifting my free hand to brace against the wall as aftershocks shudder through my body.

"That was sexy," a quiet voice says from behind me, and I spin to find Alice standing in the doorway, her fingers white knuckled as she grips the doorframe, her eyes fixed on my hand around my dick.

"You like watching me fuck my hand over how wound up you've got me?"

Her nod is slow and a tiny smile tips at the corner of her lips. "Will you? Can I watch you sometime?"

Smiling, I chuckle. "If I get to watch you touch yourself too."

Her nod is fast and decisive, and I flush the toilet and wash my hands in the sink before crossing the room and cupping her face in my hands. "I fucking love you."

She blinks, but I press a soft kiss to her lips and move past her, not waiting for her to reply. She's not there yet and that's okay, she will be once she understands that my love isn't on a timescale, it's not dependent on her independence or behavior. All I want it her, however she comes, I want it all and I won't settle for less.

Huck insists on coming with us when we go down to collect Cora, so instead of having my girl in the seat next to me, the seat where only hours earlier I fucked her pussy until she came all over my hand, I have my brother, while Alice sits quietly in the backseat.

Pulling up right outside the store, I kill the engine and we all climb out. I take Alice's hand and lead her into the store, smiling at my brother as he makes a beeline for his pregnant fiancé, scooping her off her feet as he kisses her passionately.

"Go look around," I say to Alice, reluctantly releasing her hand as she starts to move tentatively through the racks of clothing. Nothing I can see screams 'Alice' to me, but all I've seen her wear so far has been simple jeans and sweaters. I'd happily take her out in those, but if a new outfit makes her feel better, I'm all for it.

Huck and Cora finally come up for air and she glances at me over Huck's shoulder. "Hi Granger."

"Hi Cora, I'm taking Alice out for a date and she wanted to find something new to wear."

"Ohhh," Cora says gleefully, shoving Huck away from her as she marches toward Alice, grabbing things from racks as she moves, her pregnant belly almost pulling clothes off rails as she walks.

Huck laughs, watching Cora go, a smirk plastered across his lips that are shiny from Cora's lipgloss. "She loves this shit, just don't do a Beau and try to tell Alice what to wear like he did with Bonnie," he says as he moves to stand next to me.

"I don't care what she wears, I'm not letting her out to a bar on her own, so no one but me is gonna get a chance to go anywhere near her," I growl.

"The girls will drag her out eventually, doesn't matter that Cora's as big as a house, she still needs 'girls' night', apparently," Huck rolls his eyes.

"I think Bonnie and Cora will be good for Alice, she needs decent girl friends and just like you and Beau, I'll be a fucking stalker and watch her from the shadows," I laugh.

"You look happy," Huck says, slapping me on the shoulder.

"I am. I'll be even happier when I get a ring on her finger," I say lowly so neither of the women can hear.

"You there already? It's been what, three days?"

"I'd have asked her ten minutes after I saw her, I've waited as long as I can."

"Think she'll say yes?"

"Wasn't planning on asking, just telling her that's the way it's gonna be."

"Bro," he chuckles. "Can I be there when she kicks

you in the balls?"

"She isn't like Bonnie and Cora, she needs me." With a smirk in my brother's direction, I head for my woman, pulling my arms around her waist from behind and dragging her into me. "I need to make a quick call, I'll just be outside. Okay?"

Twisting in my arms, she turns and looks up at me with worried eyes.

"I'll be five minutes and I'll be right outside the window."

"Of course, take as long as you need." Her words are all bravado and more for Cora than me or her.

Leaning down, I press my lips to hers. "I love you." Some of the tension in her shoulders falls away and I pinch her chin between my finger and thumb and squeeze. "Five minutes."

Walking quickly out of the store, I position myself in the middle of the window in clear view in case she starts to panic, then I pull out my cell and open my contacts to the new one I only added today.

Serenity.

The urge to speak to Alice's sister, to find out how she could just walk away from her sister and never look back is so strong that when Alice was in the bathroom earlier, I found her cell and copied her sister's contact details into my phone.

Should I be contacting her behind Alice's back? No, I fucking shouldn't. Am I going to do it anyway? Hell fucking yes, I am.

Clicking call on her name, I lift the cell to my ear and listen to it ring and ring. After the fifth ring I assume she's not going to answer, when a soft feminine voice says. "Staff Sergeant Lowe."

"Hi, is this Serenity Lowe?"

"Speaking, who am I speaking with."

"You don't know me, but I'm a friend of your sister's." The word friend burns on my tongue, but boyfriend sounds juvenile and saying I'm her sister's fiancé before I tell Alice we're getting married is probably a mistake.

"Alice." Panic laces her sister's name. "Is she okay?"

"She's fine."

"Okay. Can I ask how you got my number?"

"I took it from her cell, she doesn't know I'm calling you. But I'm in love with your sister and I need to know why you left her all those years ago."

"Look I have no idea who you are, I've never heard my sister mention you before so I'm not sure why you think you can call me—"

"Have you spoken to your sister recently?" I interrupt.

"That's none of your business."

"See, I think it is my business, especially when it's affecting my woman."

"Your woman," she says indignantly.

"Yes, *my fucking woman*," I snarl. "Why did you just leave?"

Her sigh is so loud it sounds like she's standing in front of me, not hours away on the other side of the country. "I was eighteen."

"She was thirteen."

"I wasn't her parent. It's not my fault that our mom is a man hungry waste of space, I needed to be a teenager, I needed to live my own life and Alice, she just..." she trails off, her voice softening.

"She what?"

"She... I just couldn't be everything to her, I needed to breathe, to live, to be."

"So you left," I scoff.

"Look, you don't know the details, you don't know how it was."

"I know you left a kid broken, that she thinks she ruined your life, that she thinks she's toxic and poisonous to those around her," I'm shouting; but speaking to her sister has made me unreasonably angry. Teddy was only a kid when our dad died, but there's no way any of us would have just left him. How could she have left Alice? Tiny, sweet, innocent Alice.

"I'm not her mom," Serenity says brokenly.

"No, you were her sister, and you left her and you

never looked back." Not bothering to give her chance to reply, I end the call, shove my cell into my pocket and try to calm down. I can't go back into the store and face Alice like this, she'll think the worst and I won't do that to her. Inhaling slowly, I force my hands out of the fists they've been forming and stretch them straight out, shaking my arms as I try to relax.

It doesn't matter that Serenity is a bitch who doesn't give a shit about her sister, I'm taking care of Alice now, that's my job and I won't run from it, I'll embrace it, because she's my life now and I'll do whatever it takes to make her happy.

SEVENTEEN

ALICE

"Oh, you could totally wear this, or this," Cora says, holding clothes up against me, her head tipped to the side as she assesses me. "How do you feel about dresses? We have some gorgeous new stock that came in today."

"I don't wear them too often, but I'm not against them," I say distractedly as my eyes move yet again to Granger. Just like he said he would, he's standing with his back to the window of the store, his cell to his ear, but his body is tense, his free hand clenched into a tight fist where it hangs at his side.

"I'll go grab some so you can have a look," Cora says,

but I'm barely listening, all of my attention is on him. Is it pathetic that when he said he was going outside, I wanted to beg him not to leave me? I know it is, but whenever I try to put some emotional distance between us, he knocks down all my walls and pulls me closer, like he's deliberately encouraging all of my issues to dissolve into him.

If I could help myself around him, I would, but I think I'm almost as addicted to him as he's obsessed with me. Six times he's told me he loves me, and every time it gets more and more amazing to hear. I don't know if what he feels is real, it's far too quick, but even if he's lying, I don't care. I want to take a bath in the lie if it feels as good as it feels when he says those three little words to me.

I watch as he angrily shoves his cell into his pocket and slowly uncurls his fists, stretching all his fingers out as if he's actually having to stop himself from clenching them again. I can hear Cora's heels clipping across the floor but I don't look away from him. I'm not sure I could if I wanted to.

"It's impossible not to stare at them, isn't it?" Cora says from directly behind me.

Startled at how close she is, I spin around and face her, dragging my eyes from Granger and hating it. "What?"

"They have this pull, all of them do, but when you become the object of their desire it's like you're physically connected to them, and no matter how much you fight they just keep reeling you in." Her voice is wistful, but she's smiling.

"Is that how it was for you?"

"Honestly, at the start I never really fought it. I tried to pretend I could keep it casual, just use him for his dick, but he wasn't having any of it and I never stood a chance. I only ever fought when I thought he'd given me no choice." Her hands rub over her pregnant belly. "This wasn't planned and for a little while I really thought I hated him. I didn't of course. I haven't forgotten how he manipulated me, but somehow, the way he loves me overshadowed the lies. These men they consume you with their love, and I doubt there's a soul alive who could truly walk away from them once they've decided you're theirs."

I feel my lips part on a silent exhale, because her words feel so incredibly true.

"Could you leave him? Now you know how it feels to be loved by him, could you walk away and never feel that again?" Her focus isn't on me now, as she looks over her shoulder at where Huck is casually leaning against the counter, his cell phone in his hands, his fingers moving across the screen.

"I thought I could," I whisper.

Turning back to me, she smiles. "It's easier to accept

their love than it is to try and run from it. Granger's a good guy, quiet, but he has this steady strength to him, that some of the others don't have. I don't know you that well yet, but I promise he'll look after you, if you let him."

"I just need to figure out if I can risk letting him," I say so quietly I'm not sure she even heard me.

Her laugh is soft and sweet. "I don't think he's going to give you a choice."

His arms wrap around me before I have a chance to reply, his lips finding my neck as he buries his face against my skin. "I missed you."

"It's only been a couple of minutes," I smile, my chest feeling a little lighter with him wrapped around me.

"Exactly, forever," he groans. "Let's shop so we can go home."

"We can go now if you want."

"Nope. We're shopping."

Then Granger takes over, encouraging Cora as she brings out dresses, skirts, pants, jeans and shirts, hustling me into the changing room and forcing me to try on outfit after outfit, all of which somehow make me feel more beautiful than the last. Or maybe it's just the way Granger looks at me when I show him.

An hour later, I'm exhausted and somehow, I have enough new clothes to fill one of those closets from MTV cribs. "I can pay for my own clothes," I say again, as Granger snatches my credit card from my fingers and pushes it into his pocket, handing his own to Cora in its place.

"Alice, just let him pay, you won't win," Cora laughs, taking his card and running it through the machine.

"Granger, it's nearly a thousand dollars' worth of clothes," I argue.

"So?"

"So that's a lot of money."

"I have money."

"So do I," I argue again.

"Huck, can you put these in the trunk while this pair hash this out?" Cora says, handing off arm loads of bags to her fiancé who scowls at her.

"I thought I told you not to get lifting stuff," he scolds.

"It's a bag with clothes in, sweetie, it's not like I'm lifting ten ton bags of gravel or something." Cora rolls her eyes, then smiles when Huck is no longer looking.

"I'm paying you back, I don't want you to spend your money on me," I tell Granger, crossing my arms over my chest and glaring at him.

Backing me against the counter, he curls one arm around my back and grabs my ass with the other. "Do I need to spank some sense into this ass again already, honey?"

"You can't threaten to spank me, I'm not talking bad

about myself. I just don't want you to spend this much money on me when I can more than afford to pay for them myself. I work a lot and live a cheap lifestyle, I can afford to buy myself clothes, I just never had any need for anything beyond work clothes and sweats."

"I can spank this ass whenever the fuck I want to," he chuckles lowly. "I can also spoil my woman whenever I want to, so just say thank you, kiss me and stop arguing."

Shaking my head, I push up onto my toes and press my lips to his. "Thank you," I say grudgingly.

"That's better. Now come on, lets go home and chill for a couple of hours."

Taking my hand, Granger leads me out of the store and into the car, practically lifting me into the passenger seat despite my protests about Huck being more comfortable up front.

"Huck's gonna want to be wherever Cora is, that fucker's already trying to get her pregnant again, before his baby's even born."

Granger and Huck insist on carrying all of my new clothes straight through to Granger's bedroom when we get back to the house, refusing to allow either me or Cora to help. Grabbing my arm, Cora tows me into the kitchen, takes two wine glasses from the cupboard and pours wine into mine and juice into her own. Lifting the wine bottle to her nose, she inhales deeply. "God I miss wine, and I wasn't even much of a wine drinker before I got pregnant."

"How far along are you?"

"Six and a half months, but it feels like I've been pregnant for a year already," she says, rubbing at her stomach absentmindedly.

"Do you know what you're having?"

"Yes," she whispers. "But don't tell Huck I know, we agreed we wouldn't find out."

A giggle bursts from my lips and I almost slap my hand across my mouth to hide my reaction. Cora is kind of adorable, nothing like the girls I knew in high school. So far, both her and Bonnie have been nothing but nice to me, and neither seem to hate me yet.

"You're not on the oral pill, are you?" she asks randomly.

"Err, no, I have the implant."

"Oh good, I was just going to warn you not to let Granger anywhere near it," she laughs, waving her hand. "I could do your hair for tonight if you want?"

"It's okay, I'm sure you have plans."

"I really don't, Huck's being an over protective pain in the ass, he won't let me and Bonnie go to the bar without him and Beau, and I've been banned from axe throwing since I threatened to cut Huck's dick off the last time we were there."

"Axe throwing?"

"There's a place not far from here, it's a bar but in the back room there's axe throwing booths, with like targets and stuff to aim for. The boys all love it, what with Beau, Teddy and Huck being lumberjacks. The last time we all went, Huck pissed me off being all insane and territorial even though I'm obviously pregnant, wearing his engagement ring and I was sitting on his freaking lap. Well when it was my turn, he said something to piss me off and I kinda pressed an axe to his junk and warned him to stop being an asshole. The manager said I can't go back till after I have the baby."

I try really hard to stifle my laughter, but Cora just looks so proud and amused that I can't help myself, and a moment later I'm outright laughing. Cora joins in and when the guys come back into the living room, my stomach hurts and there's tears in my eyes from laughing so hard.

"Peaches, stop fucking laughing, you'll end up shaking the baby out," Huck says, cradling Cora to him and wrapping his hands possessively around her swollen belly.

"See," Cora says imploringly. "Let me help you get ready so I can get away from his insanity," she pleads.

"If you really don't mind." I'm reluctant to accept her offer, but she just seems so genuinely nice. Maybe it's time to put myself out there again and try with people, it's been years since I have, except with Granger and he is, well, Granger's just everything.

"Yay," she claps. "Then tomorrow, you, me and Bonnie are going out for dinner. I want to get to know my new sister better."

"No," both Granger and Huck say in unison.

Spinning, I look at Granger in shock, expecting an explanation, but his dark brows are furrowed, his expression dark and unhappy.

"We don't—" I start.

"Yes, we do," Cora interrupts me. "We're three grown ass women going out for dinner, we're not going to a party, or a club or an orgy."

"Cora," I hiss, when Granger's expression gets angrier and angrier.

"You're pregnant," Huck snarls.

"And why's that?" Cora snaps, poking her finger into Huck's chest accusingly.

Granger slides his arm around my waist and lifts me from the stool I'm sitting on, grabbing my wine glass with his free hand while he half leads, half carries me back to his bedroom.

"I don't have to go out with Cora, it was her idea," I say quickly the moment he closes the door behind us.

I expect him to look relieved, but instead his brow

furrows even further until there's a deep line between his eyes. "I'm being an asshole."

"No you're not. This is your family."

Conflicted eyes snap to mine and he closes the distance between us until I have to tip my head back to look at his face. "I don't want to share you with them."

"I don't understand?" I tell him.

"You're mine and right now I have you all to myself. If you go out and bond with my sisters, I'll have to share you and I want to be a selfish fucker and keep you all to myself."

Staring up at him blankly, I try to make sense of what he's saying, but it doesn't make sense, he wants me to get to know his family, he wants me to like them, for them to like me, that's what he said, so what's changed?

"The moment they get to know you, they'll adopt you. I want you to want me, to need me for everything and the moment you have them, you won't need me as much." His words feel like the confession they are, falling heavy and loud in the quiet room.

"You're worried because you think they'll want to be friends with me?" I ask slowly. "I thought that was what you wanted."

"It is what I want. Fuck, I want you to have good friends, good sisters. But I want you to need me more."

"I—"

"Fuck," he hisses, lifting me off the floor and carrying me to the bed, laying me down and immediately climbing on top of me, parting my legs so he can settle his huge body between them. "I know you're not as far into this as I am. I know this is harder for you, because it's more difficult for you to trust that I feel the way I feel. But I need you to need me."

"I do."

"Not just for sex, not just because you think I'm the only person who doesn't hate you. I want you to need me for air, for every breath. I want you to need me to be happy, to be fulfilled."

"Granger."

"I know I sound fucking crazy, I feel fucking crazy, but I'm obsessed with you. You're mine, I love you and I don't want to lose even a little bit of you to them."

His lips are on mine before I can even formulate a response. What do you say to that anyway? A normal person would probably freak out, but I'm not normal. I love the way he wants me. I love that, for once, someone else seems almost as crazy as I feel most days. Instead of pushing me away, his declaration makes me want to curl up in his strong arms and live there forever.

Maybe we are meant for one another, maybe my crazy calls to his crazy.

His tongue pushes its way into my mouth and he

deepens the kiss, his fingers tangling with my hair as he keeps me in place. When he pulls his lips from our kiss, he doesn't lock his eyes with mine, instead he buries his face in my neck and inhales me, his large body resting on top of mine.

"I like your crazy," I whisper, running my fingers through his dark hair.

"I like your crazy too."

Rolling to the side, he gathers me in his arms and pulls me so my head is resting on his shoulder, my body facing his. We don't say anything as he holds me close, pressing kisses to the top of my head every now and then.

"If you don't want me to go, I won't."

"I want to want you to go."

I laugh, I can't help it.

"I take you, I pick you up. No bars, just dinner and promise me, you won't like them more than me," he snarls, his tone counteracting his childish words.

"I promise," I giggle.

"Don't laugh at me, woman." His fingers find my sides and he starts to tickle me.

"No, stop, I'm not laughing," I laugh, squirming and wiggling in his arms.

"How long do you need to get ready?"

"I haven't been on a date in years. I'd say about thirty minutes, but I have the feeling Cora's going to say I need significantly longer than that," I sigh.

"Let's soak in the tub for a while, then I'll get out the way so Cora can invade. I want to pick what you wear though."

I nod, and he kisses me quickly, then rolls out of bed and heads to the bathroom, and the water starts a few minutes later.

What feels like hours later, my butt is numb and my hair is full of bouncy curls that seem to float around my shoulders like I've just walked out of a shampoo commercial. After our bath, Granger picked out a cute, long-sleeved red dress that clings to the waist then flares into a skater skirt that swishes mid-thigh. When Cora saw the dress, she gave me a pair of black pantyhose and a black fitted leather jacket, then proceeded to dry, then curl my hair, and now she's putting the finishing touches to my makeup, that I'm not sure I actually remember asking her to do.

Cora truly is a force of nature, but I can't help liking her. When Granger said she'd adopt me, he wasn't lying and since she marched into the bedroom, she's treated me like we're the best of friends, including me in all future plans that apparently I'm obligated to attend.

As much as I've tried to be stoic and revert back to my monocyclic one word answers, Cora has just refused to allow it, asking question after question until we were chatting like I haven't done with a girl since before my sister left.

Sweeping a fluffy brush over my cheek, she takes a step back, looking down at me where I'm perched on the edge of the bed and smiles. "You look beautiful. You don't need the makeup, but it makes your eyes look huge, like a gorgeous Disney princess."

Standing cautiously, I make my way into the bathroom, which is where the only mirror is in Granger's room, and assess my reflection. The dress is a lovely deep red that somehow makes my blonde hair look even blonder. The makeup is light, but Cora's right, my eyes do look huge and yet I don't feel made-up, more like a polished version of myself.

"I have black heeled pumps you can borrow, but I'm gonna guess you're not much of a heel girl, so wear the flat black over the knee boots you got today, they'll go great with the dress."

Turning away from my reflection, I find Cora, leaning against the doorframe, smiling sweetly at me.

"Thank you."

"For what?"

"For helping me, doing my hair and makeup, everything."

She waves a hand. "I love this stuff, helping make people feel beautiful is my favourite part of my job.

Making my new sister feel beautiful is even better," she winks. "Dinner tomorrow. We have to keep the Barnett boys on their toes, and reminding them we have lives beyond them is a big part of that."

"Granger wants to take me and pick me up and he made me promise I won't end up liking you and Bonnie more than him," I say a little sheepishly.

Cora laughs. "Huck's insisting him, Beau and Granger come too. I told him that they could go have a drink at Barney's while we have dinner. They're all the same, all insecure cavemen." She lowers her voice and leans forward slightly. "I think maybe that's part of what we love about them, but don't ever admit it, or they'll play up how much they need us and we'll never get to leave the house without them again."

Walking forward, she loops her arm through mine and leads me back into the bedroom, opening the closet, finding the boots and handing them to me, then opening the door and motioning for me to follow. "Let's go show that man of yours how hot you look. Best to do it out in the open or you won't end up going on that date," she giggles.

Before he handed me over to Cora, Granger changed into jeans and button down, but seeing him now, sitting on one of the stools at the breakfast bar, chatting to a brother that is either Penn or Cody, I notice again how beautiful he is.

The navy-blue button-down shirt is stretched taut over the muscles in his arms, the sleeves rolled up to the elbows as if he can only stand to be so formal and having the cuffs done up was just a step too far. His jeans are fitted in all the best places, showcasing his huge thighs, but his dark brown boots are worn and rugged. His hair has been styled into a disheveled mess, that somehow makes him look even more rakish and feral than he does when we're naked and sweaty and his hair is a mess from where I've grabbed it with my fingers while he's fucked me into a screaming mess.

A sigh of pure feminine appreciation falls from my lips and as if he can sense me swooning over him, he turns and looks at me, his dark eyes swirling with want and need and something else that I can't quite identify.

Rising predatorially from his stool, he prowls toward me and my core clenches and tightens, eager to be hunted, caught and claimed.

"Fuck, honey, you look…" He pulls his bottom lip into his mouth as his eyes rake over me, taking in the dress that clings to the few curves I have, and the boots that make my legs feel thinner and longer at the same time. "Fuck."

I'm pressed against his chest, his palm on my back, dragging me into him so I can feel the hard length of his dick pressed into my stomach.

"We need to go, else I'm gonna rip those pantyhose off you where they're hiding my pussy from me, bend you over and fuck you right here, right now. You look fucking delicious, honey, and I want to eat you all up."

A shudder runs through me and I swear, if he wasn't holding me up, my legs would buckle. Half carrying me, half cuddling me, he leads me toward the door, ignoring all of the catcalling and comments from his family as he ushers me outside and into his car.

His hand stays on my thigh the entire drive down into town, his thumb rubbing small circles, not touching me in an intimate way, just the warmth of his palm heating me. Parking in a side street, he kills the engine, then turns. "Wait, I'll get your door."

A moment later, he opens my door, leans into the car and unclips my seat belt before taking my hand and helping me out. I'm more than capable of getting out alone, but there's something proprietary about the way he's treating me that makes my core tighten in appreciation.

Not releasing my hand, he locks his car and then leads me down the street toward a restaurant with large glass windows and a low warm light emanating from inside. Holding the door open for me, he releases my hand, only to immediately place his hand at the base of my spine to guide me into the building.

A hostess steps forward with a warm smile. "Good evening, Granger, this must be your girlfriend. I'm Claudia, it's so nice to meet you."

"Hi Claudia, this is Alice, we have a table for two booked," Granger says, stepping as close as he can get behind me."

"You surely do, follow me and I'll show you to your table and get you set up with some drinks," Claudia says cheerfully.

She shows us to a table for two in the window, a flickering candle in a small hurricane lamp lights the space, giving it a secluded, private feel even in the middle of the busy restaurant. "What can I get y'all to drink?"

"I'll get a beer please, Alice?"

"White wine please," I say quietly.

"Did you like the wine you were drinking earlier?" Granger asks, all of his attention on me.

I nod.

"A bottle of pinot grigio please."

Claudia nods, hands us both menus, then fills our water glasses before she turns and blends into the hustle of the restaurant.

I'm silent for a minute, taking in the ambiance of the room, the candle light making it feel private, like we're the only people in the entire world. "I'm a lucky bastard," Granger smiles, reaching over and taking my hand in his, lifting it to his lips and pressing a kiss to the back.

"Why?"

"Because you're mine."

Rolling my eyes, I try to hide my smile, at some point since we met, his insistence that I belong to him has gone from an outrageous claim to an affectionate gesture and even though I won't admit it, I like it when he goes all caveman. "I don't remember the last time I went on a date, it's been years."

"I'm glad you don't remember, thinking about some asshole taking you out thinking you were his, makes me want to hunt him down and kill him," Granger growls.

"When was the last time *you* went on a date? Should I be the one on the hunt instead?"

"I've never really dated, not like this."

"I know you haven't been a monk, so you must have dated."

"I've fucked women, but sharing a bed to sate a need isn't comparable to what we have. You're the stars in the sky, those women were the earthworms in the soil, you know they exist but you forget about them a moment later. You're the fucking stars, Alice, meant to be stared at, admired, coveted."

My lips fall apart and I laugh. "That's kind of poetic for a caveman," I tease.

"I can drag you back to my cave by your hair and beat

my chest to warn off all the other cavemen who might want to steal you for themselves, if that's better?"

Flushing red, heat fills my cheeks and he chuckles, kissing my hand again as Claudia reappears with our drinks. The rest of the evening passes in a daze. Granger is the perfect gentleman, the food is delicious and by the time we get back to the car, I'm relaxed and a little tipsy.

On the way to the drive-in movie, Granger's cell starts to buzz in his pocket and he pulls it out, glances at the screen, then silences it and shoves it back into his pocket again. "Work," he says with a shrug, and I forget about the call as we pull into the small outdoor theatre and park next to one of the rows of speakers.

"What film are we watching?" I ask.

"No clue, they don't advertise the film, everyone just turns up and watches whatever's playing," Granger tells me, pressing the button to lean back first my seat, then his. "We should have bought Huck's car, that's got bench seats."

"There's people on either side of us," I chide.

"So, they can't see."

"They can too," I argue.

"Good job I thought to bring a blanket then." Leaning into the backseat, he pulls out a massive fleece blanket and proceeds to cover both of us with it. "Take off your pantyhose and panties."

"No."

"Honey, do as you're told."

My cheeks are burning as I glance out the widows at the truck parked on one side and the station wagon on the other.

"I won't let them see. Take them off, then give me your panties," he orders.

Shuffling around, I kick off my boots, then wiggle to free myself of the pantyhose and then my panties, before lifting my knees up and grabbing my panties from around my ankles. Gripping them tightly in my hand, I free them from the blanket and drop them into his waiting palm.

Smiling wickedly, he works them in his fingers, then lifts them to his face and inhales. "They're wet, I can smell your desire. Are you wet for me, honey?"

I nod, unable to find the words to agree.

"Lift your knees, rest your heels on the seat, but make sure the blanket's still covering you."

Doing as he says, I hold the blanket around me while I part my legs and plant my bare feet onto the cool leather. The film starts, the sound startling me, but I'm not paying any attention to what's happening on the screen, my entire focus is on the wetness pooling between my thighs as I wait for him to touch me.

When his fingers finally find my core, I startle, jumping as he caresses me, stroking his fingertips through the wetness, spreading it over my clit and lips, then down to my ass, coating me in my own arousal.

He doesn't speak as he dips a single finger into me, slowly fucking me with it.

"More," I pant.

Amusement tips at the corner of his mouth, but he slides a second finger into me, teasing me with the slow glide, in and out, never getting faster, or deeper, never touching my clit like I need him to.

Frustrated, I push my hand beneath the covers and find my clit, rubbing at it in earnest.

"Stop. I didn't say you could touch my pussy, hold onto the door with one hand and the seat with the other, if they move, I'll stop and leave you like this till we get home and I fuck you."

"Granger," I snap, annoyed.

"I'm serious, Alice," he growls, pulling his fingers from inside of me as if to punctuate his point. "This pussy belongs to me and I want to play with it, get your hands on the door and seat. Now."

Glaring at him, I grip the door handle with one hand and squeeze the other around the edge of the seat. "Good girl," he praises smugly, then shoves his two fingers deep inside of me in one thrust and start to fuck me roughly. "See what happens when you do as you're told."

"Oh god," I gasp.

"God's got nothing to do with it, this is all me," he boasts, curling his finger and finding that spot inside of me that sends stars to my eyes and pulses of building pleasure through my core.

A third finger slowly fills me and I lift my butt from the seat, struggling to take it as he stretches me wide.

"Relax," he croons, "My dick's bigger than this and your pussy swallows it so fucking perfectly. I want to take you hard tonight and I don't want to hurt you, so I need this cunt to be weeping and ready for me."

By the time he's fucking me with all three fingers, I feel stretched, but it's not painful and an orgasm is quickly growing inside of me, ready to splinter out and explode, then he slows, letting the pleasure ebb.

"Granger," I whine.

"Don't worry, honey." Slowly, he plays with my sex, keeping me on the verge of an orgasm as he teases, fucks and taunts until I'm a writhing mess of need, wiggling into his touch, begging him to make me come, to push me over the edge.

I haven't watched any of the film, it's nothing more than background noise. How can I focus on anything else when all I can feel is him, all I can smell is my own arousal and all I can taste is the lingering sweetness of his kisses on my lips?

"Fuck it, I can't wait any longer," he hisses and the

car bursts to life as he steers one handed, his fingers still buried deep inside of me. "Come on my fingers, honey, I want you to gush all over my hand."

I don't know what he does, but a second later, all of the built up orgasms he's stolen from me in the last hour explode in one cacophony of sensation, and I come and come and come. When my vision finally returns, we're pulling into the drive for his house and his hand is still slowly playing with my sex.

He doesn't speak, his lips pursed into a firm, hard line as he kills the engine, throws open his door and stomps around to me. Grabbing me, he unclips my seatbelt and lifts me from the car, keeping the blanket over my bare legs as he carries me to the house, only pausing long enough to close and lock his door.

My back hits his bed a second later and his tongue finds my clit, eating me with a fervor he's never shown before. Three fingers plunge back into me and I feel a pressure rising as he licks and fucks and eats, and this time when I come, my back arches from the bed and I scream and... pee?

Oh my god, liquid gushes from me and I think I peed. Oh fuck, I peed on him. I peed on Granger.

My body stills and I go ramrod straight, mortified that I just peed when I came. "I... I... am so sorry," I stammer.

"What?"

"I just" I can't bring myself to say the word, to admit what just happened.

"Honey, that is the sexiest thing I've ever fucking seen."

"What?" I shriek. "I peed."

"No baby, you squirted."

"I what?"

"You squirted, honey."

"I don't know what that means," I say, mortified, trying to pull my legs away from him, despite his firm grip on me.

"It's female ejaculation, honey, and it's the hottest thing I've ever seen in my fucking life."

"So I didn't pee? It felt like I was peeing."

"No, you didn't pee. You squirted."

"And that's good?" I say cautiously.

"So fucking good. Did it feel good?"

"Yes, until I thought I peed on you."

Leaning down, he runs his tongue over the wetness coating my pussy, thighs and ass and hums appreciatively. "I want to try and make you squirt again, but my dick is so fucking hard I'm pretty sure if I don't get inside of you my dick is going to explode."

Standing, he quickly strips out of his clothes, until he's naked and I'm still spreadeagled on the bed, the sheets soaking wet beneath me. "Come here, honey," he beckons, offering his hand for me to take.

Helping me stand, he drags the comforter off the bed and dumps it on the floor, pulling my dress up and over my head and disposing of my bra until I'm just as naked as he is. "Perfect," he whispers reverently. Sitting down on the end of the bed, he turns me so my back is to him, then guides me back, spreading his legs with mine as he fists his cock with one hand and drags me back with the other, slowly impaling me onto his hard dick until I'm spread wide over his thighs and stuffed full of his dick.

"Fuck," he groans. Slowly lifting me on and off his dick, thrusting his hips up and filling me completely with each movement.

In this position I can't do anything but hold on as he fucks me on and off his cock, helpless but to take whatever he wants to give me. Suddenly he lifts me off his dick, bends me at the waist, planting my feet on the floor as he drags my hands behind my back and slams his dick back into me with enough force that I'd have fallen if he wasn't holding me still with my arms yanked behind my back.

My head is hanging down, my hair in my face as he uses my pussy, slamming in and out of me with a ferocity he hasn't shown me until today. An orgasm sneaks up on me and I come, clamping down on his dick, but he doesn't give me a moment, slamming in and out of my clenching core as he fucks me through my release.

Releasing my wrists, he lifts me, dumping me over the edge of the bed as one hand forces me down and the other grabs my hair and yanks, lifting my face off the sheet as my fingers scramble to find purchase, he starts his furious pace again, fucking me so hard, my feet almost come off the floor with each punishing thrust.

Grunts and snarls fall from his lips, intertwined with declarations of possession and praise for how tight my pussy is, how good it feels wrapped around his dick, what a good girl I am to take his rough fucking. His dirty words only urge me on and I come a second time, screaming his name as he slides his thumb into my ass, using both my holes as he fucks me until he comes with a roar that sends me over the edge into a third orgasm.

I don't try to move when his heavy weight collapses over my back, his dick still inside me as I clench and squeeze him, his cum and mine dripping down my legs.

EIGHTEEN

GRANGER

By the time morning comes I've lost count of how many times I've fucked her, but somehow my dick is still hard, leaking precum that begs to be inside her sopping wet cunt. I'm insatiable and I know I should give her exhausted body a rest, but I just don't seem to be able to give her the peace she so desperately needs.

Serenity has called me three times since I spoke to her outside Cora's store yesterday, and I've rejected the call each time. Contacting her was a mistake and somehow, I need to confess to Alice what I've done, but I need my ring on her finger and the paperwork signed before I do.

We have an appointment at the courthouse at ten

in the morning tomorrow to get married. Alice has no fucking clue and I have no idea how to broach the subject with her. I don't know if telling her we're getting married will make her happy, or send her running in the opposite direction, but either way it's happening and I don't plan on taking no for an answer.

Her tired body stirs beneath me. She's covered in my cum; her pussy and legs sticky with it. I should clean her up, but I like knowing that she's coated in the evidence of how much I own her. Reaching between us, I slide my fingers into her sex, her cunt stretched, wet and ready to accept me after how many times I've been in her since we got home last night.

For the first time, I fully understand Huck's reasoning for getting Cora pregnant and if I could dig out Alice's birth control implant and put a baby in her right now, I absolutely would. Owning her doesn't feel like enough, keeping her doesn't feel permanent and her belonging to me doesn't feel like I'm binding her deeply enough.

For the first time since I laid eyes on her, this inbuilt knowledge that she's mine feels more like a curse than a blessing. I know I won't ever let her leave me now I have her, and the edge of insanity that's coursing beneath my skin scares me a little.

I've told her I'm obsessed with her, but I'm not sure she truly understands what that means. She's mine and

I'm not sure what lengths I'll go to keep her, whether she wants to be kept or not.

Rolling her beneath me, I replace my fingers with my dick, sliding into her and fucking her while she sleeps, her body reacting to me even through the thick haze of her exhaustion.

"Granger," she moans groggily. Her hand lifts from where it was curled beneath her chin and wraps around my neck, even as her eyes stay tightly closed.

"I couldn't help it, honey, your pussy called to me and I had to be inside you," I whisper against her ear as I slowly push into her, then pull back, keeping my thrusts slow and even as she wakes.

"You're gonna wear my vagina out, I didn't need to make up for the sex I haven't been having the last five years in one night."

Chuckling, I thrust a little deeper, smiling into her neck as she arches into me like a kitten, lifting one leg and hooking it over my hip to spread herself a little wider for me. "I'm not letting you out of this bed today, we're gonna eat, fuck and sleep. We're gonna turn off our cells, lock the door and binge on each other, no interruptions, no distractions, just you and me."

Her eyes are still closed but her lips tip into a smile that lights me up from the inside out. "Okay," she laughs, until her laughs turn into moans and cries and the first of many orgasms I plan on giving her today.

**

We stay in bed the rest of the day, gorging ourselves on pleasure and the joy of just being together. It's probably one of the best days I've ever had and by the time we fall into an exhaustion induced sleep, there's not a person alive who could convince me she's not mine in every way but legally.

I kissed, licked, touched and fucked every inch of her body, wringing orgasm after orgasm from her, taking every little thing she so willingly gave me. My dick probably needs a month off to recover, but I'm hard the moment I wake up and feel her naked, sticky skin pressed against mine.

The air in my room is saturated with the heady scent of sex, even though it's been about five hours since she finally pushed me away, warning me she was too exhausted to feel even another ounce of pleasure. We didn't bathe yesterday, too wrapped up in each other and if it was anyone but her cradled in my arms, I'd feel disgusting with all the dried sweat and bodily fluids coating my flesh.

Glancing at the clock, I see it's barely seven in the morning. I should be at work, she should be leaving, but neither of those things will be happening today. We're getting married this morning, thanks to the courthouse digitalizing their booking system last year. Back then, no one could understand why in a town this small you'd need to book an appointment at the courthouse online, rather than walking your ass into the building itself and making your appointment with Shirley, the same woman whose held the calendar for the last twenty years. But right now, I'm grateful as fuck for it.

I know I need to get up, to feed her, bathe her and tell her what we're doing today, but the thought of moving from beneath her is almost physically painful to me. My bladder protests and I slowly, reluctantly pull away from her and get out of bed, padding naked and a little stiff into the bathroom. After using the toilet, I set the taps to run for the bath, adding some of the bath oil I stole from Cora the other day to make the water smell nice.

Leaving the tub to fill, I pad back into the bedroom and stare at my beautiful women. Without me there to hold her, she's rolled to her side, curling into a ball in the middle of the bed. She looks small and vulnerable and a surge of protectiveness unfurls inside of me.

It's impossible for me to imagine that only a few short day ago I didn't even know she existed, now I can't picture a moment without her. The ring I bought her is in my dresser, and I slide the drawer open and pull out the small innocuous box. The yellow diamond twinkles at me in the early morning sunlight, the simple gold wedding bands I picked for us sitting on either side. In a few hours, she'll have these on her finger and Alice Lowe will be gone forever. She'll be Alice Barnett, mine legally as well as in every other way possible and I can't wait.

Putting the box back into the drawer, I close it, then sit down next to her on the edge of the bed, running my finger over the apple of her cheek. "Morning honey, come take a bath with me," I say quietly, pressing my lips to her mouth.

Humming sweetly, she turns into my kiss. Even asleep, she seeks my touch.

"Let me take care of you, sweet girl," I croon, sliding my hands beneath her and gently lifting her from the mattress and into my lap. Immediately nuzzling into me, she rubs her cheek against my chest and sighs.

"Love you," she whispers, the words barely audible, but I hear them and my heart swells to twice its size. It doesn't matter that she isn't awake and saying it back to me, she's saying it when she's in this happy, comforted state and for now I'll take it.

Something settles in my chest and I know I'm doing the right thing, that not giving her the choice to run is exactly what I'm meant to be doing. I could spend months, years even showing her with time and baby steps that I love her, that I want to care for and protect her, but ultimately the outcome will be the same. She'll still be mine, she'll still be in our bed every night, she'll still have my last name, so what's the point in delaying? I can have everything I want today, and we can just spend the time we would have wasted, being happy, loving one another and getting started on all those babies I want her to give me.

"Granger?" she says sleepily.

"Morning honey." Standing with her in my arms, I carry her into the bathroom and then step into the tub, lowering us both into the water.

"Humm," she purrs as the warm water laps over her skin.

"Does that feel good?"

"So good," she says, not lifting her cheek from where it's pressed over my heart.

"I love you so much, thank you for letting me take care of you. I want to do this every day for the rest of forever."

She doesn't say the words back, but that's okay, I know she feels it now and someday, hopefully soon, I'll hear the words from her lips as she looks at me, I can wait.

Like a sleepy little kitten, she lets me bathe her, then shampoo and condition her hair. Once we're clean, I lift her from the tub and wrap her in a towel, lifting her onto the counter and sitting her there while I put toothpaste onto her toothbrush and hand it to her. She starts to brush her teeth, but her movements are slow and, in the end, I take over, brushing her teeth, then my own before I claim her mouth in a long, slow kiss.

"You wore me out, I need to go back to sleep," she yawns.

"We'll take a nap later, I need to feed you after all the calories we burned yesterday." Lifting her from the counter, I take her hand and lead her into the bedroom. I grab underwear for both of us, pulling my boxers over my hard dick, ignoring the surge of need to be inside her, I won't allow myself to take her again until she's legally mine.

Her movements are sluggish as she drops down onto the end of the bed and covers my pussy and tits with the pretty panties and bra I gave her to wear. When I start to strip the sheets from the bed, she helps me and it doesn't take long for us to replace the sweat and cum stained ones with fresh white ones, clean and ready to be dirtied up again later.

"Put this on while we get something to eat, then we can get dressed properly once we've eaten."

"Don't you need to work today? I should probably find out what's happening with my RV," she sighs, as if she's not ready for real life to encroach on us yet.

"Fuck your RV, you aren't going anywhere so it doesn't matter when it's fixed, I'll take care of it."

"I need to work, Granger, this weekend's been great, but we can't just spend the rest of our lives fucking like bunnies and pretending the real world doesn't exist."

"Sure we can," I snap, grabbing one of my t-shirts and dragging it over her head.

"Granger." She sounds weary and I hate it.

"Tomorrow we'll deal with real life, today we're staying in our bubble, okay?"

"Okay," she nods, laying her head against my chest, letting me absorb all the stress I can feel in her.

"Come on, lets go eat." The living room is empty and quiet for the first time since I bought Alice home. Everyone else is back at work now the long weekend is over and I enjoy the solitude. I love living in this crazy mess of a house, but for the first time I'm looking forward to our wings being made so we can all have some private space away from each other. Now that I have Alice, I don't want her to have to worry about getting dressed every time she wants to get a snack or a drink, which is why our wings will all be like contained apartments, connected to the main house.

There're two covered plates on the kitchen side and I pull one toward me and lift the foil, smiling at the pile of pancakes and fluffy eggs. "I'll heat these up, do you want to pour us some coffee?"

We go to work and five minutes later, we're on the sofa, the tv playing some mindless game show as we eat. This is what I crave with her, more than just the sex, but the intimacy that comes with sharing a life with her. I can't wait to do all the boring things with her, as well as the great stuff. I just want our lives so bound together there's no Granger or Alice as single entities, only Granger and Alice, together, connected, bound.

Once we've finished eating, she loads our plates into the dishwasher and sets it to run as I grab a hairbrush and position her between my legs, brushing out the knots from her damp hair. I still haven't turned my cell back on, so I glance at the clock on the mantel, seeing it's nine thirty and time to get ready.

"I have an appointment in town in half an hour, so we need to get ready."

"I can stay here, or go check on my RV," she suggests sweetly, although from the downturn of her lips, the idea of being separated holds as much appeal to her as it does to me.

"No, you're with me. We're still in our bubble, remember," I smile.

Opening our closet, I pull out jeans and a white button-down shirt for me and a pretty emerald green dress that I think Cora called a tea dress for her.

"We're getting dressed up?" Alice asks hesitantly.

"It's an important appointment," I deflect, winking at her. I know I should tell her we're getting married, that I should give her the choice to argue and try to say no, but

I don't want to. My brothers all know what we're doing today, but they're all just as crazy as me and I asked Beau and Huck not to tell the girls. I'll give Alice the wedding of her dreams as soon as we can plan it, if that's what she wants, but today is just about cementing what I already now. That she's mine.

Alice pulls the dress over her head, smoothing it down her body as I grab sheer stockings, that Cora picked out when we were shopping, and hand them to her. Her hair is dry now, a shiny waterfall of blonde falling down her back. She looked beautiful after Cora covered her face in makeup, but she's stunning now, natural and smiling at me, she doesn't need anything to make her more beautiful.

Unable to help myself, I go to her and pull her into my arms, pressing my lips to her and basking in this woman and how grateful I am to have found her. "I love you so fucking much, you've made me happier in the short time I've known you than I have been my entire life so far, and I can't wait to spend forever with you."

A tear pools in the corner of her eye, but I wipe it away before it can fall.

"I..." she faulters, but I don't press her.

"I know."

"You do?" she asks tentatively.

"I feel it." Grabbing her hand, I press it over my heart.

"Right here. I can wait for the words."

Pushing up onto her toes, she kisses me and I swear the beating in my chest doubles in speed, I'm the luckiest mother fucker in the world.

"Grab your shoes, we need to get going or we're going to be late."

I hand her the black boots she wore on our date and she takes them, disappearing into the living room. Quickly, I move to the dresser and grab the ring box and her ID that I found when I unpacked her stuff. Shoving them into my pocket, I unplug my cell, turn it back on and immediately silence it, there's nothing more important than exactly what I'm doing right now.

Alice is more animated than ever on the drive into town, she's like a different person to the one I met that day by her RV. No longer the girl who wouldn't look me in the eye and made it her mission to answer each question with as short a response as physically possible. When we get to the courthouse, a beautiful red brick building with a clock tower and impressively large wooden doors, I find a space right outside and park my car.

"So, who are we meeting?" Alice asks

"Come on, let's get in there," I say, avoiding the question.

Opening her car door, I offer her my hand, squeezing her fingers a little too tightly as I help her out and lead her into the building. Shirley smiles and nods in greeting from behind her small desk as I hustle Alice down the hallway to the small glass window that Eric Hilderman is sitting behind. Releasing Alice's hand, I turn to the window. "Morning Eric, we have an appointment with Judge Cooper."

Eric's bony finger runs over the huge ledger in front of him, all of the names hand written in ink, despite the impressively large printer sitting a few feet behind him. Eric is old school and even though the courthouse might have embraced the twenty-first century, apparently Eric has not.

"I see you filled in all the paperwork on the interweb. I'll just need to see some ID," he drawls, his voice slow.

"Here you go," I say, pulling Alice's from my pocket, then taking my own from my wallet and sliding it through the gap in the window.

Eric stares at it for a moment, then grabs the license he's already got prepared from somewhere beneath his desk and painfully slowly adds some more detail to it with his old-fashioned fountain pen, then stamps it with a rubber stamp covered in ink.

"Here you go." He slides the license and our ID back to me, and I exhale a shaky breath of relief. It's not that I thought our license would be denied, but with it in my hands, all I have to do now is tell the bride that today is her wedding day.

NINETEEN

ALICE

G ranger is acting strangely.

When he turns away from the small window, he's clutching a rectangle of paper in his hand, but I can't read what it says and before I have a chance to look, he's taking my hand and towing me down a corridor and out a door into an enclosed courtyard filled full of winter flowers, that are still in bloom despite the cold weather.

"Honey..." Granger starts, spinning around to face me. My hand is in his. He always holds me tight, as if he thinks I'm going to make a run for it the first time I have chance, but today he's holding me a little tighter than usual.

"Are you okay?"

Reeling me in, I fall into his chest and he immediately kisses me, his lips parting mine, his tongue dipping inside, reaffirming his claim on me, as he likes to do, especially when we're out and there are people to see.

"I love you."

His words are like a balm to my soul and I wish I could push my own words out, words to tell him that he's become everything to me, that I'm not sure I even exist without him. But I just can't. He sees the truth though; I wonder sometimes if he doesn't know what I'm thinking before I do.

"Tell me the truth, do you belong to me?" he asks.

Looking up at him, I see this isn't a game, this isn't his caveman act where he asks me who owns me and I tell him he does and then he fucks me until the only noises I'm capable of making are screams of pleasure and his name.

"Alice, honey, you own me body, mind and soul and I own you too, so do you belong to me?" His voice is low and rough and it sends vibrations of pleasure humming through every cell in my body.

"Yes," I whisper. "Yes, I belong to you. I never thought it was possible, never thought anyone could ever want me like this. But if I'm going to give myself over to anyone, I want it to be you," I confess.

A shaky breath stutters from his lungs and he visibly relaxes, his eyes falling shut for a moment. When they open again, they're brimming with emotion, raw and intense and undiluted. Then he grabs my hand, drops to one knee and pulls a small box from his pocket. "I'm not going to ask you to marry me, because that would suggest you have a choice and you don't. We're getting married today, because I can't go another hour without giving you the entire world, starting with my last name. I never thought I'd find my one, my woman, and then there you were and I knew right at that moment that until you were mine in every way conceivable, I wouldn't be able to rest. I love you more than I realized it was possible for a man to love a woman. You are the stars in the fucking sky, Alice. Say yes, because I won't take no for an answer."

A choked laugh bursts from me as I look down at my crazy caveman on his knees in front of me. This is madness, pure and simple. A man I met four days ago just told me we're getting married and instead of running, I'm laughing, because it's so him, so us.

I should say no, I should fight, claw, run, but why would I? I can't think of a time when I've ever been happier than I am right now. Granger doesn't see my issues as flaws, he embraces them and me. He wants to solve my problems, be my anchor in a storm and I want to let him, not because I need him to look after me, but because my life is full and happy for the first time in years, and it's all because of him.

"Yes."

He's off his knees, the ring is on my finger and his lips are on mine in half a second. I don't try to look at the rock I can feel on my finger, jewelry is pretty, but this man is the true gift, the one I barely feel like I deserve, but that I'm not sure I know how to survive without now.

"I love you," he laughs, spinning us around. "Now let's go get married."

We're on the move again, out of the courtyard and through the corridors to where a familiar group of people are all standing. Cora and Bonnie break away from the men as soon as they spot us, their expressions a mixture of hope and concern.

"You don't have to do this if it's not what you want," Bonnie says quietly, ignoring the growls of protest from both Granger and Beau.

"You can stop this, if he's strongarmed you into this," Cora says, lifting her head and glaring at Granger, daggers almost manifesting from her eyes. "The men in this family have a way of telling you what's happening, but forgetting to ask if this is what you actually want."

"This is what I want," I assure them, even as Granger drags me into his chest and physically holds me to him, preventing my escape even though I'm not trying to get away.

"Enough," Granger snaps, loud enough to shock Cora into silence and to have me freezing in his arms. "Huck, sort your woman out, because right now she's not behaving like my sister."

Cora's face pales and she gapes at Granger as if she has no idea who he is right now. "I…"

"We're getting married, right now. You can either come and watch, or you can leave, but no matter what you choose, I am making Alice my wife, today."

Steering me away from his family, Granger marches me down the corridor and into the small room, where a judge and a clerk are waiting for us.

Granger is so tense, his shoulders look ready to crack as the clerk asks us a series of questions, taking the small piece of paper Granger offers her, that I now realize is in fact a marriage license, and then motions for us to take our places at the front of the room as the judge steps into position.

The ceremony is short, the judge taciturn, the group of Granger's family behind us quiet. It's not exactly what I imagined my wedding would be like when I was a fanciful little girl, dreaming about marrying my price charming.

"Do you Granger Brooks Barnett take Alice May Lowe to be your lawfully wedded wife, to have and to hold from this day forward as long as you both shall live?" The judge asks, his expression serious.

"I do," Granger responds immediately, sliding a gold band onto my finger

"Do you Alice May Lowe take Granger Brooks Barnett to be your lawfully wedded husband, to have and to hold, from this day forward as long as you both shall live?"

For the hint of a second the words die on my tongue, then I look up into the face of this man, that I only met days ago, but who makes me feel understood and cherished and I know, I just know that even though it's crazy and fast, it feels right.

"I do."

"By the power vested in me, by the state of Montana, I now pronounce you man and wife."

I don't hear anything else he has to say as Granger steps forward, curling his arm around my back and yanking me into his chest. Then his lips are on mine, his kiss consuming, branding, claiming as his fingers tangle in my hair keeping me in place. "Mine," he whispers against my lips.

"Yours," I whisper back, smiling into his mouth.

"Alice Barnett, my wife, mine to keep."

Finally, the world around me seeps back into the bubble his kisses had sheltered me in and the sound of applause and cheering from behind us becomes apparent. I don't even have time to process it as he ushers me to a table, the clerk handing me a pen and pointing to the place I need to sign.

Beau and Teddy step free from the group and sign the paperwork after Granger does, and then the judge is shaking our hands, congratulating us.

His family surround us. I'd forgotten they were even here. They sound happy for us, but neither Cora nor Bonnie seemed that way before. But they weren't questioning Granger's compliance, they were checking on mine. They were worried he had forced me into it. Is that something they really thought he'd do? I mean, he didn't really give me a choice, but then would I have said no if he had? Would I have told him he was insane and dismissed this idea out of hand if he'd have suggested we get married this morning before he bought me down to the courthouse?

This was planned, the appointment was booked, the license already applied for. When did he do this? We've only known each other for less than a week, surely this stuff takes time.

Suddenly a barrage of doubts hits me and I wonder what the hell I just did. I just married a stranger, a stranger whose own sisters were worried he was coercing me into this.

Granger's face appears in front of mine, his smile so wide it's contagious and I find myself smiling back at him, even though behind my façade I'm a mess of worry and doubt.

"Mrs. Barnett," he croons, wrapping his arms around me and lifting me off the floor, spinning us around as he kisses me passionately. "You have made me the happiest man in the world."

"When did you plan all this?"

"Saturday."

"We'd known each other a day."

"And I already knew you were mine," he growls, his voice taking on that sexy husk that makes my core clench appreciatively. "I want to take you home and fuck you so bad, but my family want to take us out for brunch."

All of his tension from earlier is gone and there's a lightness in him now that I hadn't realized wasn't there before. "Fuck, wife, I love you so much. I know a courthouse wedding probably wasn't what you've dreamed about, so start planning a big do if that's what you want. Whatever you want, I want you to have it all, I just couldn't wait another moment without you being mine."

His words settle some of the tension sitting low in my belly, his enthusiasm and happiness so consuming I find myself pushing up onto my toes and kissing him.

Before long we're all moving along the sidewalk as a group, me, my husband and what I suppose is now *our* family. A sudden burst of joy at having a family again almost stops me in my tracks. Today I got married. Today I gained six brothers and two sisters.

I have a husband.

Granger is my husband.

Instead of the shock and fear I'd expected to feel, I'm surprised at the joy that starts at my toes and works its way up my body to my heart. This man is overwhelmingly good to me, he gets me, accepts me, loves me. All of the doubts that have plagued me vanish and all I feel is all consuming, mind numbing, love.

I love him. I love the way he doesn't care that I'm insane, likes it even. I love how he can make all of my thoughts turn to him the moment he walks into the room. I love how he sets my body on fire every time he touches me. I love how he takes all of my faults, my insecurities, idiosyncrasies and fears and shoulders them for me. He's sweet and kind and sexy and gorgeous and… mine. This man is mine, my husband, mine to keep, mine to cherish. He's the antidote to my poison.

Unable to wait even a moment to tell him, I stop walking and pull on his hand where our fingers are entwined. We're in the middle of the sidewalk, not exactly a romantic location, but the words are bubbling up my throat, unwilling to be stifled.

"Honey?" Granger asks, stopping with me.

"I love you," I blurt.

His eyes light up and his full lips part as he looks at me like I'm a mythical creature that he's never encountered before. "Say it again," he demands.

"I love you."

"Again."

"I love you so much."

His arms are around me, his lips on mine as he dips me like we're in a scene out of a romance film. I giggle even as I kiss him back, losing myself in my man, my antidote, my husband.

I barely hear the words of congratulations and welcomes to the family from his brothers, in fact the whole brunch is a blur as I focus on my husband beneath me. He pulled me into his lap the moment we were seated at the table in the bright restaurant, refusing to let me take my own seat, despite my protests that people would stare.

"Let them stare, I want my wife in my lap, so everyone knows you're mine," he laughs, his spirit so light and buoyant as he alternates between playing with the rings on my finger and kissing me breathless. "I guessed the size, we can get them resized if they need it though."

"They're perfect. What stone is this?" I ask, touching the large yellow stone at the center of my engagement ring.

"It's a yellow diamond, the same color as your hair." His huge palm curves around my neck and under my hair as he pulls me onto his waiting lips, kissing me for the hundredth time since we woke up this morning. "I never thought I'd get married, then I met you and it drove me crazy not to own you as legally as I do in every other way. It's been an hour and I already can't imagine you ever not being my wife. You're mine now, Mrs. Barnett," he chuckles.

When the food comes, he insists on feeding me. Decadent bites of almond cream cheese filled crepes, creamy eggs benedict interspliced with sips of crisp champagne. When we've finished, we leave as a group and Granger holds me tightly to his side, not letting me go for a minute.

"Right newlyweds, go home and celebrate while there's no one in to listen to you making your wife scream, then tonight we're going to Barney's and I'm gonna start searching for my woman so I can look as happy as you fuckers do," Penn announces, laughing.

My cheeks instantly heat, even as Granger's deep chuckle reverberates through his chest into mine. "See you later, assholes."

"Granger, Alice," Cora calls, moving toward us, Huck a step behind. "Look, I just wanted to say I'm sorry. Granger, as much as I love you, you're my brother but you have to admit that you guys have a do what you want first, ask permission later attitude, especially when it comes to us women. Alice is my sister now too, I needed to make sure you hadn't bullied her into this wedding, because of your Barnett caveman bullshit."

As apologies go, it's not a great one, but given what she said about the way Huck and Beau behaved I guess I can see where she's coming from.

"Thank you for looking out for Alice, but Cora, you ever try and come between me and my wife again and we'll have a fucking problem. I love you, you know I do, sis, but just because my brother is a manipulative asshole, that doesn't mean the rest of us are," Granger says sternly.

"I know," she says, tears streaming down her face.

"Fuck, don't cry," he says, pulling her to him and pressing a kiss to the top of her head.

"I'm sorry and I'm really happy for you guys," she says, pulling back and wiping her tears away with the back of her hand. "Welcome to the family, Alice." Then her arms are around me, her pregnant belly stopping us from getting too close.

"Thank you for caring, Cora, it really does mean a lot to me that you'd go against your brother to make sure I was okay." My voice breaks, fuck, now I'm gonna cry.

"Jesus, enough," Huck says, pulling Cora away. "Go fuck, I can't deal with my own woman crying, I definitely can't cope with my woman and my sister crying at the same time."

Gathering me close, Granger presses a kiss to the top of my head and turns me, opening the car door for me and ushering me inside. His hand is on my thigh the entire drive back up to the mountain to his, or I suppose our house now and by the time we slow to a stop, I can feel the palpable tension filling the car.

"Wait," he warns when he opens his door and climbs out, immediately rounding the hood and opening my car. Leaning in, he unclips my seatbelt then scoops me out of the car like I weigh nothing, carrying me to the front door and then across the threshold. "Welcome home, Mrs. Barnett."

I giggle, the sound feeling foreign from my lips as I cling to his neck.

When my back hits the bed I expect him to follow me down, but instead he pauses, standing at the end of the bed, his eyes fixed on me.

"I want you naked, wife. I want to see you in nothing but the rings that I gave you." His voice is so rough and low he sounds inhuman.

Sitting up, I tug my dress up and over my head, leaving me in my bra, panties and the sheer stockings. Granger's eyes heat, but he doesn't move forward, his feet planted to the spot as he watches me, the bulge in his pants getting larger by the second.

Unfastening my bra, I let the straps fall down my

arms, but hold the cups in place for a moment, feeling confident and wanting to tease him a little, like I'm the one in control, even though we both know I'm nothing more than a puppet to his master.

Releasing the bra, it falls forward and I wiggle my arms free, not covering my breasts, or nipples that are pebbled and eager for his touch.

Sliding my thumbs into the sides of my panties I push them over my hips, trying to be as graceful as possible while I'm half sitting, half lying down and somehow manage to pull off a semi sexy reveal of the goods, taking my stockings with me, until I'm completely naked, apart from the beautiful gold rings adorning my finger.

"Come here, wife," he beckons with an arrogant crook of his finger.

Maybe I should play hard to get, make him work for it, but I don't have enough game to pull that off, or any desire for him to not see I'll do whatever he asks me to do. So I roll to my hands and knees and crawl off the bed, taking the final step until I'm in front of him, offering him all I have to give. Me.

"Tell me," he demands, his voice ragged.

"I love you."

"Again."

"I love you."

"Who am I?"

I wrinkle my brow for a minute, trying to understand what he wants me to say, then it dawns on me. "My husband."

"Yes, I fucking am." His smile is so gloriously wide that it instantly shatters the sexual tension that had filled every molecule of air. His arms wrap around me and he lifts me off the ground, kissing me as he spins us until I'm breathless and giggling.

"Undress me, wife," he playfully orders, smacking my butt cheek.

He plays with my nipple as I unbutton his shirt, unlatch his belt, then unzip his jeans and push them down his hips, where he kicks them off. He's commando beneath his pants, his dick hard, bobbing against his stomach, a pebble of precum pooling at the head.

"I want to see your lips stretched around my dick."

Dropping to my knees, I look up at Granger as I reach out and wrap my hand around his hard cock. I'm not hugely experienced, this is only the second blowjob I've ever given, but my mouth's watering with the need to taste him. Parting my lips, I lick the bead of precum from the head, keeping my eyes on his as I feed the head into my mouth and suck.

His eyes roll and an animalist groan slips from his parted lips, his hand finds my head, fingers tangling in my hair. Using my limited knowledge of blowjobs, mainly from books, I release the head with a pop and lick down the length of him, using my hand to grip him at the base while my other cups his balls and squeezes lightly. Taking him back into my mouth, I try to take as much of him as I can, widening my lips and pushing my head forward until I gag and have to immediately pull back, sucking at the head again like he's a lollypop and I'm seeing how many sucks to get to the center.

Whatever I'm doing, he seems to like it. His eyes stay on mine and his grip on my hair tightens as he guides my mouth on and off his dick, praising me as I work him with my fist at the same time as my mouth, wanting him to fall apart the way he makes me whenever he touches me.

"Enough," he snarls, dragging me off. "I don't want to come in your mouth, I want to be buried deep inside of you." Lifting me from the floor, he turns us then climbs onto the comforter, laying back as he urges me to follow him down. "Sit on my face, I want to lick you until you scream."

I do as he asks, crawling up his body until my core is straddling his face. I stall, unsure what to do, but he drags me down, his tongue finding my clit and eradicating all rational thought from my mind as he makes me come twice in a matter of minutes, his fingers filling me as his tongue works my body into a frenzy.

I call his name as I tip over the edge for the third

time, my muscles wilting from all the pleasure. But he's nowhere near done with me. "Straddle my dick, wife, I want to watch my cock spread your pussy wide as it takes every inch, then I want you to ride me until I fill you with my cum."

His dirty talk reignites me and with his help, I straddle his hips. "Put my dick in you," he orders, his eyes firmly fixed between my legs as I grab his dick and guide it to my soaked entrance.

"Slowly."

So slowly it feels like agonized torture, I lower myself onto his cock, feeling my pussy stretch around his girth until I'm sitting in his lap, panting with the need to move, to come, to scream. His hands find my hips, and he helps guide me until I get into a rhythm rising and falling, griding my hips until his dick is scraping over that elusive spot inside of me with every thrust. Despite the illusion of control he's giving me, he's most definitely topping from the bottom, his hands moving me the way he wants me, controlling the pace, slowing me when I try to go faster, taunting me with an orgasm that stays frustratingly out of reach.

"Please," I beg.

"Please what?"

"Make me come, I need to come."

"Tell me."

"I love you."

"Again."

"I love you. Please, please, Granger. Please."

My begging finally makes him relent and a moment later, I'm beneath him, his dick still inside of me, his body above me as he grabs my legs and lifts my butt from the mattress and into the air.

"Mine. My wife, my woman, mine," he chants as he fucks me hard, ruthlessly claiming me, slamming me into an orgasm that makes my ears ring and my vision blur as he reminds me over and over again that I'm his now, that I belong to him, that he's keeping me. When he finally comes, I feel the heat of his release inside of me, feel it dripping down my thighs, and I love the weight of his body as he collapses on top of me.

"I love you."

"I love you too."

TWENTY

GRANGER

I'm the king of the mother fucking world!

The luckiest bastard that ever lived.

Hashtag fucking blessed.

Alice. My wife. My motherfucking wife, is naked, asleep and covered in my cum beside me, her blonde waterfall of hair a tangled mess strewn across the pillows, her kiss and blowjob swollen lips, parted slight in her sleep.

I've fucked her twice more since the first time. Once with her legs wrapped around my neck, the second bent over the end of the bed with my thumb in her ass while she screamed so loud she went hoarse. My wife. Fuck I love saying it, thinking it. My wife is fucking perfect.

I expected her to argue, maybe to even run, but instead she said yes and then confessed that she loved me. This woman is my fucking world and I'm not sure how I even got through each day without her.

Maybe this need I have for her will settle, but right now that doesn't seem likely. Even letting her go to the bathroom seems like too much space between us. Fuck knows how Beau and Huck cope with Bonnie and Cora working, there's no way I can let Alice work away from me for hours on end, I'd lose my mind. No, she needs to be with me, all the time.

I'm married. The thought doesn't evoke the panic I expect, because Alice is my wife, not some random, faceless woman. Now I have the ring on her finger, I just need to put a baby in her belly and I'm pretty sure I'll be the happiest man alive.

If I could just get Alice's sister to stop calling me, everything would be perfect. Contacting her was a mistake, there's a reason she's not in Alice's life and instead of letting my anger with her family overtake my thoughts, I should have considered what exactly would happen.

I assumed Serenity would have no interest in her sister, and given they've had practically zero contact in the last ten years, that made sense. But now her sister won't stop calling and I'm worried that I've opened a fucking can of worms that should have stayed shut.

Admitting that I don't want her to have contact with her family makes me sound like an asshole, but maybe that's what I am, because I refuse to share her with anyone else, it's bad enough that my family all want to claim her as sister. Apparently I'm not the type of man who knows how to share when it comes to the most important thing in my life.

Her sister is a potential threat to me. Serenity was Alice's surrogate mother most of their childhood, if she tells her sister that she should leave me, would she? The fact that I'm not sure is the reason why I'm awake and stressing out, instead of asleep curled around my beautiful wife.

My cell buzzes for the second time today and I know without looking it'll be Serenity again. I consider blocking her number, but I'm worried that if I do that, she'll start lighting up Alice's cell instead and right now, I really don't want them to talk before I figure out how to tell Alice that I got in touch with her estranged sister behind her back.

Alice might be submissive and willing to let me be firmly in control of our lives, but I worry that dredging up a painful past for her might ruin what we're building here. I can't allow that, won't allow that. She has me now and a crazy house full of siblings, her sister hasn't been there for her for years, she picked herself over her kid sister. That was her choice, but I refuse to let her try to sabotage mine and Alice's happiness.

Pressing the red button, I send Serenity to voicemail again, but she hasn't left any messages so far. Alice stirs beside me and all of my attention immediately goes to her, my cell and Serenity all but forgotten in favor of my beautiful naked wife.

"Hey," she says sleepily.

"Hey honey, you hungry?"

She shakes her head, her tongue bobbing out and wetting her full bottom lip. Unable to resist I run the pad of my thumb over it, going from side to side. "Your lips are swollen," I smile.

"Wonder why?" she smiles, her eyes still closed as she reaches out across the bed until she's touching me.

"I like it. Maybe everyday should start with you sitting on my face, then you on your knees with my dick in your mouth."

"You're so dirty."

"That's not dirty, honey. If I was being dirty, I'd say that each morning should start with me fucking your face, then sinking my dick into your tight ass and filling you with so much of my cum it's dripping out of you for the rest of the day."

Her eyes snap open and her lips part on a shocked

gasp before she snaps them shut again.

Chuckling, I use my thumb to part her lips, pushing the tip between her teeth until it's resting on her tongue. "You look horrified, but I don't think you're as appalled by that idea as you're pretending to be."

She tries to look suitably upset, but I can see the amusement in her eyes. "I see how it is. You marry me, lulling me into a false sense of security, and now I'm your wife you show me how much of a sexual deviant you are."

"Only for you, wife, I was purely vanilla until I saw you then all my deviant tendencies surged to the surface. I can't wait to spend the rest of my life doing dirty, dirty things to you."

Her giggle is pure music to my ears and I can't help myself, I pounce on her, flipping her to her stomach and smacking her ass, before my dick finds her hot, wet entrance and fills her in one deep thrust.

I can't get enough of my wife and it turns out, I don't want to try.

***

The next week is pure bliss. Alice and I fall into a routine of spending every moment of our days together and I've never been fucking happier. I know to some people the way I insist she come with me to work, the way I refuse to let her out of my sight might seem odd, possessive and stifling, but it doesn't feel that way to us.

I like Alice with me all the time and when she's with me, her brain never has a chance to spin, feeding her toxic thoughts. It works for us and that's all that matters. Her RV is still down at Bay and Penn's shop, still broken, the repair forgotten. I plan to sell it eventually, but for now I'm content that she hasn't mentioned it since before we got married.

Her life revolves around me now and I fucking love it. We wake up together, bathe together, eat together, work together, we're co-dependent to the extreme and I've never been fucking happier. She says she has her own money, but I never let her spend any of it. She could have millions in the bank, but I don't give a fuck, she's my wife and anything she wants or needs, I'll be the one paying for it.

It's perverse, but I need her to need me almost as much as she needs me to be the one to take the lead in our marriage. She looks to me for everything and even though it may seem fucked up to outsiders looking in, it's what keeps us both sane.

My family adore her, especially now she's started to come out of her shell around them. It'll take her time to truly understand that she isn't a bad person, that she doesn't have a trace of poison in her, but I know she'll get there eventually and she's already a thousand times calmer and more settled since we defined our relationship and what we both need from the other.

I want to be her world and she needs me to be her anchor, we sink or swim together.

Beau is still trying to get her to go and work for him, but her eyes widened with panic when he suggested it at dinner last night. Afterward she spent the night withdrawn and silent, until I stripped her naked and consumed her mind with pleasure, pushing away all of the negative thoughts.

Her fucking sister stopped calling the day after the wedding and I'm grateful, contacting her was a mistake. We don't need her in our lives, all Alice and I need is each other and the family I desperately want to start with her.

I hate that fucking implant in her arm, but I can't figure out how to get it out without her agreeing to it. It's not like I can fuck her into exhaustion, then remove it, it needs a doctor's office and minor surgery to get the godforsaken thing out.

Every day I tell her I love her, that I want her, need her. That I own her and want to see her belly swollen with my kid, but I can tell from her indulgent smile that she isn't taking me seriously. I've registered her with our local doctor's office and arranged an appointment to have it removed next week, I just haven't told her about it yet.

"You okay, honey? You're quiet this morning," I say when I pull my car to stop outside my workshop.

"Just tired," she says around a yawn.

"I'll get the heat cranked up and you can go take a nap."

"Okay," she yawns again.

When my furniture business started to take off, I contemplated renting a work space, but paying rent seemed like a waste of money, so when I saw this old mill come up for sale, I decided it made more sense to buy. It was crumbling when I got it for a song, but it didn't take long for me and my brothers to get the place fixed up and made into the perfect workspace for me.

Unlocking the door, I push it wide and Alice steps into the main workshop, full of my tools and benches full of pieces of furniture at various states of completion. Behind the shop is an enclosed booth that I use to varnish and lacquer, and a storage space where I store all my completed pieces. On the first floor is a kitchen, a small bedroom I use when I need some space, or if I'm working long hours to finish a piece, and my office. The ceilings are high, with the center of the workshop being double height, the upstairs rooms accessible by a walkway that circles the perimeter.

Most of the time when I'm working, Alice keeps me company, helping out if she's bored. At her request, she tidied my office and organized my piles of paperwork. Mainly she's just here because that's where we both want her to be.

Following her in, I close the doors behind me to keep out the cold, crisp winter air, and turn the heating on at the control on the wall. I never let it get too cold in here, so the frost doesn't get a chance to affect the wood, but I've been turning it up higher since Alice started coming in with me every day.

"I'll go turn the coffee machine on," she says, climbing the stairs up to the kitchen as I turn on all my machines, getting ready to work.

I hear her footsteps come back down the stairs and she stops beside me. She's still hesitant to be the one to initiate touch between us, even though I've told her a thousand times that I'd have her in my arms permanently if I could. "Come here, honey," I croon, opening my arms. She walks straight into them, burying her face in my chest as I wrap my arms tightly around her.

"I'm so tired. You need to let me get some sleep tonight."

"I can't help it, I need you."

"You woke me up three times last night, Granger."

"My dick needed to be inside you," I snap, a little annoyed that she's making it sound like me fucking her is an inconvenience.

"Well tonight my pussy is off limits after 9pm. I need to sleep."

Grabbing her ass, I haul her up my body, lifting her off the floor, my hands supporting her weight. "Then maybe after that I'll take your ass instead. That belongs to me too and I've only had my fingers and tongue in there, it's about time my dick claimed you there too."

She stiffens, but doesn't try to pull away.

"Do you want my hard dick in your ass, honey? Do you want me to own all of your holes? Because the thought of your ass spread tight around my cock makes me want to strip you naked right this minute."

"It'll hurt, you're too big."

"It'll fit just fine, your body was made for me and I'll stretch you out good first, until you're begging for me to fuck you."

I'm slowly grinding her against the hardness in my pants as I let my words settle over her. She loves it when I talk dirty to her, and I love telling her all the depraved things I plan to do to her body. "Tell me you want me to fuck your ass, Alice."

"Granger."

"Nuh huh. Tell me what you want me to do."

"Fuck me."

"How baby, how do you want me to fuck you?"

Her hips roll against me, her eyes half lidded as she dips her tongue out and licks her lips.

"Tell me," I say more forcefully.

"I want you to fuck my ass. I want you to own every part of me." Her words are breathy and a little desperate, but I hear her and a sadist smile weaves its way across my lips. This woman is fucking perfect in every way.

"Tonight honey, I promise, you're gonna scream so fucking hard as your ass rides my dick. But first you need to come, then you need to take a nap."

"No, now," she protests, lost to the lust I've built up in her.

"Now you get my fingers, later you get my dick." Releasing her with one hand, I slide it between us, pushing it beneath her jeans and panties, to her cunt that's wet and slick after my dirty teasing. Pushing three fingers into her cunt, I grip her ass tight with my free hand, holding her to me as I quickly fuck her pussy, thrusting my fingers in and out of her as she lets her head rest against my shoulder, her hips baring down on me as she chases her release.

Her body is like my playground and I already know just how to make her come fast and how to drag it out, keeping her on the edge until I want her to fall. Right now, I want to feel her cunt tighten around my fingers, a shock and awe orgasm, guaranteed to leave her drained and ready to sleep. Scissoring my fingers, I curl the tips, finding her g-spot and rubbing at it with each thrust, until the rhythm of her hips becomes erratic and I feel her teeth clamp down on my shoulder as she stifles the sounds of her pleasure and comes around my hand, gripping me tightly as she wrings every ounce of pleasure from the orgasm I just gave her.

When she settles, her breath puffing out of her in a ragged exhale, I slowly pull my fingers free, lifting them to my lips to taste her release on my skin as I carry her spent body upstairs to the bedroom. Sitting her down on the edge of the bed, I unfasten her jacket, pulling it from her arms. Unbuttoning her jeans, I drag them down her legs, leaving her in one of my thick knit sweaters and her damp panties.

"Sleep," I tell her, kissing her hard and fast before I hold up the covers and wait for her to climb beneath them. Covering her over, I fight the urge to climb in with her, but if I do she won't be getting any sleep, my need for her body too great to resist.

"Leave the door open," she says sleepily, her eyes already closed.

"I'm right down stairs. Love you."

"Love you."

Leaving her, I walk to my office and plug my cell into the docking port on my desk, setting my music to play quietly on the speakers downstairs, then I pause at the bedroom door, she's asleep already.

Three hours later, she's still asleep and I feel like an

asshole for waking her so many times during the night. I need to take better care of her and allowing her to be exhausted just because my dick is constantly hard for her, isn't good enough. I need to do better.

My cell starts to ring through the speakers, but I'm in the middle of gluing legs onto the chair I'm working on, so whoever is calling me will have to wait.

"Granger, your cell's ringing," a sleepy Alice says, walking out of the bedroom half dressed and rumpled from her nap.

"Can you answer it, honey? I can't let this go right now." I gesture down to the chair leg I'm holding in place.

She nods and pads to the office.

"Hello?" her voice comes through the speakers.

"Alice."

That voice, so alike Alice's, but not at the same time.

"Serenity?"

"Hey Alice."

The speaker suddenly goes silent and my eyes move to where Alice is walking out of my office my cell clutched to her ear, her eyes wide and full of horror and betrayal as she listens to her sister on the other end of the cell.

For the first time since she became mine, Alice turns away from me, walks back into the bedroom and closes the door behind her. Choosing to put distance between us, choosing to block me out.

TWENTY ONE

ALICE

"Serenity, what's going on, why do you have Granger's number?"

"He called me last week, who is this guy?"

"What? He called you? Why?" I don't understand what's going on, why would Granger call my sister? How did he even get her number?

"He called wanting to know why I left. Where are you? What's this guy's deal?"

"I don't know why he did that. I'm sorry he bothered you, I'll make sure he doesn't contact you again," I say, my voice sounding robotic even to my own ears.

"Alice." Serenity's voice evokes emotions that I'd

rather not deal with. She left and I understand why, I don't even blame her, but being here with Granger I'd forgotten why I live the way I live, why I keep myself distanced from people and from hearing that tone in her voice. The tone that's so familiar from my childhood. The way she'd say my name before she stepped in and cleaned up whatever mess I'd made or problem I'd caused makes me flinch. "I'm fine. I'm sorry he got in touch. Take care."

"Alice." She calls my name but I'm already ending the call and lowering Granger's cell to my lap. My fingers move across the screen and I delete the call history, noticing that she's tried to call him more than once, then I delete her number from his contacts.

Why would he do this? Why would he contact her, maybe he's sick of me already, maybe he was hoping she'd swoop in and take me off his hands, rescue me like she did when we were kids.

The door flies open, hitting the wall behind it with so much force that it bounces off the exposed brick and swings back, almost hitting Granger as he storms into the room, his chest heaving, his face a mixture of worry and anger.

"Why the fuck did you shut the door? What did she say to you?" he demands.

"You called my sister." It's not a question, it's a statement, my voice flat and lifeless.

"I did." He's not at all repentant.

"Why?"

"I wanted to talk to her."

"Why?"

"I wanted to know why she left."

"That's none of your business."

"Everything about you is my business, you're my wife," he roars, making me flinch with the intensity of his words.

"I told you who I am, I told you what I do to the people around me. Why would you call her? My life isn't her problem. I don't do that anymore; I don't force my problems onto other people. Why would you do that?" My voice breaks a little at the end, making the lack of emotion seem even more apparent. I'm broken, two minutes on the phone to my sister and everything here feels fake, like a façade I've created for myself. Suddenly this room is too small, his presence is too big and I feel like I'm suffocating.

My pants are on the floor and I grab for them, shoving my feet into the fabric, frantically pulling them up my legs, my fingers fumbling with the zipper and button.

"What the fuck are you doing?" Granger snarls.

"I need some air, some space."

"No." He shakes his head, his arms cross across his chest, his jaw tense and firm. "You're not going anywhere."

"Get out of the way, I'm not a fucking prisoner and I need some air."

"No. Only way you're leaving this room is with me, holding my hand, you want to go somewhere that's fine, I'll go with you. Now take my hand."

Shoving my feet into my boots, I ignore him, striding to the doorway and attempting to barge past him, but his hands come up and stop me, restraining me and preventing me from leaving. "It's not happening, honey; I'm not letting you walk out on me. You give me your problems and I'll solve them, you don't deal with them alone anymore. So tell me what she said."

"She didn't say anything, and right now my problem is you. How do you plan on dealing with that?" I question, lifting my eyes to his for the first time since he stormed his way into the room.

"This isn't about me, your eyes are dead, like they were when you got to town. I want to know what the fuck she said to make you look like that and I want to know right fucking now." His voice is just below a yell, somehow intimidating and infuriating both at the same time.

"She said you'd called her asking why she'd left. I apologized for you contacting her, told her I'd make sure it wouldn't happen again. That's it." I sound dead, lifeless, but I can't help it, I feel empty.

"You don't fucking apologize to her," he shouts.

"You called her, a complete stranger, and started demanding answers to questions that you have no right to ask. Of course I apologized. I also deleted her contact from your cell and erased all the call logs too. You had no right to intrude on her life."

Attempting to pass him again, his hold on me tightens. "Take my hand and we'll go wherever you want."

"I just want some air on my own."

"You don't get to be alone anymore, we're married, we're fucked up and co-dependent. Where ever we go, we go together."

"So that's it, you just get to decide that I never get to go anywhere on my own ever again," I snap, trying to pull myself free from his grip.

"Yeah, you gave me that gift, you gave yourself to me and I'm not giving you back. Now take my hand and tell me where you want to go."

"Forget it," I say robotically, twisting and trying to move back to the bed. "Are prisoners allowed to sleep."

"You're not a fucking prisoner," he yells, hauling me off the floor and throwing me over his shoulder. The stairs are a blur as I bounce from my prone position, my head hanging above his butt as he kicks open the front door and unceremoniously drops me to the floor beside his car, my one hand still held tightly by his. "You wanted air, I'll give you fucking air."

Sullenly, I refuse to look at him, even though I can feel his eyes on me. The urge to close in on myself, get in my RV and run hits me like a wrecking ball. For the first time since I accepting this thing between Granger and I, the life I had before him suddenly feels wistful instead of lonely. If I'd never met this man, my husband, I'd have just carried on as before, but I did meet him and I was happy, so why did he do this? Why did he dredge up the past and force all these emotions that I was doing so well at ignoring to the surface?

If he wanted to get rid of me, why would he have married me? Why to go to these lengths to make this permanent?

Confused and hurt and sad, I close my eyes, tip my head back and let the cold air surround me. "Stop watching me, go work."

"No."

"I'm not a child, I don't need to be supervised."

"Two hours ago, you couldn't stand the thought of putting a door between us and now you want me to go away."

"Yes," I exhale, hating how broken I sound. The melancholy that's settled around me feels like a weight I'm just too tired to carry. How can a two minute conversation with my sister do this? Probably the same way a two-week relationship with Granger made me forget who I am.

Only I remember again now. I remember the look on her face when she told me she needed to live her own life, that she was leaving me. With my eyes closed, I see the faces of everyone who I've infected, the varying looks of disgust, pity, revulsion. The whispered jabs, the blatant curses, all of them the same, all saying how pathetic, how weird, how needy I was. My life plays on a loop behind my eyes and I remember it all. Why I need to be alone, why I move so often, why I never allow myself to make any ties.

"Alice." Warm hands cup my face, but I don't open my eyes. I already know what he's going to say, but I can't face it, so I pull away from his touch, needing distance, a chance to re-build the walls he's shattered around my heart. "I shouldn't have called her." His words suggest he's apologizing, but his tone says he doesn't give a fuck, that he's just saying what he needs to placate me.

"I just need some space," I whisper, forcing my eyes to open.

"No. You'll run, I can see it in your eyes and I won't let you go, I'll chase you down and bring you back, so why bother. You're mine now, you're not going anywhere." He means every word, it's there in the intensity in his eyes, the stern line of his mouth, he won't let me go and I'm partially relieved, partially terrified of the truth.

"I won't run. I couldn't even if I wanted to."

Granger's cell starts to ring again and he tightens his hold on my hand as if he's worried I'll disappear in the time it will take him to glance at his phone. His brow furrows. "I should take this, I don't recognize the number, but it could be a customer."

I nod, trying to free my hand from his grip but he just squeezes me tighter.

"Hello."

A line appears between his brows as he listens to whoever is on the other end of the line. "She's here, she's fine. I'll ask." Lowering the cell from his ear, his eyes lock with mine. "Your sister would like to talk to you."

"Why?" I ask, panicked and confused.

"I don't know, honey. Do you want to talk to her?"

"I don't... I don't know."

"I think you should talk to her. Let's go back inside where it's warm, you don't even have a jacket on."

I nod, because it's easier to just let him take over rather than it would be to make decisions for myself.

He lifts the cell back to his ear and speaks. "Sorry, just give us a minute, we're just gonna go somewhere a bit warmer." Tugging on my hand, he leads me inside and back up to the bedroom I was happily sleeping in. Climbing onto the bed, he pulls me to sit between his legs, curling his arm around my waist and pulling me back to rest against his chest, while he taps at the screen of his cell and sets the call onto speaker.

"Hello."

"Alice."

"Hi Serenity, are you okay? Why have you called back?"

"Because I'm freaking the fuck out, Alice. This guy that I've never heard of calls me out of the blue, telling me he loves you and wants to know why I left home ten years ago. Then when I speak to you, you tell me nothing apart from saying you'll make sure he doesn't call again. Of course I'm gonna call back."

"I already told you I was sorry he called, I don't really know what else you want me to say?" Pulling my knees up to my chest, I curl myself into a ball as memories of rejection and loss hit me all over again.

"I want to know where you are, who this guy is."

"Why?" The word slips from my lips before I can help it. As angry as I am with Granger right now, his constant reassuring presence behind me is making me feel brave.

"Why?" she parrots back.

"Yeah, why? I think it's been three years since I last heard from you and that was a text wishing me a happy birthday."

"You're my sister."

"I don't even know your boyfriend's name. I've never met him. I don't know your address."

"You know his name," Serenity sighs, like I'm a child asking the thousandth stupid question of the day.

"I don't, but that's okay, your life is none of my business."

"Phillip, Phil, his name is Phil."

"Granger is my husband, we got married a week ago."

"Married." The single word is a screech that echoes through the phone and bounces around the room. "You got married and didn't tell me. Does Mom know?"

"I haven't spoken to Mom in years. It took her six months to notice I'd moved out."

"I don't care. You don't get married and not tell your family. What the hell, Alice? Where are you? Give me details and I'll get on a plane."

"Why would you come here?" I know I sound dense but I'm genuinely baffled by her reaction.

"Because you've obviously gotten yourself into a mess. You're married to a man none of your family have even met."

"Fuck you," I shout, immediately silencing her.

"Excuse me." Her tone is indignant.

"I said, fuck you. You don't get to start telling me I've gotten myself into a mess when you have chosen to have nothing to do with me since I was thirteen years old. I don't need your approval, I don't need anything from you, which is exactly what you wanted, isn't it? You wanted to live your own life and I've respected that. But you need to respect the fact that I'm a grown woman, I've been on my own for years. If I want to get married that's none of your business. If I want to divorce and get married a dozen more times it's still none of your business. If I have ten kids and move to a commune it's still none of your business. So yes, *sister*, I said fuck you."

Her silence is the loudest noise in the world.

"I'm... You're right, I'm sorry. God, I'm so fucking sorry."

"It's fine. You leaving was right, it was good, it helped me understand who I was and to make sure I didn't do to other people what I did to you."

"What do you think you did to me?" she asks quietly.

"I was needy and clingy, I made you solve all my problems, I ruined your life, stole your childhood. It's my thing, I'm not a good person to be around..." I trail off, hating that Granger is listening to this conversation, even though I've already said all this stuff to him.

"Is your guy there?" she asks, her voice barely above a whisper. "Hand him the phone."

"He's listening, you're on speaker."

"What can I do for you?" Granger asks, his grip on me so tight I can barely breathe.

"Where are you? Like what state?"

"Montana, small town up in the mountains called

Rockhead Point."

"Okay I'm gonna get the first flight out. I'll text you the info as soon as I know when I'm gonna be there."

"Okay," Granger answers while I sit there, gob smacked and stunned to silence.

"See you soon."

The call ends and I stare down at the cell in my hands. My sister who I haven't seen in years, is coming here.

"What just happened?"

"Apparently your sister's coming to town for a visit."

"Why?"

"I'm not a hundred percent sure, but if I had to guess, I'd say she wasn't happy about all the bullshit you just gave her about you being needy and clingy and ruining her life."

"I don't understand?"

"Honey, I love you. But you've got shitty, blinded views about yourself. Most of the garbage that comes out of your mouth is utter bull crap, but you've convinced yourself that you're a terrible person and as much as I'd love to, I can't change that in a couple of weeks."

"Granger."

"No. Just fucking listen, because I've got a feeling once your sister gets here, you're gonna be hearing the same off her. You are the most amazing person I've ever met and that's not only because I love you. You're sweet and kind and gorgeous and there's no way in the fucking universe that you could ever be toxic, or poisonous or any of the bullshit that you've been feeding yourself to try and help you get over the way your sister abandoned you."

He lifts his hand into the air to stop me from arguing with him.

"No honey, she might have had her reasons and they might even be good ones, but you were a kid, with an absentee parent and she abandoned you."

I shake my head. "It wasn't fair to expect her to spend her life fixing me."

"She wasn't fixing you, Alice, she was being a parent and I agree it wasn't fair that your mama didn't step up to the plate to look after you both the way she should. But that isn't your fault. Our daddy died when Teddy was really young, so all of us stepped up to be dad when he needed us to be. We don't resent him and he doesn't resent us. He's our baby brother and we're just glad as hell that he turned out so good as he did, he's the best of us. I get why your sister left, but she did a shitty job when she did because she let you think it was your fault that she wasn't happy and that's bullshit, all that blame lies solely at your mama's door."

"No, I did it. I needed her too much, I do it to anyone who's around me. I'm doing it to you."

His palms cup my cheeks and he turns me to face him. "There is never going to be a time when you need me too much. My life is you, I breath when you breath, smile when you smile, hurt when you hurt. You need me and I need you just as much. If there is such a thing as me without you, I don't ever want to know what that's like again."

Tears spill from my eyes. How is it that even when I'm angry at him that he knows the perfect thing to say to disarm me completely and fall in love with him all over again. Ours might not be a conventional love, but it is love. Powerful, all consuming love.

"I'm pissed at you," I say through my tears.

"I know you are, honey."

"I really love you though."

His smile is so wide I swear the winter sun feels brighter. "I know you do. Let's go home. Let me take care of you, honey."

I nod and he sighs, tension I hadn't realized he'd been holding escaping from his body as he relaxes behind me, turning me completely so I'm draped across his thighs. "I love you."

Wrapping my arms around his neck, I bury my face into his shoulder as he clings to me, showing me for the first time just how vulnerable I make him. Since we met, it's felt like he's always the one holding me up, but right now he needs me.

I'm not sure how long we sit there, holding each other, but eventually we pull ourselves apart, close down the workshop and go home. Because it is home, even if we share it with his family, because my home is where ever he is.

TWENTY TWO

GRANGER

Serenity sends me a text later that night with her flight info.

Serenity

Our flight lands in Bozeman at
11.00am, we'll rent a car and drive
to Rockhead Point.
Any decent hotels in town?

When I show Alice the text, she squirms uncomfortably. "I don't know why she's coming."

"Because she wants to see you," I say with a roll of my eyes. "We can invite them to stay here, we have the space if you want."

"No," she says immediately. "No, I..."

"Okay honey, I'll send them a link to the Buffalo Inn, it's not the ritz, but it's clean and reasonably priced."

Me

> The Buffalo Inn is about the best we have to offer; I'll ring and book you a room. How long do you think you'll be staying?

Serenity

> We both had leave owing so we don't have to be back on base for a week.

I wince when I read her reply, a week is a long time if the girls don't manage to get things sorted, plus I don't want her sister to think she can barge in and take over my woman's life.

Me

> Alice and I can take a few days off work, so I'll book you a room for three nights, then you can decide if you want to stay for the rest of your leave.

Serenity

> Okay, see you tomorrow, I'll text you when we get into town.

Alice is a mixture of nerves, fear and anxiety for the rest of the day and in the end, I drag her to bed and fuck her until she's so exhausted she passes out on top of me. I know it'd be better to have spent the night talking out the issues she has with her sister, but she's spent so many years building up her walls to protect herself from hurting people the way she hurt her sister, that I don't think she'll be able to truly confront her feelings until she sees her sister in person.

When we get up the next morning, I expect the house to be empty, everyone having gone to work, but instead our entire family is waiting in the living room.

"What's going on? Why aren't you at work? Is everything okay?"

"We all wanted to be here for you and Alice," Teddy says from where he's sitting at the dining table. "We know it's gonna be a big thing for you to see your sister again and we wanted you to know we've got your back. If things don't go so well, then fuck her, you've got six brothers and two sisters who love you and will always be here for you."

My family fucking rocks. I've always known that, but seeing them stepping up to support my wife, who they barely know, makes me feel like the luckiest bastard in the world. But this is what the Barnett's do, we're there for each other, we're family.

I'm not sure what I expect from Alice, she's tense beside me, she's not used to having anyone in her life, let alone a ready made tribe all waiting to embrace her. Stepping forward, she rushes into Teddy, slamming her body into his and hugging him tightly. "Thank you," she says, her voice almost breaking with emotion.

My baby brother scoops her up and holds her tightly. "It's okay, sweetie, you're not alone anymore."

Now she's hugged one, they all fucking want to hug her and I end up standing on the side while my brothers steal my woman. They all welcome her to the family and assure her over and over that they have her back, that we're Barnett's and that we look after each other, that we're a family. By the time the girls get to her, they squish her in the middle of the two of them and I'm fucking swallowing down the lump of emotion that's blocking my throat.

I'm a lucky fucking bastard. The perfect wife and the best family a man could ever ask for.

Prying Alice free from Cora and Bonnie, I bundle her close, pulling her to the dining table then down into my lap. The others all crowd round us, filling our huge table to capacity. "We're gonna need a bigger table."

"Why? We all fit," Cody says.

"We won't once you all find your people. Plus, we're gonna have the kids too. We definitely need a bigger table."

Cody's eyes get wide and he stares at me like I've got two heads. "I'm happy single, bro, don't throw the curse my way."

"Throw it mine," Penn announces. "I'm ready for some happily ever after. I want a taste of what you fuckers have. I'm ready for my woman, screwing around is losing its appeal."

Bay and Cody look horrified, while I notice Huck and Beau nodding in agreement. None of us would give up what we've got with our women to go back to mindless sex with random women. Tightening my hold on Alice, I press a kiss to her neck. "I love you," I whisper, only loud enough for her to hear.

"I love you too," she whispers back.

***

Serenity texts to say she's in town just after lunch, and I watch as Alice physically braces herself.

"You want us all to come with?" Teddy offers in the calm, quiet tone he's taken to using with Alice.

"Maybe," she bites her lip.

"How bout we all go to Barney's, that way we can get some lunch and a few drinks. It's a nice relaxed environment, but we can be there if you need us," Beau says.

I look to Alice, fighting the urge to take control of the situation, but needing Alice to be the one to take the lead on this until I assess if I need to step between her and her sister. I won't allow Serenity to be a problem, but I also don't want to discourage my wife from addressing the person who's affected her life so dramatically for the last ten years.

Alice's gaze finds mine, and I know right then that she's begging me to take over, her eyes are pleading with me and I can't resist. She needs to be strong, but that doesn't mean that I can't be her strength. "Barney's sounds good. You guys can come say hi, then you can leave if Alice and her sister need some privacy."

Beau nods, then turns his attention back to Alice. "We're always here if you need us, little one."

Fuck, why do I feel like I'm going to fucking cry? Beau is my big brother, since Dad died, he's the one we've all looked up to, the one we all wanted to be when we grew up. I didn't realize I needed to know I had his support until he just said it.

"You ready, honey?"

She nods, but it's not convincing.

"You want to come home, you say the word and we come home. You want to tell her to go fuck herself again, you do it. You want to hug her and tell her you love her, you do that too. Nothing is wrong, okay, and no matter what happens, later we'll come home and you'll be surrounded by family. You are not alone anymore. You have me and you have all your brothers and sisters. Soon we'll start a family of our own. You'll never be alone."

"What if you get sick of me?" Her words are broken and ragged.

"Impossible."

"Impossible?"

"What if you get sick of me?" I smirk.

Her smile is soft and slow. "Impossible."

"Let's go see your sister."

The drive into town is slow, I take Alice in my car, while the rest of the family pile into the huge minivan we use if we want to all go out together, although once Cora has the baby we won't all fit in one anymore. Alice is quiet beside me, I can feel the tension emanating from her. My girl is stressed, and apart from turning around and taking her home, I'm not sure what I can do to help her. Telling her everything is going to be okay will only go so far, especially as I'm really not sure everything is going to be okay.

Her hand is held tightly in mine, my thumb rubbing circles over her skin as I drive one handed down the familiar mountain roads. I want to say something to calm her, but I have no idea how this reunion with Serenity is going to go down.

Alice wants to take all the blame, but I refuse to let her. Fuck, maybe it's me she should be worrying about, not her sister. How the hell am I going to keep my mouth shut if Serenity says something that pisses me off?

Parking in a side street behind Barney's, I wait for Bay to park behind me, then I turn to face Alice. "I love you. I'm glad your sister is here, but her presence doesn't change a fucking thing. You're mine and I won't ever give you up. No matter what she says, I know who you are. You're mine."

As I watch, she swallows thickly and nods. Reluctantly releasing her, I walk around to her door and open it, unclipping her seatbelt as I like to do and help her out of the car. She wraps herself around my side and I curl my arm over her shoulder, holding her to me as I follow the rest of my family down the street and into the bar.

We settle into a long banquet of tables with built in seating on one side and chairs on the other, and I text Serenity the name of the bar and a map tag so she can find us. I should probably offer to go fetch them, but I want her to come here and see all of us and the support we give her sister so she knows to watch what she says. It's a fucked up intimidation tactic, but I want Serenity to be at a disadvantage, so she knows not to fuck with her sister.

The waitress comes and we order a round of drinks. I order a soda for myself and a beer for Alice, then wait while the rest of the table orders. We're positioned at the end of the table so there's somewhere for Serenity to sit without her having to ask Alice to move, which I wouldn't allow. I want to know exactly what she has to say to my wife and I refuse to be excluded from the conversation.

Alice is so close beside me, she's practically on my

lap, so I lift her up and pop her on my thigh instead.

"Granger, I can't sit on your lap," she protests weakly.

"Why?"

"Because we're out in public, at a bar."

"I don't give a fuck where we are. You started to the relax the moment I put your ass in my lap, so fuck it, your ass stays in my lap."

She giggles and I grab her chin and lead her lips to mine. More of the tension drains from her as she gives herself over to me, her body melting into mine, the way it always does when I touch her and claim her in the way we both love.

"Alice."

Alice freezes against me for a split second, then she pulls back and turns her head slowly to look at the woman and man that are standing by the table.

"Serenity."

Even before she said her name, it was obvious that this is Alice's sister, they look incredibly similar, only where Alice is all broken edges and fearful eyes, Serenity is quiet control. They share the same straw blonde hair color, but where Alice's is loose and flowing to her shoulders, Serenity's is cut into a short crop against her head. She's slim, but toned, taller than Alice and with an obviously military air to her. The guy to her left is tall, dark haired and given his expression, not too impressed about being either in this bar or Montana at all. I take an instant disliking to him, but he's also staring at my wife, so maybe it's just that.

The girls stare at each other, so I use my initiative and lift Alice off my lap, standing her in front of me, her back pressed to my chest, then I lean over her, offering my hand to her sister. "Hi, I'm Granger. Nice to meet you."

My movement spurs Serenity into action and she immediately takes my hand and shakes it. She's got an impressively firm grip and I fight the urge to squeeze back. If she wants to compare dick sizes, mine's bigger.

"Serenity. This is Phil."

I offer my hand to Phil and he shakes it too. His grip is weak and a little limp, it doesn't make me like him any more.

"Take a seat, let's get you a drink," I suggest, sitting back down and puling Alice into my lap again, she comes willingly, holding onto my arm where it's wrapped around her waist. The waitress immediately appears with our drinks, handing them out before taking Serenity and Phil's orders and leaving.

"This is the rest of our family. Beau and his wife Bonnie, then Teddy, Cody, Huck and his fiancé Cora, Bay and then finally Penn," I say, pointing to each of them in turn.

"Your family?" Serenity asks.

"I'm one of seven, nine now with Bonnie and Cora."

"And you all live here?"

"Yeah, we're all born and bred right here in Rockhead Point," I tell her, not missing the hint of derision in her tone.

"Wow, small town life. You never thought of moving to a city?" Phil asks.

"Apart from the girls, we all went away to college. We've lived in cities, Teddy went to school down in Florida, but we all came home. We like our roots," I say, making sure to maintain eye contact with him.

"Alice, how did you end up here?" Serenity asks her sister.

"I was just passing through, the RV broke down and Granger stopped to help. Bay and Penn own a garage so they came out and towed it back to town."

"RV? Dad's RV?"

Alice nods. "Yep."

"How is that heap of junk still running? It was a pile of crap when I left for basic training," Serenity asks, with a wistful smile.

"I've kept it going, it's got me where I need to go the last five years."

"And where was that?" Serenity asks.

"All over."

"So where's home?"

"Here, now," Alice says, squeezing my arm.

"And before here?"

"Lots of places.

"Stop being so evasive, where have you been living?" Serenity snaps, using a voice that like a stern mother scolding her kid.

I don't like it, so I reply. "She's been living in her RV, moving from state to state depending on the seasons. Winter in the mountains, summer at the beach, fall in new England, spring in a city along the way."

Serenity's eyes widen. "I don't understand."

"What's not to understand?" Alice asks, genuinely confused.

"What did Mom say about you living like a gypsy?"

"The last time I spoke to Mom, she called me and asked me to get bread and milk and make sure there was groceries in the house. I told her I'd moved out six months earlier. She asked me if I could still get her some groceries, and when I told her I was on the other side of the country, she cursed me out and said she supposed she'd have to get her own milk."

I cringe listening to Alice's words. I hate that my mom is gone, if she wasn't she'd have doted on my wife, she'd have spoiled her rotten with the kind of love only a mom can give. Alice never had that. From what she's told me, once her dad left, her mom stopped showing any interest in being a parent and left Serenity to look after the girls.

"What about boyfriends, friends? You never considered moving into a place with anyone?"

Alice shakes her head. "No."

Serenity turns to Phil as if he can help her, but he just looks back impassively, then she turns her attention back to her sister. "Why didn't you come to West Virginia, you could have stayed with us?"

"I would never invade your life, besides I was fine on my own."

"You're my sister, why wouldn't you come to me?"

Alice looks to me and I nod, urging her to say whatever she needs to say. "Serenity, when you left, you told me you needed to do something for yourself for once. I respected that. I know I made you take care of me, to fix my problems and look after me when you should have been out drinking and being a teenager. I ruined your childhood, I wasn't going to dump myself on your life and ruin the future you'd made for yourself too."

"I never meant—" Serenity starts.

"I saw what I did to you, and then I realized I did it to other people too. I cling, I'm needy, I go from person to person trying to find someone to dump all my baggage on and ruin their lives, just like I did you and it's not fair. So I decided to stop. I got in my RV and I left, I drove and moved and I've been doing that ever since. Until Granger."

Serenity's gaze moves from her sister to me, she looks over the way I'm holding Alice, the possessiveness in my touch, and her nose wrinkles. "When did you get married?"

"Last week. We just went down to the courthouse, but we're going to plan a proper wedding once Alice decides what she wants," I tell her.

"How long have you known each other?"

"Not long. But when you meet your person, you know. Alice is my person, I knew the moment I saw her."

"What do you think about the load of garbage my sister just spewed?"

"Which bit do you consider garbage?" I ask carefully.

"The bullshit about her being needy and clingy and ruining people's lives."

"You ought to wait till she gets to her toxic and poisonous personality. She really believes it too. She's been alone for ten years because she really thinks that's what she does to the people she allows herself to spend time around."

Serenity reaches blindly for Phil's hand, squeezing it tightly as I stare right at her, silently telling her that she did this, that it's her fault.

"Alice."

"I don't really want to talk about this. Can't we just get drunk, then you can go home and we can arrange to meet up in another ten years?" Alice says, wearily, sighing as she rests her head against my shoulder and turns to look at the rest of the people at the table. "You guys wanna get drunk?"

Teddy smiles back at her. "Sure sis, what's your poison? To-kill-ya shots or girly pink shooters that sneak up on you until you're rolling on the floor drunk."

"Definitely pink girly shots. I want to see Beau drink something pink."

Unable to resist it, I smile to myself, glad that she's looking to our family for support.

"Alice, we didn't come all the way here to get drunk," Serenity snaps.

"Then what did you come for? It's been ten years, Ser, I think I've had four or five texts from you in all that time. I've told you why I stayed away, so what's your excuse? I know I ruined your childhood, but I was a kid too. So why now? Granger started this, he should never have contacted you, but you could have just ignored his call and you didn't, you kept calling back. You didn't even ring my cell, you rang his. Was it to warn him, to tell him I wasn't worth his time? Why?"

"I…" Serenity's lips part, then snap shut and she stands from the table, pulling Phil up with her. "Look, maybe we should do this another day when we're all calmer."

"I'm calm," Alice shrugs. "You came all this way. You

came here, I didn't chase you, so you must have had some idea about what you planned to say to me. Why are you running away now?"

I swear I'm so fucking proud I could shout it from the ceiling. I hoped she'd confront her sister, but honestly, I expected her to cower and right now she's proving me wrong in the best way. Maybe it's just time, or maybe it's having a table full of people who all love and support her, or hell, maybe it's just being here in my lap and taking all the love and strength I can give her. Whatever it is, my wife is kicking fucking ass and her strong, controlled sister is wilting right in front of us.

"I just—" Serenity starts.

"You just what? You thought I'd be the same person I was at thirteen? You thought I'd be alone and pathetic? I was alone. But I'm not anymore. I met a great guy, we got married and I gained an amazing new family who all took the day off work today to be here to support me. I am a truly terrible person, I know that. But somehow, I found Granger and he makes me better. He doesn't care that I'm a mess. In fact, he challenged me to throw all my shit, my baggage, my issues at him and let him carry the burden for me. He loves me, in spite of who I am. I'm poison, but he's my antidote."

"You're not poisonous," Serenity snarls, shocking me with the ferocity of her words.

"I am," Alice laughs. "But I don't think that matters anymore."

Serenity bursts into tears, covering her face with her hands as she turns into Phil, who wraps his arm around his girlfriend's shoulders and holds her to him. "Look, I think maybe she's had enough for today. It was a long flight and she's been a fucking mess since the first call last week. Can we meet up tomorrow? We could come to you, or you can come to the hotel?"

"Sure, why don't you come for breakfast at our place? I'll send you a map link, we live about half way up the mountain."

Phil nods, then leans over and holds out his hand to me. "See you tomorrow." Then he looks at Alice. "It's nice to finally meet you. You probably won't believe me right now, but your sister talks about you a lot. We'll see you in the morning." Turning, he nods to the rest of the family who are all trying to pretend they're not listening, then he guides a still sobbing Serenity from the bar.

TWENTY THREE

ALICE

I watch my sister until Phil guides her out of the door. She was crying. I don't think I've seen my sister cry since Dad was arrested and our life started to spin out of control. Why was she so upset? My mind whirs as I try to understand her behavior.

She's here, which is weird enough to start off with.

She bought her boyfriend who I haven't met before, but who isn't at all what I expected.

Now she's crying.

I really just don't get it.

Granger wiggles beneath me, his lips finding my neck. "I'm so fucking proud of you, honey. You stood up to her, you called her on all her shit. I love you so much."

"Was I too mean?" I ask, suddenly worried.

"No. You weren't mean at all, you were honest. I'm guessing you guys have never talked about her leaving before?"

"Yesterday was the first time I've actually spoken to her since she went to basic training," I say with a nonchalant shrug. "I don't want her to be upset, I just don't know what she's doing here and why she was looking at me the way she was."

"I'm gonna guess that your sister probably has as many unresolved feelings about you as you do about her. I was worried about her coming here, but now I've seen the two of you together, I think you both need this."

"Shots," Teddy calls from beside us, taking the huge tray of pink, sparkly shots from the waitress and smiling widely at me. "These pink enough for you?"

I giggle. "Definitely."

He hands me one, then offers them around the table, smiling widely as he passes one to a reluctant Beau who eyes the pink, glittery concoction like it might actually poison him.

When everyone except Cora, Granger and Cody have shots, Teddy raises his glass toward me. "To our new sister. Now you have six new brothers and two new sisters, know that one of us will always be there to drink pink, sparkly shots with you."

Everyone cheers and I smile, saluting my new family with my glass before I throw it back, humming in approval as the sweet and fruity bubblegum flavored liquor hits my throat. Lowering my empty glass to the table, I watch as the rest of the glasses are drained, till only a still grimacing Beau is left. "Only for you, little one. This shit smells disgusting," he says, throwing the shot back. "Fuck, I think I just discovered what unicorn shit tastes like."

I can't help it, I laugh and I don't stop laughing for the rest of the afternoon. We drink, eat bar food and talk, and for the first time it dawns on me that I'm truly one of them now. I'm a Barnett. I have an amazing husband and a wonderful new family. I'm not alone and it feels liberating.

"Come on, honey," Granger coos, as he reels me in, my fingers entwined with his as I weave down the sidewalk back to the car.

"I want you to fuck me on the hood of your car," I announce a lot too loudly.

"Woohoo," one of the guys hoots from behind me, reminding my drunk brain that we're not alone.

"It's too cold to fuck you outside," Granger laughs.

"Don't we have a garage? You could park your car in the garage and then fuck me on the hood."

"No, honey, we don't have a garage."

"We should get a garage. Hey Cody, can you build us a garage?" I shout, trying to turn my head to look behind me, but every time I do, my whole body turns and I almost fall.

"I'll build you a garage, sis, I'll even put heating in it so you guys can fuck in the warm," Cody says, obviously amused.

I nod, like that makes total sense. "Will it be done by the time we get home?"

"Nah, sorry, you guys are gonna need to fuck in your bed tonight."

"That sucks," I say sadly.

"Hey, what's wrong with our bed?" Granger teases.

"Nothing. I just think it'd be hot for you to spread me out over the smooth metal and eat me, then fill me up with your cum." I sigh wistfully.

"Jesus, honey," Granger groans, pulling me to him and slapping his hand over my mouth. "You need to stop talking, my dick is hard and you're gonna be passed out or puking by the time we get home."

"Nuh huh, I can hold my drink. I never get drunk," I protest.

"You're drunk now, sweetie," Cora calls. "I fucking hate not drinking, it's the worst bit about being pregnant."

"I'm glad I'm not pregnant, pink shooters are fun," Bonnie says from where she's being carried over Beau's shoulder, her hair hanging down over her face.

"Don't worry, baby girl, we're gonna work on changing that when we get home. I want your belly full with my kid," Beau growls, reaching up and smacking her ass.

"Can we just do anal instead? I don't wanna get pregnant when I won't remember the sex," she whines.

"No. I'm gonna fuck you over and over till I knock you up," Beau snarls, spanking her again.

"If finding your woman means turning down anal, then I hope I never fucking find mine," Bay says with a dramatic shudder.

We reach the cars and the conversation quiets as Granger bundles me into the passenger seat, leaning over me to clip my seatbelt into place, taking care of me the way he always does. "I really love you," I tell him, my words sounding a little slurred, which is weird.

"I love you too. But I need you to tell me if you're gonna puke, so I can pull over."

"I'm not gonna puke, I'm not that drunk," I protest.

"Honey, you're as drunk as a skunk. Just remember to tell me if you're gonna get sick."

I nod, wiggling in my seat to get comfortable, my eyes starting to feel a little heavy. Maybe I am a little sleepy. I should have a power nap, that way I can be awake and refreshed for all the sexing.

Sexing with Granger is fun.

His soft chuckle is the last thing I remember as sleep pulls me under.

***

I'm hot, my mouth tastes like ass and my stomach is churning when I wake up, disoriented. I'm in bed, my head rested on Granger's lap, the low hum of the tv playing softly.

"Morning sleepyhead," he says from above me, his fingers stroking my head as I blink the sleep from my eyes.

"Morning." Pushing myself upright, I shuffle over so I can curl into his side, instead of lying with my head resting on his dick.

"Here," he says, holding out two tablets and an open bottle of water for me.

Taking the pills, I swallow them down with the water and try to piece together what happened before we got home last night. "Teddy was right, pink shooters are dangerous," I say, my voice gravelly.

"They are when you have six of them between rounds of beer. I'm actually amazed you didn't puke."

"Is everyone else okay?"

"Bonnie's in bed, she started throwing up as soon as we got back last night, Beau's taking care of her. Teddy and Penn looked a bit worse for wear this morning, but this isn't any of their first hangovers."

"What time is it?"

"Just after eleven."

"Weren't we supposed to have breakfast with Serenity and Phil?"

"I text them already, they're coming for lunch instead."

"Oh," I say quietly, burying my face into Granger's naked chest and trying to ignore the anxiety that bursts to life in my stomach.

"It's gonna be fine. Come on, let me take care of you before they get here."

I nod, my eyes closed as I nuzzle a little deeper into his chest.

Laughing softly, he lifts me into his arms and carries me to the shower, climbing in with me once the water is warm enough. He washes my skin, then my hair, running conditioner through it and even offering to shave my legs, which I'm happy I can decline, before he lifts me from the shower and wraps me in a huge fluffy towel, sitting me on the counter while he brushes my teeth and combs the knots out of my hair.

I'm more than capable of doing all these things for myself, but my hangover mixes with the need to have someone care for me the way he does, is too much temptation to resist.

"I love looking after you like this," he says as he helps me slide my feet into the panties he's picked out for me.

"Do you, or are you just saying that to make me feel

better?"

"No honey, I fucking love it. I hope you always need me like this."

"I love it," I confess. "I love you."

"I love you too."

When I'm dressed, he offers to blow dry my hair, then laughs when I wince at the thought of the noise. "Come on, let's go make brunch. I'll make you one of my hangover smoothies, you'll feel better in no time."

"It doesn't have raw eggs in it, does it?" I ask, feeling queasy just from the thought.

"No," he chuckles, leaving me at the breakfast bar while he pulls ingredients from the refrigerator, chopping stuff and dumping it into a blender. "Cover your ears."

I do as he suggests, lifting my hands to cup my ears as he turns the blender on, turning whatever he's put in there into mush. A couple of minutes later he turns it off and pours the purply, green liquid into a glass and hands it to me.

Taking it, I lift it to my nose and sniff cautiously. "What's in it?"

"Best not to ask, just drink it, it tastes good and it'll make you feel better. I'll get lunch started."

Exhaling, I lift the glass to my lips and take a tentative sip. It tastes weird, but not bad, so I keep sipping it while Granger moves around the kitchen. "Do you want me to help?"

"Can you cook with a hangover?"

"No, but then I can't really cook without a hangover either," I shrug.

"I'll teach you when you're feeling better."

An hour later, I feel almost human and Granger has cooked up a feast. The guys have a schedule for the chores around the house, which I haven't been added to, but according to Cora and Bonnie, it took them months to get the guys to add them to it, so it makes sense that I haven't been given any weekly jobs just yet.

Bonnie and Beau left to go over to her dad's ranch a while ago, so it's just Granger and I in the house as we wait for my sister and her boyfriend to arrive. I'm nervous, but not as fearful as I was yesterday. I think Granger is right, we both need to have this conversation that's been brewing for a decade. I'm just not sure if it will end up with us trying to reclaim our relationship or ultimately cutting ties for good.

A knock at the door pulls me from my thoughts as I jump up from my spot on the couch and move to open it. "Hey," I say to my sister and her guy, opening the door wide. "Come on in."

Granger wipes his hands on a towel and moves to me, curling an arm around my waist as they move into the living room, their eyes moving over the space and taking in the details of the house.

"This is some place."

"Thanks," Granger says, reaching out to shake Phil's hand. "My daddy built this place."

"Wow, is it just you guys that live here?"

"No, we all live here, we're just renovating and creating private living spaces and extra bedrooms for any kids that come along."

"So like a mountain commune," Serenity snips.

Granger's laugh is soft and amused. "No. This is our home, and none of us wanted to move out. Once the girls started to move in, we figured it made more sense to just build on to this place rather than knock the house down and build seven separate homes. This way we all have our own space, but this will be communal space so we can all spend time together as a family."

"How many of you are there?" Phil asks. "I know you introduced us yesterday, but it was a big day."

"Beau is the oldest, he's married to Bonnie, then Bay, Cody and me, then Huck who is engaged to Cora, Penn, and Teddy is the baby."

"Wow, I'm an only child, the idea of having six siblings is crazy to me," Phil says, obviously trying to fill the silence.

"Can I get you a drink?" I ask, suddenly feeling like I need to play hostess. "Coffee or juice, soda? I'd offer you a beer, but honestly I'm still hungover and I don't think I can handle smelling any alcohol for a while."

"Coffee would be great."

"Cream, sugar?"

"Both for me," Phil says.

"Serenity?" I ask, looking at my sister for the first time since she came into the house.

"Black please."

Granger releases me and I pad over to the coffee machine, pulling mugs from the cabinet and adding cream and sugar to Phil's, then making mine and Granger's how we usually take it. They're all sitting at the dining table now, and I place the drinks down in front of everyone and then take my seat beside Granger, opposite Phil and my sister.

"This table is amazing. Did you have to have this commissioned? It's much bigger than you can buy from a store," Phil asks, running his hand across the smooth polished surface.

"I made it, I'm a carpenter, I make bespoke furniture," Granger says.

"Wow, that's fantastic, and this is just beautiful," Phil praises again.

"What do you do? Alice said she thought you were in the military too?"

"I'm a civilian contractor, I'm actually an accountant. Serenity and I met when she moved to Camp Dawson seven years ago."

My eyes flit to Serenity. Her boyfriend is an accountant? For some reason, I expected her to be with a marine or something. The idea that she'd settle down with a guy who looks at numbers all day, probably in a cubical or something just doesn't seem right.

"Phil, wanna help me grab the food?" Granger suggests, pressing a kiss to my temple as he moves from beside me, obviously giving me a little space to talk to my sister.

"So what do you think of Montana so far? Is this your first time out here?" I ask in an attempt to make small talk.

"It's pretty."

"Yeah, and it only gets prettier the more snow there is. This would have been my third winter in the mountains, but I broke down before I got a chance to get to one of the bigger ski resorts."

"You worked at a ski resort?"

"Yep."

"Doing what?" she asks.

"One winter I was a maid in a hotel, another a barista in a coffee shop."

"So you don't have a job?"

"No, not really, there's always casual jobs available in the winter."

"So that's been your life for the last five years. You've

just moved from place to place working as menial labor?" There's a sneer in her tone that I really don't appreciate.

"Look, I don't appreciate your attitude, you don't get to judge my life."

Clenching her jaw, she looks away, breathing deeply. "Look I had to leave. I had to. I couldn't stay any longer else I'd have never gotten out."

"I get it. I don't blame you for leaving," I say simply, because I don't. It devastated me at the time, but I understand.

Her brow furrows, and she examines my face like she's searching for the lie in my words, but she won't find one. "I left you."

I shrug.

"You were a kid and I knew that mom wouldn't take care of you, and I still left you."

"You were a kid too. I don't blame you for going, it wasn't your responsibility to take care of me, to shoulder that burden."

"You weren't a burden, you're my sister." The words sound like they've been ripped from her, but I don't understand why this seems hard for her. It was ten years ago, and her leaving did me a favor.

"Look, I don't think we need to drag up things from ten years ago. Why are you here now? If this is some misplaced guilt, then please know you have nothing to feel guilty about. You leaving helped me. It made me realize some stuff about myself that I might never have figured out if you hadn't. I haven't spent the last decade miserable, I've seen the country, literally driven through almost all fifty states and worked in some of the most beautiful and interesting places in America. My life's been good," I shrug.

She gapes at me, like I literally have two heads. "How can I not feel guilty? I left, and you decided you're this terrible person who is clingy and needy and toxic." She practically chokes the words out. "I did that, I left, and you blamed yourself and you should hate me, why don't you hate me?" There're tears falling down her cheeks again and I can't stop staring at them. My sister doesn't cry. She didn't cry when Mom made us leave Gram Gram and Pops, she didn't even cry when Mom left us in the trailer in Florida for two weeks after she moved us there and went cross-country with her new boyfriend. She didn't cry when we moved again and again. No, it was me that cried, and she was the one who comforted me. So why is she crying now?

"Look, it wasn't fair of me to expect you to put your life on hold and take care of me. You were a kid too and I stole that from you and I just kept doing it. You didn't get to be a normal kid, you didn't get to be a teenager, I took all that from you and the more you gave, the more I took.

It's me who should be the one feeling guilty, not you. So let yourself off the hook. I'm fine. I'm here, I'm happy, I'm married. Go and be free and live your life. You don't owe me anything."

I expect to see relief, an unburdening in her expression, but instead she starts to cry harder, until Phil finally moves to comfort her, while I stare on in confusion.

"I don't know what to do," she says to Phil between sobs.

Plates of food are set out in front of us on the table, but I didn't even notice them arriving. Granger sits down beside me, placing his hand on my thigh and squeezing.

"Alice, Serenity has always felt a lot of guilt over leaving to join the army," Phil says.

"But she shouldn't," I say quickly.

"She's pushed it down and not dealt with it all these years, until Granger called the other day and some of the things he told her, coupled with the things you've said have just brought everything to the surface."

"She has nothing to feel guilty for," I say again, trying to reassure both him and my sister. "She moved on and started living her life for the very first time without having to deal with me and all my bullshit issues. I've never been anything but happy for her."

"Oh god," Serenity's sobs get louder.

Looking to Granger, I'm surprised to find his brow

drawn low, his eyes full of sadness and anger.

"I don't understand what's going on," I sigh.

"Honey," Granger starts. "Imagine if I told you that the way I need you, the way I love you was toxic and evil. How would you feel."

"I'm toxic, not you," I say slowly, my breathing becoming erratic.

"Calm down," he coaxes, pulling me onto his lap and wrapping his arms around me. "I love you."

"I know," I nod.

"The way you see yourself, the way you think you impact on other people is warped."

"No, it's not. I've seen the way people react to me. I didn't imagine that."

"Have I ever reacted that way?"

"No," I shake my head.

"Has my family ever reacted that way?"

I take a moment to think, then realize that no, they've never shown any signs of hating me, of getting sick of me. "No."

"Do you know why that is?" he asks me slowly.

"Because you love me and they love you," I tell him.

"I'm sure they'd make a real effort to love you if that was the only reason. But, honey, it's not. The reason I love you, the reason my family all love you, is because you're an incredible person."

I shake my head, rolling my eyes as I dismiss his words.

"What happens if I hear you talking bad about yourself?" Granger warns, and my butt cheeks clench in response to the memory of him spanking me.

"I didn't say anything bad."

"I can hear your thoughts," he chides. "You are fucking incredible, Alice. I knew it the moment I saw you and I fucking hate that you think you're this terrible person, because it couldn't be any farther from the truth."

"You weren't a needy kid," Serenity says, her sobs subsided until her voice is just ragged and tiny tremors run through her shoulders.

"Yes I was," I laugh. "I needed you for everything."

"No, you didn't. By the age of ten you basically looked after yourself. You made us both lunches, you cleaned the house, took yourself to school, you raised yourself."

"That's not true. I came to you for everything."

"You never ever came to me until you'd done everything you could to sort whatever it was you needed on your own. When you started your period, I was on an overnight fieldtrip from school and you waited until I was home and unpacked before you even told me and asked me what to do. When we moved to Florida, you were eight and you were so terrified of being alone in the trailer at night and you wet the bed, you stripped the bed and changed the sheets rather than wake me up and ask me for help. You are one of the most self-sufficient people I've ever met."

"No," I shake my head.

"Yes. When I joined the army, I hated myself for wanting to leave, so I told you that I needed to do something for myself, I made you think you were the reason I was going and it was bullshit. I broke up with my boyfriend and I was angry at Mom and Dad, it was never about you, I just needed an excuse to go and so I said all those things to you. I never imagined you'd believe them. I never dreamed that you wouldn't see through all the lies. I've spent the last ten years thinking you hated me for spewing all that shit to you and that's why I stayed away. I was so ashamed of what I did, I didn't think you wanted to have anything to do with me. You never called or visited and I didn't think I deserved to ask you to come, or to expect you to want to talk to me, and until Granger called me, I had no idea that I should have been hating myself for ruining your life."

My lips part and I stare at my sister, but I can barely see her through the haze of bewildered confusion that's settled over me. "No," I say. "No, that's not true. You didn't lie. I'm needy, I'm clingy and dependent and people hate me as soon as I they get to know me."

"People love you, they always have. You were always surrounded by friends and I was jealous at how carefree you were because I was so angry all the time."

"I don't have friends, people don't like me," I argue, jumping up from Granger's lap.

"Come here, honey, you need to eat, so let's just all take a time out while we have lunch. You guys can talk some more after we eat," Granger says, twisting his fingers with mine and not letting go. It's his way of reminding me that I don't get to walk away, that he's here so I need to stay too. Instead of feeling restrictive, it calms me and I let him pull me back down into his lap, uncaring if my sister or her boyfriend are bothered by me sitting with him.

Lunch is awkward to say the least, even though the food is delicious. Granger and Phil somehow manage to fill the strained silence with inane chatter, and even though he's not exactly who I expected my sister to be in a relationship with, it's clear that he's a nice guy. When we've all eaten our fill, there's nothing else delaying me and my sister delving into our apparently much more messed up than I realized relationship.

"Look, I'm not sure what rehashing all this stuff is meant to be doing. You have your side of things and I have mine," I say, just wanting to be an ostrich and stick my head in the ground. "Why don't you explain what made you come now?"

"You got married," she chokes out.

"Okay," I say slowly.

"You got married."

Blinking, I wait for her to say more, but she doesn't and Phil finally clears his throat and speaks. "I've been trying to get Serenity to marry me for the last five years and she's refused. She said she couldn't get married without you and she couldn't just call you after ten years to come to her wedding."

"Oh." My lips snap shut and I swallow thickly. "So you want to know if I'll come to your wedding?"

"No, you fucking moron," Serenity screeches, jumping up from her seat. "I want a relationship with you, I want my sister back. I want you in my life and I want to know what I can do that will ever make you forgive me for being such a selfish bitch and messing you up completely."

Granger chuckles, and I elbow him. "Why are you laughing?" I question.

"Because the two of you are so similar. You assume the absolute worst about yourselves and you've forgotten the most important thing."

"Which is?" Serenity snaps, her arms crossed across her chest defensively.

"That all this stuff that put a wedge between you happened when you were kids. Alice, you were thirteen and Serenity, you were barely eighteen. If you had parents who gave a shit about you this would all have been sorted out within a week of it happening, but instead it's been left to fester for the last ten years and it's molded both of you into who you are now. Theres a lot of water under the bridge, more than you can hash out over lunch, but this is just a starting point. Neither of you is going to just accept what the other is saying and move on, I think too much has happened to both of you for that to happen. So maybe you should just try to get to know each other as who you are now, as adults."

"I agree," Phil says. "You can't fix the past, but you can move forward."

"I don't need you to fix me," I say to my sister.

"I just wish I didn't break you in the first place."

Rolling my eyes, I start to tell her yet again that I've always been this way, but Granger covers my mouth with his hand, silencing me. "I love you," he whispers into my neck.

I melt into him, my man, my husband, my antidote.

EPILOGUE

ALICE

My cell rings, but I ignore it. My head's resting on Granger's chest, both of us damp with sweat, his cum dripping down my thighs. Today is our six-month anniversary. I know it's not something most people celebrate, but Granger and I seem to be able to find an occasion to celebrate whenever we want to escape and have a night of crazy, intense sex.

All of the building work is finished on the house now, and we have our own self-contained three bed apartment that connects to the main house through what used to be Granger's bedroom door. But sometimes it's nice to get away, so we bought a tiny fishing cabin an hour away from

Rockhead Point where we can run away to when we want some time completely alone.

When I think back on the day my RV broke down, I can barely take in how much my life has changed. Back then I was happily alone, moving with the seasons, a gypsy never making any roots, always on the move. Now my roots are so tangled to this man and our life, that I know trying to free myself would end with me withering and dying.

Our relationship is unique, and for a lot of people it probably wouldn't work. Neither of us likes to be without the other, so we still work together and spend all our time together, and I wouldn't want it any other way. Granger's business has really flourished, and as well as doing custom pieces we opened a showroom at the mill where customers can come and buy his one off pieces.

My relationship with my sister is getting better all the time. She still feels like she needs to fix whatever she thinks she broke all those years ago, but we speak at least once a week now, and the whole family are going down to West Virginia in a couple of months for Serenity and Phil's wedding.

Sometimes I wonder if Granger's idea of us being fated to be together is actually true, because what are the odds that my shitty old RV would break down, here in the town he lives in, on a day where he was driving through town, and that he'd stop and check I was okay.

No matter what twist of fate or serendipity or whatever brought him into my life, I'm grateful for it. Granger owns me heart, body and soul and I wouldn't change a thing. I'm still needy, clingy and dependent, but these days I know the only person I act that way with is Granger, and that's because he needs me to be needy, he likes that I'm clingy and he loves me to be dependent.

I know who I am, and that's okay, because I might be poisonous, but he'll always be my antidote.

Claimed By The Mountain Man
Montana Mountain Men #4
Coming Soon.

Acknowledgements

This story isn't how it was supposed to happen. If you were looking for mindless smut, then I'm sorry, but the emotion just wouldn't shut up and so it is what it is. This book is deeper than a puddle, but I promise I put all the orgasms in to try and balance it out.

I am having such a blast writing this series. I mean, when else would I get a chance to write about a man who wants his woman by his side 24/7 and not have someone screaming ABUSE at me. Never, that's when.

Granger was supposed to be the quiet brother, but if you've got this far, you'll know he's definitely not the shy and retiring type. I actually think that he might be a bit crazier than his brothers, you just don't expect it, because he's not beating his chest and behaving like a caveman for anyone but Alice.

Every time I write my little love story at the back of each book, I sit there and remember that this is my life, that I do this for a living and I swear it makes me tear up a bit each and every time. I am literally living the dream and it fucking rocks.

If you guys have read any of these before you'll know my bestie Sarah always gets a mention in my books. She mentioned the other day that she's not really been as involved in this series as she has in the ones that have come before it, and I suppose that's true. But here's the reason why... My bestie is living her own dream and she's smashing it. She's at college, taking her future by the balls and calling it bitch and I'm so freaking proud of her. You've got this, hun, and in a few years' time, you'll be a fully qualified midwife and up to your elbows in vaginas and baby goo.

To everyone at Hudson Indie Ink, you guys are awesome, thanks for supporting me while I spend my days writing about horny, insane mountain men.

To my wonderful and very, very patient cover designer Kerry Heavens at Rebel Ink Co. I'm so sorry. I know I've been the nightmare client with this one, but I promise not to be for the rest of the series.

Sarah my wonderful editor, you make my words all pretty and shiny, thank you for getting me and recommending my books to everyone, including me lol.

As always, to my fabulous readers, thank you for reading my words, loving my heroes and embracing the worlds I've created. I'm grateful for each and every one of you.

There're still four more Barnett brothers to come, so watch this space for Claimed By The Mountain Man coming soon.

ABOUT THE AUTHOR

Gemma Weir is a half crazed stay at home mom to three kids, one man child and a hell hound. She has lived in the midlands, in the UK her whole life and has wanted to write a book since she was a child. Gemma has a ridiculously dirty mind and loves her book boyfriends to be big, tattooed alpha males. She's a reader first and foremost and she loves her romance to come with a happy ending and lots of sexy sex.

For updates on future releases check out my social media links.

ALSO BY GEMMA WEIR

The Archers Creek Series

Echo (Archer's Creek #1)

Daisy (Archer's Creek #2)

Blade (Archer's Creek #3)

Echo & Liv (Archer's Creek #3.5)

Park (Archer's Creek #4)

Smoke (Archer's Creek #5)

*

The Scions Series

Hidden (The Scions #1)

Found (The Scions #2)

Wings & Roots (The Scions #3)

*

The Kings & Queens of St Augustus Series

The Spare - Part One

(The Kings & Queens of St Augustus #1)

The Spare - Part Two

(The Kings & Queens of St Augustus #2)

The Heir - Part One

(The Kings & Queens of St Augustus #3)

The Heir - Part Two

(The Kings & Queens of St Augustus #4)

*

The Montanna Mountain Men

Property the Mountain Man

Owned by the Mountain Man

Kept by the Mountain Man

OTHER AUTHORS AT HUDSON INDIE INK

Paranormal Romance/Urban Fantasy

Stephanie Hudson

Sloane Murphy

Xen Randell

Sci-Fi/Fantasy

Brandon Ellis

Devin Hanson

Crime/Action

Blake Hudson

Mike Gomes

Contemporary Romance

Gemma Weir

Ann B. Harrison

Elodie Colt

Lightning Source UK Ltd.
Milton Keynes UK
UKHW011547291221
396337UK00003B/676